THE

WIDOW'S

WATCHER

ALSO BY ELIZA MAXWELL

The Grave Tender
The Kinfolk
The Unremembered Girl

THE
WIDOW'S
WATCHER

ELIZA MAXWELL

Published by Lake Union Publishing, Seattle

www.apub.com

Amazon, the Amazon logo, and Lake Union Publishing are trademarks of Amazon.com, Inc., or its affiliates.

ISBN-13: 9781503901049
ISBN-10: 1503901041

Cover design by David Drummond

Printed in the United States of America

For Isabel,
my wild, willful, wonderful child

1

"You didn't have to leave the dog behind."

Jenna kept her eyes on the road, wheels between the lines.

"I did, Cassie. You know I did." An undertow of weariness dragged at her limbs.

"The first rule of writing: make your protagonist relatable. Likable, even. Abandoning the dog with strangers? Not so much."

Jenna sighed.

"I'm not a protagonist, Cass. This isn't a novel, and the Davises aren't strangers."

"They're strange all right. Especially their creeper son."

Each word dripped with teenage derision. It wore on Jenna like sand against stone. It was always there, rubbing. Given enough time, it could take down mountains.

"He's not a creeper."

"Beckett doesn't like him," Cassie said, as if that were the final judgment of the universe. "Beck likes everybody."

"I don't want to talk about this. Beckett's fine. You know I couldn't bring him."

In the span of silence that followed, Jenna hoped her eldest daughter had let it go. The relief was short-lived. Cassie merely changed her tactic.

"Opening a book with the main character driving a car is a cliché, by the way."

Jenna clenched her jaw and bit back a retort. *Breathe,* she thought. *Just like the nurses told you during childbirth. Breathe.*

Who knew that was intended as a life lesson?

When the nurse had laid Cassie in her arms, Jenna had laughed, wide and openmouthed. Warriors in battle the two of them were, she and her brave, howling daughter. They'd fought valiantly, shedding blood and coming up victorious on the other side. Her laughter blended with Cassie's cries, their voices rising together.

"I know, love," she'd whispered to the little life in her arms. "This is new for me too. We'll figure it out. We'll figure it out together."

Such confidence. Such naivety.

"Where are we going anyway? Do you have the faintest idea?"

"Cassie, lay off. Please."

"A scene should have a point, Mom. Cause and effect, a drive toward a goal. Wandering aimlessly with no apparent destination isn't going to cut it."

"Enough!" Jenna said. Her breath quickened, her anxiety cranking up at the badgering. "Enough now, Cass."

I have a goal, Jenna thought. *Just not one I intend to discuss with you, thank you very much.*

As Cassie had grown, Jenna had slowly but inevitably discovered that this child, her child, wasn't an extension of herself.

"They spend their whole lives walking away from you," the kindergarten teacher had said on her little girl's first day. "Your job now is to be there when they look back."

Jenna's eyes had searched her daughter out as she introduced herself to a little boy, the two of them launching into an animated discussion about whatever pressing matters five-year-olds discuss.

But Cassie never looks back, Jenna thought then as she stood in the doorway waiting to wave goodbye to a child who'd forgotten she was there.

Oh, but the stories. The stories were the flickering light of a lone star in an inky-blue sky. The fantastical, sweeping stories that had begun before Cassie could even write them.

This, Jenna had thought. *This is it. Tangible evidence my DNA runs somewhere through this kid.*

There'd been times she'd wondered. Was it possible the child had been switched in the hospital? Had some sly nurse slid into her room while she dozed and slipped a changeling into her arms, then snuck away into the night with her real daughter?

What had become of the daughter Jenna always thought she'd have? The shy, studious girl who would hide when visitors came? The child who would pull the bottom drawer out of her dresser, dump out the contents, and snuggle into her self-made nest with a pillow and a picture book?

That daughter came later. They named her Sarah, their second born.

But Cassie wasn't her sister, or her mother, and never would be.

Accepting that made it easier for Jenna to appreciate and celebrate the daughter she *did* have. The wild, willful, wonderful daughter.

"Unless your goal is to end up stranded on the interstate in the middle of nowhere—which is fine if you're going for horror, but not really your style—you need to put gas in the car, Mom."

"Thank you, Cassie, for that astute observation. I don't know what I'd do without you."

"Neither do I."

If the stories were a star in the sky, Jenna had been tracking that star her entire life. From a practical distance. She'd majored in journalism. Journalism was a marketable skill.

A springboard, she'd told herself. *I'll write that novel one day. When the time is right.*

When Matt had encouraged Jenna to take a hiatus from her job and write the book she'd always planned, she'd hesitated.

"If not now, then when?" His optimism confounded her.

Cassie had other plans.

"I've decided to self-publish my book," her daughter had declared at dinner a few months later.

"Wait . . . what?" Jenna's fork stalled midair.

"Have you considered how to do it?" Matt asked. Cassie launched into a surprisingly well-researched discussion about platform and distribution, marketing and cover design.

The glob of pasta on Jenna's fork lost its balance and plopped onto her plate. Her insides felt similarly flattened.

"It's crazy," she whispered to Matt that night while she massaged lotion onto her face. Her skin had started to show wear and tear approximately the day Cassie was born.

"I don't know if *crazy* is the word I'd use."

"What would you call it, then?"

Matt shrugged, his back turned as he pulled off his T-shirt. "Proactive? Enterprising?" He walked toward her and put his hands on her shoulders. He pulled her into a hug. "I'd call it brave."

His chin rested on the top of her head. She listened to his strong, steady heartbeat.

"You don't understand. You're supposed to toil and shed blood and paper your walls with rejections. You learn from that, and they're hard lessons. *That's* how you become a writer."

Matt shrugged again. "I guess Cass decided to do it her own way, Jen."

"But what if the book's not ready? What if *she's* not ready? What if it's not good enough and she's buried under the failure?"

Jenna backed up to look her husband in the eyes as she shared her real fear.

"She's so talented, Matt. And so young. What if she gives up?"

Matt managed to hide the smile lurking beneath the surface, but Jenna knew it was there.

"Then she'll deal with that. And we'll be there to help her. But, honey . . . our daughter? She's not the kind of girl that gives up. She's not that fragile."

He didn't say it, didn't mean it, didn't even consider what Jenna would hear in those words. Despite his intentions, *not like her mother* rang clearly in her head.

Jenna's fears were unfounded. They often were. Cassie's book was good. Could she see her daughter's youth in places? Sure. But there were also glimpses of the woman Cassie would become—strong, decisive, and confident in herself and her words.

Cassie was destined to become the woman Jenna aspired to be.

And every vestige of that was gone now.

Jenna's eyes were drawn to the passenger seat of the van, to the old wooden box that had been her grandmother's.

It was all gone.

Jenna jerked the wheel and drove the minivan she no longer had any use for onto an exit ramp.

Everything was gone.

She was left with nothing. Nothing but her eldest daughter's voice in her head and a carved wooden box that cradled the ashes of the family she used to have.

2

The restaurant next door to the service station drew Jenna in. She wasn't hungry, though she couldn't remember the last time she'd eaten. Nebraska, maybe.

But the nearly empty parking lot lured her with a promise of quiet and coffee. A chance to catch her breath, settle her nerves.

Jenna stared, unseeing, out the window of the restaurant. For how long she couldn't have said. The sound of children broke her reverie. The coffee had gone cold.

A boy of about twelve, wearing a hooded sweatshirt and earbuds, sat slumped in a chair across from his mother. His face shone with the artificial light from the tablet in front of him.

Two little girls half his age—twins from the look of them—ran back and forth between the vintage coin-operated mechanical horse and their mom.

Their chatter was bewitching.

The woman, deep in conversation on her cell phone, held up a hand to ward them off while they took turns clamoring for attention. Lips pinched, the mother tapped her fingers against the table. When the waitress offered menus, she managed a tight smile and a nod.

"No, Frank, that's not going to work. The sitter canceled, remember?"

"Mommy, Mommy, can we have some quarters?" asked the little girl in blue. Her sister was clambering onto the top of the horse, yelling, "Giddyup!"

"Lainey, stop. Mommy's on the phone," the woman said.

"Pleeease," the little girl whined.

"Lainey, go play with your sister."

"But, Mom, we need quarters." The child tugged on her mother's sleeve and moved into her line of sight.

"Lainey, not now!"

The woman pulled her arm back and turned away from the girl. The boy slid farther down his seat.

Jenna didn't think as she rose and walked toward them.

Her eyes skirted the edges of the little girl seated on the back of the horse, as one might avoid looking directly at the sun. She dropped two quarters into the slot for the machine.

The second girl ran by Jenna to climb on with her sister when the tinny mechanical music began.

"Thanks, lady!"

Jenna's hand came up of its own accord, presumably to ruffle the girl's hair as she passed, but she stopped short of making contact, her hand floating disconnected at her side.

Meeting the eyes of the mother who'd witnessed what she'd done, Jenna read the indecision there. Part of the woman probably felt judged, which wasn't Jenna's intention.

Good manners won out, and the woman put her free hand over the mouthpiece of her phone, her lips forming the shape of the words *thank you* in Jenna's direction.

She inclined her head in reply. A smile was impossible.

Jenna was halfway back to her booth, straining with the effort not to run, when she stumbled and hung her head. She gripped the back of an empty chair to keep from falling. She had no plan, no ulterior motive. Yet her feet had an agenda of their own. She doubled back.

Sliding uninvited into the empty chair between the mother and her son, Jenna placed both hands flat on the table.

"Put down your phone," she said to the woman, whose name she didn't ask.

The woman's eyes widened. She glanced at her son, who looked up, interested in something other than his electronic lifeline for the first time since they'd walked into the restaurant.

"Excuse me?" The woman rotated the phone from her mouth while keeping the other end next to her ear.

"Put down your phone," Jenna repeated.

A man was speaking on the line, his voice muffled and indistinct.

"I'm sorry, do I know you?" the woman asked.

Jenna felt her control spiraling dangerously away.

"No. But I know you. I *was* you."

"Frank, I'm gonna have to call you back." Frank was still speaking when the woman ended the call, her eyes never leaving Jenna's.

"Lady, I don't know who you think you are, but—"

"You can do better. Put your phone down and pay attention. Listen to what they're saying. Listen to what they're *not* saying." Jenna nodded toward the silent preteen watching the exchange with bulging eyes.

The woman's shoulders squared and she leaned away from Jenna, her mouth opening, then closing, as she searched for words.

"You're going to regret it. One day, when you're living in an empty house and this is all a distant memory, you'll have nothing left but regret." Jenna's eyes pleaded with the woman, this stranger she'd never see again.

"Of all the . . . ," the woman sputtered, looking from Jenna to her son, who shrugged. "I don't have to sit here and listen to this. Girls!" She held out an arm to usher her younger children toward her. They ignored her.

Jenna sighed. Some rational part of her regretted the way her words sounded.

"Don't go." Jenna struggled for composure as she rose from her seat. "Enjoy your meal. Look at them. Listen to them. Love them. Then love them some more. I'm leaving anyway," Jenna said with a catch in her voice as she turned and hurried out of the restaurant.

She crossed the deserted parking lot, indifferent to the snow that had started to fall, and listened to the thing locked inside of her rattle its cage. She couldn't hold it in forever. She was running out of time.

"I'm leaving anyway," she whispered to no one.

3

The silence was suffocating inside the vehicle. Jenna considered the radio, but the idea of chipper, disembodied voices pushing opinions into her space was worse.

Lost in her graveyard of memories, Jenna drove on as the minutes ticked past. She hadn't made it back to the interstate but meandered for miles down roads in and out of towns she neither knew nor cared to know the names of.

City blocks gave way to rural farm-to-market roads, but the destination Jenna was moving toward had no requirements for time or place. One was as good as the next.

Field after field passed, sitting empty and fallow for the winter, waiting for spring to come. A different world than the concrete Houston suburb Jenna had left behind.

She turned the van right, then left, then right again, eventually snaking along a curvy road that wound down a hill into the shadowy embrace of a stand of evergreens. The houses, modest and neat, sat far from the road, nestled snugly in their places.

The airy flakes of falling snow added to the shameless charm. A break in the trees flickered past, and she caught a glimpse of a lake illuminated by the early-evening light of the dying sun.

"When all else fails, you can always rely on a fantastic setting," Cassie said, serene and matter-of-fact.

Jenna pulled the minivan to the side of the road. She paused to take it in.

There was no traffic. There was no sound at all, save the call of geese flying in formation overhead, heading south in the direction Jenna had come from. Even their passage was muffled.

"Yes," she whispered. "Yes."

Quickly now, her decision made, Jenna glanced around the interior of the van. She'd brought nothing from home but the wooden box and her soft leather messenger bag. She grabbed the bag and turned its contents out into the footwell. Gum packets, receipts, wallet—detritus of a life interrupted.

Slowly, with more care for the contents of the box than she'd had for the bag, Jenna made sure the lid was secure, then slipped the box into the now empty satchel.

There, she thought, as she slid the shoulder strap across her torso. *There.*

With the box safe by her side, Jenna opened the door of the van and shivered against the sharp bite of the wind.

It's time.

4

Jenna had been shaking on the inside for so long, she welcomed the cold seeping through her skin. To shake on the outside as well felt right.

She wondered if anyone was home inside the faded brown bungalow-style cabin she passed as she walked down an unknown homeowner's driveway. Perhaps, but it didn't feel that way.

The world had paused, holding its breath. Everything except the snow, which blew on the wind like fairy children on holiday.

Even Cassie remained silent.

The driveway ended, after bending left where an olive-green truck sat that must have been as old as she was. She continued past the truck, past the bend, and through the gathering snow, which crunched beneath her feet. She walked through a stranger's yard, toward the lake she'd seen from the road.

The yard sloped sharply downward, and Jenna followed a set of ancient concrete steps built into the hill.

The steps were slick with ice and snow and varied in height. She concentrated on her footing. Once at the bottom, she found herself on a small landing that stopped abruptly at a man-made retaining wall that had seen better days.

Jenna's eyes swept across the partially iced body of water stretching before her, hidden from the rest of humanity, tranquil in its anonymity.

"Incredible," Cassie said.

Jenna's face remained impassive. She had the vaguest sense her expression had frozen the day she'd received the call, as if the voice on the line had somehow reached through the airwaves and severed the connection between her face and her heart. Between everything and her heart.

"Smile, Jenny," her mother used to scold. "Pouting is unattractive. Your face is going to get stuck like that."

Jenna's lips tried twisting at the irony and failed. There was finally something her mother had been right about.

She pulled in a deep, cold breath and spared a moment to at least acknowledge the natural beauty surrounding her, so bold and life sustaining. Two things Jenna no longer was.

Is there anything so empty as something that's once been full?

She bent to lower one leg, then the other, over the retaining wall. Snow had gathered along the edge of the frozen lake, but it gave way beneath Jenna's weight. Four inches, then six, her foot sank before she found resistance. She had no way to know how strong the ice beneath the snow was or how deep the frigid water beneath.

There were places farther out with no ice at all.

"Stay with me," she whispered, reaching for her daughter, the only thing she had left.

Jenna closed her eyes. Sensations washed over her. Heat from tears not shed. The comforting weight of the box against her side. The imagined warmth of Cassie lacing her fingers through her own.

"I've got nowhere else to be," Cassie said.

Jenna took a step away from the wall. Her foot pressed through the snow again before it met the ice below.

This was her destination. This was the place she'd driven thousands of miles to find. Someplace, any place, with no ties to the family she no longer had, or the life she would never live again.

Any lingering hesitation drained away, along with the little warmth left in her body. She took another step away from shore.

And another.

Her pulse raced. For the first time in a long time, something like joy stirred inside of her.

She took another step, no snow beneath her feet now. Only ice, creaking with anticipation, just as she was.

A slow smile spread across Jenna's face.

Her mother was wrong after all. The thought made her laugh, a full and deep sound, laced with the same triumph she'd had the day Cassie was born.

She took a step. And another.

The silent cocoon of the world as she made her way slowly, indelibly forward embraced her.

The universe had made a mistake. As had Jenna. She should have been with them. There was no reason, no logic, to a reality where she was expected to go on living in such emptiness, scraped hollow until nothing remained.

But it was going to be okay. The universe, with Jenna's help, would make things right.

In this beautiful place she'd never been, she would find peace.

It was time for her to leave this lovely, treacherous world. Time now to make it right.

The universe was listening. A crack appeared at her feet with a sound like a life breaking in half. It spread faster than her eye could track, showing her the way forward.

All she had to do was follow it.

Jenna took another step.

And another.

No hesitation. No second thoughts.

A whisper of warning shivered up her spine, but Jenna ignored it, her decision made.

5

Lars's first thought was that he was seeing a ghost.

"Audrey?" he whispered. His hands stalled where they held the hot cup of soup he'd pulled from the microwave. There was no one in the house to hear his slip of the tongue, or the gasp when the heat of the cup penetrated his consciousness.

He dropped it onto the counter and soup sloshed over the side, but his attention was on the wide bank of windows that faced the lake.

He stepped closer, squinting to take in the sight of a woman with long dark hair making her way slowly down his steps.

Doc Meyer had told him his heart was the problem. He hadn't said anything about his mind.

Lars shook his head. There was nothing wrong with his mind, dammit. There *was* a woman. She was right there, flesh and blood.

And she sure as hell wasn't Audrey.

"What the hell?" he asked no one.

As he stood watching, the woman stepped onto the ice along the edge of the lake.

Harmless enough, if odd. The edge was frozen through to the bottom. So long as she didn't go farther, there was no problem.

Then she did.

Without hesitation, the woman stepped out. He saw her catch her balance on the slippery surface. She didn't pause, but took another step.

Fumbling with the latch on the window, Lars cursed the arthritis in his fingers as he yanked the stubborn old double pane up with all his strength.

The blast of frigid air pushed at him. The woman had taken another step while he'd been messing about with the window. He opened his mouth to shout a warning, but before he could, a warble of laughter reached him that chilled him in a far deeper place than did the cold Minnesota air.

Understanding bloomed. He hadn't heard laughter like that in nearly thirty years, but the loose, lonely sound of a soul that's come untethered wasn't a thing he was likely to forget.

Recognition settled upon him like a shadow.

On its heels, a white-hot outrage.

6

"Whoa there, lady," came a voice like rusted hinges.

The voice grabbed Jenna's attention, pulling her back as much as the hand that clamped on to her bicep.

With a gasp, she turned to stare at the source of the intrusion.

Jenna didn't have time to register the man's face as she was yanked by the arm with enough force that she stumbled. She followed along, more from an instinct to keep her legs beneath her than because she wanted to go in the direction the man was pulling her.

Back to the edge of the lake.

Back to the emptiness she was determined to leave behind.

The retaining wall was coming closer. Jenna tried to pull away, but the stranger's grip was iron. She had no choice but to comply.

"No, sirree. Have to be blind and dumb not to see what you got in mind, but not today. No, ma'am. Not on my lake anyways."

He yanked harder. Something dark and hot bubbled up inside of her.

The interloper turned to face Jenna. To her horror, he put his hands on her waist, picked her up, then set her back down above the wall.

"How dare you—"

"Ah, save it, lady." The man lifted a leg to step over the wall himself. "I got no time for the likes of your kinda business today."

"You can't put your hands on me like that."

He'd ruined it. He'd ruined her perfect moment with no more consideration than he'd give to swatting a fly.

"Under normal circumstances, you'd be right." His face was lined and craggy where it wasn't obscured by a wiry gray beard.

"But I'd say these are hardly normal circumstances, and I won't hesitate to do it again." His face leaned close to hers. "Now get yourself outta here, before I have to do it for you."

Jenna backed up at the blaze in his stark gray eyes, an anger he had no right to. It was hers.

"Who asked you anyway?" She stepped up to meet him nose to nose. "You think you're some sort of Galahad, coming to rescue the damsel?"

"Lady, I look like Galahad to you?" His bushy eyebrows rose, two untamed animals growing out of his face. "I don't give a damn what you do, but I got no intention of waiting out the winter knowing your dead carcass is gonna float up in my lake in the spring. You take your fancy pants elsewhere, and you do it now, before I decide to call the cops."

He put his hands on her again, turning her by the shoulders so she was facing the concrete steps, and gave a small shove.

"Go on, then."

All the way up the hill the man was at her back, urging her forward. His presence stoked her fury.

"That yours?" He gestured toward her minivan parked along the street.

Jenna set her jaw and crossed her arms. It was childish, but she'd stumbled so far onto this limb it was impossible to find her way back with any semblance of grace.

The man scowled, his overlarge eyebrows moving across his face like caterpillars trying to find a comfortable spot.

"Lady, I told ya, I got no time for shenanigans. Now is that your van or not?"

"Yes," she spat out. "Yes. Fine. I'm going."

Yet she continued to stand with her legs braced apart, arms crossed over her chest.

The two of them stared at each other for a beat, then two.

One of the caterpillars got restless and rose, revealing the pale eye beneath.

"Well, then, whatcha waiting on, missy?"

Her hands clenched into fists as she briefly imagined wrapping them around his throat. She turned wordlessly and huffed her way back to her van, leaving the man standing watch over her progress at the end of his precious driveway, protecting his precious lake.

A burning animosity propelled her into the vehicle. She removed the strap of her bag, set it in the passenger seat, and slammed the door behind her. Glaring back at the man, Jenna gave the keys in the ignition a vicious crank.

The engine rolled over, and she found a tense satisfaction in the sound, a voice for her frustration. Then the noise gave out and turned to a wheezing whine of defeat. Her satisfaction withered with it.

She cranked the key again as she glanced down at the dashboard, willing the engine to catch.

But the universe had given her one chance today. It didn't care what Jenna wanted anymore. Neither did the engine of the van.

"No," she said under her breath. "No, no, no, you bastard."

Another turn of the key. Jenna heard what sounded like a death rattle, shuddering into nothingness.

"You can't be serious. Come on!" She gave another useless turn, but there was no point.

The van was done.

"Dammit!" She pounded both fists on the wheel.

She glanced toward the driveway. The old man was gone. There was nothing there now save a thickening curtain of snow. He'd disappeared, like he'd never been.

"That's great. Absolutely fantastic."

She leaned her head back against the seat and took a deep breath. "Any sage advice now, Cass?"

There was no reply. Not from the empty van. Not from the voice in her head.

"Of course not." Another breath, then she gave in to the inevitable and reached for the handle of the door. "Figures."

The frozen lake was still there, silent in the distance, but she was sure the old man was watching, even if she couldn't see him. There was no dignity in the idea of racing him back to the center of the lake.

She wouldn't do it that way. Like a woman who'd taken leave of her senses. Ending her life was the most rational decision Jenna had ever made, and she was determined to get this one last thing right.

"Even if it kills you?" Cassie asked.

Jenna could almost see her daughter, arms crossed, her head tilted in disapproval.

Ignoring her, Jenna tramped back through the falling snow, up the man's driveway once more. She plowed forward on instinct, despite the foul taste of bile in her throat, and did what needed to be done next to get her out of here.

She stomped up the steps to the weathered door she assumed he'd disappeared through.

Jenna made a fist and pounded.

He didn't answer.

She held her breath and pounded again.

"Come on, you asshole!" she shouted. "I know you're in there."

Growing more agitated by the moment, she raised her hand to pound again.

"Fine time to ignore me now! Couldn't mind your own damn business when I—"

She broke off as the door abruptly swung outward. There'd been no warning, no thudding footsteps coming from inside the house. Only the turn of the handle followed immediately by the outward push of the thick wood with such force she had to back up several steps. If it weren't for the steaming mug of what appeared to be soup in his hands, she might have thought he'd been standing just inside the door, waiting to see if she'd go away.

The old man peered at her. He didn't speak.

"My van won't start." It was an accusation, as if he were somehow responsible.

His impressive eyebrows drew together, and she bit back a few choice words as he blew onto his soup to cool it.

But when he reached out, hooked a gnarled finger around the brass doorknob, and shut the door in her face without a word, her jaw dropped.

She stood there, gaping, but the door didn't open again.

Jenna turned, then walked to the edge of the small porch, shaking her head.

"Old bastard," she murmured. "Who the hell does he think—"

The door opened behind her.

She turned to see him standing in the doorway again. The soup was gone, replaced by a cell phone, which looked incongruously shiny and smooth in his hand. He held it up without a word.

Jenna took a hesitant step in his direction. He made no move to bring it to her, and she suspected he was waiting for her to draw close only to pull it back and shut the door again.

Once she was near enough, he slapped the device into her hand.

"Thank—"

The door closed in her face.

Expletives she'd rarely spoken aloud burst across Jenna's mind, but she clamped her jaw and ground her teeth.

"Fine." She gripped the phone in her frozen fingers. "I'll just call a tow truck, then, why don't I? Get out of your damn way."

She hit the button at the bottom of the phone to light up the screen and swiped a thumb across the display to view the options.

She stared.

With a long-suffering sigh, she turned back to the door.

At least the pounding was keeping her hand warm.

When the man opened the door again, the soup back in his hands, Jenna held up the phone.

"I don't know where I am."

It was the old man's turn to sigh.

"If you ain't a boatload of trouble, lady, I don't know who is." He took the phone back, glanced over his shoulder into the darkened house, then turned to look her up and down.

"Stay there." He proceeded to shut the door on her. Again.

"And where else do you think I'm gonna go, then?" she yelled to the plane of wood standing between them.

Jenna wrapped her arms around herself and turned to watch the snow fall, seething at the predicament she'd managed to put herself in.

Cassie's laughter rang in her ears.

"Is this what they call a meet-cute?" her daughter asked. "Because this guy has leading man written all over him."

"I'm glad you find this funny."

"Ah, don't be such a grump," Cass said. "I think he's hot . . . in a geriatric, prison parolee sort of way."

"Cassandra, please." Jenna was in no mood for her daughter's wry, inappropriate humor.

Cassie's peal of amusement drifted away into the snowfall.

The cold surrounding Jenna began to seep into her consciousness. Little pinpricks to get her attention at first, which she tried to ignore. Soon, though, with the anger banking inside of her and the temperature dropping by degrees, there were great swaths of her body that began to feel they'd never be warm again.

She stamped her feet and rubbed her hands, numb now, up and down the arms of her thin jacket, designed for a friendlier climate than whatever godforsaken place she'd found herself in.

Jenna looked toward the door. There was no sign of her self-appointed savior. She tucked her fingers beneath her arms. She wouldn't knock. Not again.

Minutes crawled past as the snow wicked the color from the world around her.

Unable to resist, Jenna turned back to the house. She swallowed her pride and raised her fist to knock, but her eyes were drawn to a small window farther down.

On soft feet, feeling like a voyeur, she tiptoed across the boards of the porch and leaned her head just far enough around the window jamb to peek inside.

There were shabby lace curtains, which might have once been white, blocking most of her view, but they didn't quite meet in the middle. Jenna caught a glimpse of the man who'd pulled her from the lake, the man who'd instructed her to *stay here* in that arrogant tone, then left her to freeze her ass off.

He was stretched out in a recliner, in thick socks that had a hole in the bottom of the left one. He was watching television if the flickering light playing across his face was any indication. Next to a fireplace.

Jenna's eyes watered at the thought of the waves of heat that must be rolling off the hearth.

"You old bastard." The words formed misty smoke in the air.

Straightening, Jenna considered beating on the door again so she could tell him he was a bastard to his face, but he'd probably shut it on her before she could get the words out. If he bothered to get up from his chair.

She thought again about heading back onto the lake, longed to, but the moment was gone. The beautiful moment she'd driven across the country to find.

He'd taken it from her, and she couldn't get it back while stoking her resentment at the theft. She'd mourn the loss later, once she found a way out of this hellhole.

Looking around, Jenna weighed her options. She could walk back up the winding road that had brought her here, try to flag down a passing vehicle. But the snow was getting thicker, and she wasn't convinced she wouldn't end up frozen in a ditch before she found help.

"Not the distinguished exit you had in mind?" Cassie asked.

"Stop it," Jenna said. "I'm not debating this with you."

She stamped her feet some more, then balled her hands together and brought them to her mouth to blow on them.

The neighbors would be a safer bet.

She took a deep breath and made her body as tight and purposeful as she could manage, then braved the snowfall and headed in the direction of the house nearest the cabin.

She pictured the cell phone that had once been an integral part of her day. A lifeline to the outside world, a web of connection to her family and friends.

During the dark days after the call, each time it rang or dinged or beeped, an irrational hope carried her toward it. That unsinkable seed of possibility that this time, finally, would come the punchline of some terrible joke. Someone else's family had been taken. Not hers. Matt's voice on the other end, scratchy with distance, explaining everything away.

The last time, she'd been running a bath, alone in the silence that was no longer serene, only empty. She'd run the bath for no reason except to listen to the sound of the water filling the tub.

Sitting on the edge of white porcelain, she'd heard the cell phone chirp. She told herself she wouldn't this time. Wouldn't run for it, wouldn't get her hopes up only to have the inevitable pain crash in again.

But in a life now full of days that meant nothing, there was no distraction from the possibility that maybe, just maybe . . .

When Jenna grasped the phone from the bedside table, her breath snagged in her throat as she saw she had a message. An old friend's mother. A woman she hadn't seen, heard from, nor thought about in over twenty years.

She was so sorry for Jenna's loss. There were no words to express . . . And so it went.

The little seed of hope finally cracked under the weight of all the words that couldn't express how deeply sorry everyone was. The two halves fell open, revealing a hollow center.

Jenna had looked up to see the tub was nearly overflowing. She'd risen and shuffled slowly back into the bathroom, the phone hanging loosely within her fingers.

She dropped to her knees and turned off the tap, then listened to the groan of the pipes as she watched the water drip, drip down.

She knelt there, next to a full tub of clear, warm water, with her arms leaning over the side. She ran one finger across the surface and watched the ripples spread outward.

Beckett padded to her side. He whimpered, just once.

Jenna's fingers loosened on the phone, and she watched it fall. It splashed into the water and sank face-first to the bottom of the tub.

They weren't coming back.

She hugged Beckett to her. Too tightly, but he didn't seem to mind. She buried her face in the ruff of his neck and grieved alone in the dry, vacant place she'd been left. Kneeling on the cold tile, Jenna faced her choices. To stay and suffocate under the weight of emptiness, or leave it behind. Everything. Take matters into her own hands, in her own way.

Beckett was the only one she hadn't turned away from already. She was an only child, and her parents had been gone for many years, but it would have made little difference. She couldn't bear to look at anyone else, not her friends, not Matt's family with their sympathy and their tears. They mourned their loss, while hugging their own children tighter.

It was no choice at all.

Jenna shook off the memories. She'd never expected to need her phone again. Finding herself wishing for it was another trespass she placed at the old man's feet.

No one answered the door at the nearest neighbor's house. The place had an air of hibernation about it, a sense that no one had been there for quite some time.

Jenna walked back to the street, and it occurred to her that no one had. None of the houses in sight seemed to have vehicles in the driveways or smoke coming from the chimneys. All were shuttered against her.

Summer cabins.

She was standing on an abandoned street, looking at a row of empty summer cabins.

"No," she whispered. She craned her neck to see farther, but the place was deserted, waiting for the harshest of seasons to pass.

No wonder the old man had been so proprietary about *his* lake. It *was* his lake and his alone, at least for the foreseeable future.

"No!" Jenna shouted.

She'd have to go back.

"Bastard."

"You're overusing that word," Cass told her as she trudged up the hill toward the brown house with the fire in the hearth. "You can do better."

"Can it, Cassie. I don't need a lecture on constructing a chapter. What I need is a tow truck, so unless—"

Jenna raised her head at the sound of a vehicle beeping an alarm as it backed up, and beheld the sight of a battered truck that had probably once been red with some sort of winch attachment sidling up to her immobile van.

"Ask and ye shall receive," Cass said.

"Hey," Jenna shouted, hurrying in the direction of the tow truck, waving her arms. "Hey!"

Her carved box was still in the front seat of her van, about to be towed away without her.

Skidding around the front of the tow truck, she nearly lost her footing on the icy road, but managed to keep herself upright, just barely, by falling onto the side of the vehicle with a bang.

The truck jerked and clanked as it was thrown into park, and the driver's side door opened.

"Whoa, there, lady." The tow truck driver had the same thick northern accent as the old man. "Not so smart to be coming up like that on a man backing up a truck."

He spoke with a slow, patient cadence, like he was talking to a child.

Jenna struggled to catch her breath. The cold was taking it faster than she could pull it in.

"Where's your coat, missus?"

Jenna shook her head, unable to put together a coherent sentence.

Warmth was coming from the cab of the truck, and Jenna was shaking with a bone-deep chill.

"You can't be wandering around in the snow like this with a sorry excuse for a jacket and nothing else," the man said, shaking his head at her.

"All I have," Jenna managed to push out through teeth clenched against the chatter.

The man removed his heavy coat and wrapped it around her shaking shoulders. It smelled of engine exhaust and unfamiliar male, but she was too grateful to care.

"This your van?" The driver was younger than she'd realized. Nearer her age than the old man's.

Jenna nodded shortly, hugging the coat to her.

"I take it you're not from around here?" He raised his eyebrows at her in a way she was becoming accustomed to.

Jenna shook her head. "The old bastard called you?" she managed to ask.

His eyebrows shot up farther. "Yup."

Jenna sighed. "If he thinks I'm going back over there to say thank you, he's got another think coming."

The man shoved one hand into his pocket and used the other to push back his knit cap and scratch the top of his head.

"Lemme get this straight. You saying old Lars knew you were out here. In that laugh of a jacket. In the snow. And he left you here in the cold?"

"If by 'old Lars,' you mean the goat that lives in the brown house, we didn't exactly hit it off."

The man leaned into the cab of the tow truck and cut the rumbling engine.

"Come with me," he said, gesturing toward the house in question.

Jenna shook her head.

"No thanks, pal. I'm happy enough just to get the hell out of here."

He studied her a moment. "Right, then. You can wait here if you want."

Jenna's mouth fell open as the man turned and headed toward the door of the brown bungalow.

"Wait," Jenna yelled to his retreating back. He didn't stop, so she hurried to catch up. "Look, I appreciate the sentiment, but it's not worth it. Really."

When the man's fist, significantly larger than Jenna's, pounded on the old man's door, it sent up a demanding boom that made her wince.

"There's no need—"

"Open up. It's Owen," the driver shouted.

"Please, let's just go." Jenna placed a hand on his arm.

Her self-appointed protector patted it as a grandparent might and ignored her.

"Open up, I said," Owen shouted as he banged on the door again.

A thumping came from inside the bungalow. Jenna dropped her hand and stepped back.

The thumping was followed by the rattle of the doorknob. The heavy wooden door swung wide again.

"Keep your knickers on." The old man peered at them with nothing short of apathy.

"What's going on?" the younger man asked.

Owen, Jenna reminded herself.

"I'd think that'd be fair to obvious, boyo," said Lars.

"You'd be wrong, then."

"Woman's car won't start. Needs a tow," Lars said. "Last I checked, you run a garage. You got a tow truck. What's hard about that?"

Owen reached up and scratched his head again. "Yup, that part I can see. The part I don't understand is why you left her to freeze in the cold with nearly no clothes on her back while she waited on said tow truck. You got an explanation for that one?"

Lars took a step forward, out of the doorway, so he could give Jenna an appraising look. A flush crept up her cheeks despite the chill wind, and she looked away, unable to meet the man's stare.

"It's my house. Don't suppose I owe anybody any explanations. Least of all you."

Lars inclined his head curtly in the direction of the tow truck driver and shut the door on them both.

Owen's forehead furrowed, but Jenna couldn't suppress her relief.

"Look, I appreciate the effort, but I just want to go," she told him.

After a long glance at the barred door, Owen looked back at her.

"All right, then," he conceded. "I'll take the van to the garage, and tomorrow we'll see what's what. You staying with friends or something?"

Jenna shook her head. An unexpected wave of fatigue weakened her knees.

"Got family around here?"

"Could I bother you to drop me by a hotel?"

She hadn't slept since God knows when. Before she'd left home, and in no more than fits and starts since the call had come, if she was honest. If Jenna didn't find a bed soon, she'd likely sink to her knees there on Lars's front steps.

Serve him right to have to deal with my frozen carcass after all. But her vindictiveness had lost its edge. She was too worn out to give it the effort it deserved.

So tired, in fact, that Owen had been speaking for a while before her muddled brain had a chance to catch up.

"I'm sorry, what?"

"I said, that's going to be a problem," he repeated with a pitying look.

Of course it is. Jenna gave a mental sigh.

"Open up," Owen yelled, banging on Lars's door again.

"Wait, why?" Jenna cried. "I don't want to talk to him again. Let's just go."

Owen continued his incessant banging.

"Go away," came the muffled response from the other side of the door.

"What's your name?" Owen asked her, between bangs.

"J . . . Jenna Shaw." She glanced between his face and the door.

"Nice to meet you, Jenna. Owen Jorgensen. I said open up, dammit." He directed the last part toward the still-closed door.

Lars must have grown as tired of the noise as Jenna, because he finally flung the door open.

"What now?" Irritation was visible in every line on his face.

"Got a problem. She's got no place 'round here to stay. Hotel's still shut down for repairs."

The bushy gray brows rose slowly. The exact nature of the situation began to dawn on Jenna.

"I fail to see how that's my problem," Lars said.

"I'd let her bunk at my place, but I've only got the old couch," Owen went on. "She could have my room, but then I'd be stuck on the couch, and after a double shift, I'm beat. I don't particularly care to spend the night on the sofa, so you're elected."

"No," said both Lars and Jenna simultaneously.

"I think after leaving her out in the cold, it's the least you could do."

"The least I could do? I saved her fool life, boy. The least I could've done was let her walk off into the lake and drown," Lars spit out. "Starting to think I should have."

"This is not a good idea," Jenna said.

"I'm with the lady," Lars added.

"Look, your only other option is old Mrs. Beasom's bed-and-breakfast."

Lars snorted. Jenna resolutely refused to look at him.

"Sounds good, let's go."

Owen held up a hand. "She broke her hip three months ago, and her cats have taken over. The place stinks like urine and cat feces, and the health department wants her shut down. The ladies from the Presbyterian have been trying to help, but she keeps threatening to shoot them."

"Old bat couldn't hit a barn door with that rifle," Lars said with a roll of his eyes. "It's the only thing in this town older than she is."

"Look," Owen said to Jenna. "I know it's not ideal, but I'll vouch for him. He's got terrible manners, but ignore him when he talks and you'll be just fine here until I can get you back on the road."

He got only brooding silence in reply.

"Give me a better option," Owen said to the two of them.

Neither spoke. Jenna marveled that there'd ever been a time when she had believed herself in control. Of anything.

"That's settled, then," Owen said, turning to Jenna. "You can stay in the spare room."

"No. She can't." Lars dug in his heels.

"It's clean. Not like he gets many visitors," Owen went on as if Lars hadn't spoken.

"Can't imagine why," Jenna muttered.

Lars sent a withering glance in her direction.

"I'll give you a call tomorrow and let you know what's going on with your van."

"I don't have a phone," Jenna said desperately.

"It's all right. I'll just call the house."

"This is not going to happen." Lars crossed his arms and planted his feet.

Owen sighed.

To Jenna's astonishment, he took her by the arm and muscled the two of them past the stubborn old man, right into his warm, waiting home.

"Get out of the way, Dad," he grumbled. "Sheesh."

"Dad?" Jenna cried. "This is your *dad*?"

The two men turned to stare at her.

"Of course it is," Owen said. "You don't think I'd just walk into a stranger's house, do you?"

"Woman's not so bright, Owen. Did I mention I pulled her off the ice?"

"Did I ask you to do that?" Jenna's helplessness at the circumstances ignited her temper again.

"See what I mean? You'd think she'd show a little bit of gratitude, but no. Instead, I'm stuck in the middle of *The Taming of the Shrew*. And I don't get paid to tame shrews, Owen."

"Shrew, is it? I'm a shrew? At least I don't run around manhandling women against their will. You're lucky I haven't called the cops and had you charged with assault, buddy!"

"Ha!" Lars threw back his head with an ungracious laugh. "I'd like to see you try. Maybe you'd care to explain what you were doing wandering around on thin ice in the first place. They'd pin a damn medal on me, just for listening to you shriek and not tossing you back onto the lake."

"That's my business! Mine!" Jenna jabbed a finger at her chest.

Her pulse pounded in her throat. The old man's contempt was cracking the shell she'd been encased in for months. Everyone had been tiptoeing around, treating her like she was made of glass. Her body, her mind, her heart. Fragile, handblown glass.

"What did I tell you, son? Not so bright," Lars said, crossing his arms again.

Jenna and the old man glared at each other, neither willing to give an inch.

"Are you two done?" Owen asked from where he leaned against the kitchen counter.

They both turned their heat on him, but he seemed unmoved, if exhausted.

"Good." He straightened. "I'll leave you to it, then."

Jenna saw the resemblance now. It was in the eyes, in the set of the shoulders, and in the complete disregard for the wishes of the people around them.

Owen moved toward the door.

"Wait!" Jenna said. "My van. I have to get something."

"I can bring in your stuff for you," Owen offered.

"No, I'll get it myself." She brushed past him.

As she walked through the falling snow to gather the wooden box from the front seat of her van, she told herself it didn't matter. What difference would it make, spending the night in the old man's spare room?

She slid the box out of the bag and ran a hand over the top.

This was the only thing left that mattered.

"And if he turns out to be a psychotic killer prone to murdering middle-aged women in their beds?" Cassie sounded more curious than concerned.

Jenna pushed the box back into the bag.

"Then he'd save me the trouble, but somehow I doubt he'll be so accommodating."

When Jenna returned with her satchel slung over her shoulder, its original contents retrieved from the floor of the van, and the box held tightly in her arms, the two men glanced at the box but refrained from comment. Which was good, because Jenna had no intention of explaining what was inside.

"Dad, try to be civil, if you can manage it," Owen said as he put his hat back on. "As for you, Jenna Shaw, it was nice to meet you."

And with that he was gone. Once the door shut behind him, a split second of surreal silence followed. Jenna and Lars stared at each other. She fought against a dizzying sense of how quickly life had shown her illusions for what they were. Family. Love. Future. Control. Even her own death.

Jenna's grip tightened on the box in her arms.

She had nothing left to lose. And she was unendurably tired.

"Fine," Lars spat out. "Down the hallway, last door on the left. Bathroom's on the right."

"You could say thank you, Mom," Cassie whispered, but Jenna couldn't manage it. Not without choking on the words.

"And don't be expecting a continental breakfast, missy. I want you gone tomorrow," Lars threw over his shoulder as he stomped toward the faded recliner and flickering television screen.

"Can't come fast enough."

"I heard that."

"You were meant to." She made her way down the dim hallway to find the sleep that could no longer be denied.

7

The moments upon waking, just before full consciousness, when her mind betrayed her, were almost wholly to blame for Jenna's reluctance to sleep.

She'd yet to find a path to bring her back that didn't pull her through the minefield of belief that her family was alive and well.

Every day. Every time.

She was forced to face the loss, accept the brutal truth crashing like waves around her, then somehow find the strength to pull her unwilling body from the bed and make her way through another empty day.

This day would be no different.

But this time, the room that came into focus was different, and the sounds of life coming from down the hallway gave Jenna a reason to swing her legs out of the bed.

Lars Jorgensen. Today she had a new goal. To put as much distance between herself and Lars Jorgensen as she could.

The previous day flickered across her memory. A swell of discomfort began low in her belly and traveled upward to flush her cheeks.

She'd never behaved toward anyone the way she'd behaved to Lars Jorgensen. That wasn't who she was.

At least, it wasn't who she used to be. This new Jenna was as much a stranger to her as the old man was.

She'd fallen onto the bed the night before wearing the same clothes she'd worn for the previous few days. They were wrinkled and beginning to smell, she realized with a whiff of herself.

She dug through her messenger bag and found an elastic hair band, a brush, and a nearly empty packet of spearmint gum.

That would have to do.

Her gaze was drawn to the box she'd set upon the bedside table the night before. Uncomfortable leaving it lying about, she glanced around the room.

After an internal debate, Jenna decided to place the box in the bottom drawer of the dresser that sat beneath a window on the far wall. She was relieved to find the drawer empty, not sure how she'd feel about having to shove aside someone else's socks or underwear to make room for her family's ashes.

She placed the box inside and shut the drawer with careful deliberation.

Girding herself for a confrontation, Jenna walked down the hallway, following the scent of coffee and the sound of water running in the sink.

She heard humming, and the sight that greeted her was an ample bottom bent over a dishwasher rack. It clearly didn't belong to Lars Jorgensen.

"Excuse me," she said to the bottom.

There was no reply.

Jenna took a few steps farther into the room, but the bottom was busy keeping the beat.

She tilted her head downward and said louder, "Um, excuse me?"

The woman attached to the other end gave a start and raised her head, eyes wide. She placed one hand on her chest while the other reached to remove a set of headphones.

"Good gracious alive, girl!" the woman said. "What in the world are you doing?" She leaned heavily against the counter at her back and tried to catch her breath.

"I'm sorry, I didn't mean to scare you."

The woman, probably in her mid- to late sixties, looked her up and down. Jenna was aware how she must appear, with her slept-in clothes and bags under her eyes.

"If you're looking for the soup kitchen, it's in town, hon," the woman said, confirming Jenna's suspicions and bringing a flush to her cheeks.

"No." She shook her head. "I'm waiting on my car. It wouldn't start."

The older woman tilted her head. "Your car is at the garage?"

Jenna nodded. "I was stranded out here. I spent the night."

The woman's brows shot up.

"Lars let you spend the night. Here?"

"In a manner of speaking. His son . . ." Jenna trailed off when the woman nodded in comprehension.

"Ah. That makes more sense. Owen's a good boy. What's your name, hon?"

"Jenna."

"Why don't you have a seat, Jenna? I'm Diane." The woman closed the dishwasher and turned it on. The hum and swish it made were familiar, and oddly comforting.

"Can I get you anything for breakfast? Coffee?" Diane asked, friendlier now that she knew Jenna hadn't wandered in off the street in search of a free meal.

"Coffee, please." Jenna glanced around. "Is Mr. Jorgensen here?"

Diane shook her head.

"Never sticks around on my cleaning day, which is fine and dandy with me."

She set a steaming mug in front of Jenna.

"Are you . . . Mrs. Jorgensen, then?"

"Me?" Diane asked with a laugh. "Married to that mule of a man? I hardly think so. My last name is Downey. I'm the housekeeper."

The older woman refilled her own cup and took a seat across from Jenna.

"What brings you out this way?"

Jenna pushed her chair back, suddenly uncomfortable with the cozy scene. She'd forgotten how to do normal.

"I should call and check on my van."

Diane noticed Jenna's abrupt shift, and gave her an assessing look.

"Sure, hon. Phone's right over there." She gestured to a pea-green rotary phone that had probably been hanging on the wall since the house was built.

Jenna stood and picked up the receiver, then realized she didn't know the number.

"There's a list taped there on the wall," Diane said, watching her.

Jenna glanced over and saw a curling yellowed piece of notebook paper with faded cursive handwriting that listed Lars Jorgensen's important numbers. Owen was at the top of the list.

"Thank you," Jenna mumbled, turning back to the phone and dialing the number.

"Jorgensen's Garage."

"This is Jenna Shaw. I'm checking on my van. It was brought in yesterday evening."

"Hey there, Ms. Shaw." She recognized the voice as Owen's. "How are you this morning? Dad treating you all right?"

"He's not here. I wondered if you'd had a chance to get the van running."

An echo of machine tools whirred in the background.

"Honestly, I haven't had time to look yet, but I should be able to tell you shortly. Diane's there today, isn't she? Dad'll be over at the church.

Why don't you catch a ride with her when she's done, and I'll let you know how it's looking."

Jenna glanced at Diane, who was wiping the countertop with a soapy rag and making no attempt to hide the fact that she was listening.

"Yeah, okay," Jenna said. It wasn't like she had any choice. "I'll ask her. Thank you."

"You got it, Jenna. Just have her drop you by the garage."

When she hung up the phone, Jenna took a deep breath and turned to the housekeeper, forcing herself again to ask a favor of a stranger.

8

"Going to be a hot one today." The woman chuckled at her own joke as she drove.

There was no snow falling that morning, and the sun was out, but it might as well have been a child's crayon drawing taped to the sky for all the good it did. Jenna pulled Owen's heavy coat tighter.

"You're not from around here, are you?" Diane asked, an attempt to fill the awkward silence.

"Where is 'here' anyway?" Jenna said, sidestepping the question. She'd never been good at small talk.

Diane studied her.

"Raven, Minnesota," she said finally.

Jenna nodded.

The only difference it made was the direction she'd take when she drove out of there. The frozen north had lost whatever appeal it might have once had. *West,* she thought. Southwest, maybe, in search of someplace where the sun still had a stake in things.

She'd find somewhere new, another beautiful place where Lars Jorgensen couldn't pull her back from what she needed to do.

"I've never understood your propensity for grand gestures," Cass said inside her head.

Jenna had been alone with only Cass's voice for company for long enough that she barely stopped herself from responding aloud.

"What's the point?" Cassie continued.

Jenna shifted in her seat and stared at the reflective expanse of white rolling by outside the window.

"You don't have to overcompensate in everything you do, Mom. We know you love us. You don't need you to kill yourself in some theatrical middle finger to the universe."

Jenna squeezed her eyes shut.

She was aware her daughter wasn't actually speaking to her. Jenna wasn't crazy. Cass's voice was nothing more than a coping mechanism her brain had manufactured to deal with her grief.

Knowing the words came from someplace inside herself didn't make hearing them any easier. Her mind was made up, and nothing—not even her subconscious speaking in her dead daughter's voice—would sway her.

"Have you worked for Mr. Jorgensen long?" Jenna asked Diane, determined to mute the nagging in her head.

"Longer than I care to say." Diane gave a rueful twist of her lips.

Jenna studied the woman's expression, wondering distractedly what Lars Jorgensen had done to earn the housekeeper's disdain.

"So is there a Mrs. Jorgensen?" Jenna asked.

An innocuous question, but Diane's expression tightened. The remnants of the old Jenna must have still been in there somewhere, because her senses began to vibrate, ever so faintly, even before the housekeeper stumbled out a response.

"It's . . . well, it's not my place to . . . He doesn't really talk about . . ." Diane glanced at Jenna uncomfortably.

She needn't have worried. Whatever unease the question had raised, Jenna no longer cared about the answer. Her attention had snagged on a snapshot affixed to the visor of Diane's car.

She didn't mean to stare but couldn't seem to look away. Diane noticed her preoccupation and reached to hand the picture to Jenna.

"My grandson, Thomas. Tommy, his mom calls him." Her pride was unmistakable. As was her relief at the change in subject.

The photo was a close-up of a baby with chubby cheeks. He was chewing on a fabric toy the exact color of his big, round eyes.

Her own children had eyes that blue when they were born.

Jenna's throat was tight as she ran a thumb along the boy's cherubic face.

She handed the photo back with such speed it nearly slipped from her fingers.

"He's beautiful," she forced out.

"Do you have kids?" Diane asked, smiling as she tucked the photo back into place.

Jenna had never considered how often strangers asked that question until she no longer had an answer.

Did she have kids? *Yes, yes!* her mind screamed. Three unique, amazing kids, each with their own strengths and quirks and temperaments. Her kids, her tribe. Her life.

"No," she whispered. "No kids."

Jenna turned back to the white landscape. She didn't blink. She wondered how long she'd have to stare at the bright, sparkling snow to go blind.

9

"Days?" Jenna asked incredulously. "Plural? As in, more than one?"

Owen had the good grace to look apologetic.

"I'm sorry, Ms. Shaw. The part has to be ordered, I'm afraid, for this make and model van. I don't have it in stock."

"That's not going to work." Jenna ran her hands over her face. "I can't stay here for *days*."

She did a slow turn, looking outward for an answer, only to circle back to Owen's sympathetic face.

"Is there someplace in town I could rent a car?"

"Closest place is in Saint Peter," he said with a shake of his head.

"And how far is Saint Peter?"

"'Bout fifty miles."

She squeezed her eyes shut, told herself to breathe.

"Listen, why don't you go across the street to the café and take a load off? Get a cup of coffee, a sandwich or something. I'm kind of backed up here now, but as soon as I get a chance, I'll get on the phone and see if I can track down that part. Maybe find a supplier a little closer."

Jenna glanced around. Three people in line behind her were waiting to speak with Owen. There were cars parked around the edges of the building and a pair of legs in blue work pants dangling from beneath one of the cars in the three bays. The clank of a falling tool echoed, followed by a muffled curse.

Jenna sighed. "Okay. Thank you, Owen."

It wasn't his fault. It was no one's fault except her own. That didn't make it any easier to accept.

She began to shrug out of his coat, but he shook his head.

"You keep it for now. I know where to find you if I need it."

Her shoulders sank as she put it back on. She supposed he did.

Jenna glanced up and down the street as she crossed over to the Raven Café. The town wasn't exactly a thriving metropolis, but there were a few cars passing, the drivers of which gave her openly curious stares.

The town was small. Startlingly so.

It made her feel like a fish in a bowl.

Along with Jorgensen's Garage, she saw a Laundromat, the café, what appeared to be a general store, and a secondhand shop. At opposite ends of the street, on opposing sides, were the spires of two different churches, placed like bookends.

She'd grown up in a town eerily similar. There would be a bar on one of those side streets. Someplace for the locals to knock a few back. On one of the others, a school. A tiny one-room post office. A tinier public library, if they were lucky.

A bell rang above the door of the restaurant as she entered. Jenna wasn't imagining the lull in the conversations of the breakfast crowd.

Strangers would be a rarity here. Maybe not so much in summer, when those cabins came out of hibernation at the lake, but with winter's grip firmly in place, Raven, Minnesota, was members only.

Jenna chose an empty booth next to the window and tried to ignore the glances thrown her way. The volume picked up again as people went back to business as usual.

A waitress brought Jenna a plastic-covered menu.

"Just coffee, please." She handed the menu back without looking at it.

"You sure? How about a slice of pie to go with that?"

Jenna had her mouth open to say no, thanks, when she noticed a familiar green truck turn into the garage across the street.

"Ma'am?" the waitress asked.

"Hmm?" Jenna said, distracted by the sight of Lars Jorgensen climbing out of the ancient automobile. He slammed the door behind him before he walked into his son's garage like he owned the place.

"Pie?" the waitress prodded.

"What?" Jenna said, shaking her head. "Fine, sure."

She wasn't hungry, but it seemed to matter to the other woman more than it should.

"What kind would you like? We have—"

Jenna waved a hand, cutting her off. "I don't care," she said, biting back the urge to scream. The woman flinched. Immediately appalled at her own rudeness, Jenna managed to add, "Whatever you suggest. I trust you," along with a weak smile.

The waitress retreated behind the counter, no doubt chalking her up as a lousy tipper.

By the time the waitress made her way back with the much-discussed slice of pie and a cup she filled at the table with steaming coffee, Lars had exited the garage, looking constipated as he stomped through the parking lot. She wondered if he always looked that way. As he threw open the door of his drab green truck, she thought probably so.

"Thank you," Jenna mumbled to the waitress without looking at her.

"No," she whispered when Lars stopped, then looked in the direction of the café.

"No, no, no," she chanted as he caught sight of her in the window.

Their eyes met, and he slammed the truck door closed without stepping into it and headed her way.

Jenna straightened her shoulders and gave all her attention to the coffee waiting in front of her.

Hoping he would ignore her, she stirred a spoonful of sugar into the black liquid as the bell above the door jingled ominously at her back. She fumbled with one of the tiny prepackaged cups of cream the waitress had brought.

A shadow loomed over her as she managed to open the thing, only to have it slip from her grasp and spill across the Formica tabletop.

"What are you going to do now, eh, missy?" he boomed, paying no heed to the captured interest of her fellow diners.

Jenna narrowed her eyes at her unwelcome visitor.

"I'm thinking I'll convince you to let me spend another night at your place, then sneak into your room and smother you with a pillow. Put you out of your misery."

Lars's eyebrows shot up and he shuffled back a step.

After a pause that Jenna took an infantile satisfaction in, his mouth fell open, and she braced herself for whatever scathing commentary the man felt he'd earned the right to toss her way.

The sound that finally came out was so disconcerting she glanced up to make sure he wasn't having an attack of some kind.

He was laughing at her.

10

Lars studied the woman seated across the table. She had fire in her, he'd give her that, though it was obvious she'd taken some knocks.

Her eyes were sunken, her skin pale.

Once he'd cooled off, he'd been forced to acknowledge, privately at least, that there were things in this world that could drive a person out on that ice.

He knew that better than most.

Yet he had a gut feeling sympathy wasn't what this woman needed, with her hollow eyes and her family vehicle she drove alone.

Lars had learned the hard way that ignoring his gut was a mistake.

Despite the fact Jenna Shaw had as much interest in speaking to him as he had in a prostate exam—or maybe because of it—he slid into the opposite side of her booth.

"What are you going to do now?" he asked again.

She didn't meet his eyes but kept her gaze focused on the plate in front of her, where she was pushing around a piece of pie with her fork.

"What do you care?" She tossed the fork aside without taking a bite.

Lars leaned back and crossed his arms. "You can pretend you were sightseeing in the middle of a frozen lake all you want, lady, but I know different."

She sat back and crossed her arms as well, mirroring him right down to the surly expression.

"What's the point having my boy fix that van of yours if you're just going to take it a few miles down the road and run a hosepipe from the exhaust?" Lars asked, leaning forward and placing his forearms on the table.

The woman turned her face away and stared out the window. He marveled at how tight her jaw was, the stubborn inflexibility on display.

"Again. What business is it of yours?" she said.

"It's wasteful!"

Eyes turned in their direction. Gossip would be flying around town before the check was paid. Let them talk.

Her jaw flexed, but her expression didn't soften. *About as much good as spitting into the wind.*

Lars sighed. "Hand over that pie," he said. "No point in it going to waste."

She pushed the plate across the table, then watched as he reached for her unused fork and cut off a large bite.

She waited until he was chewing before she spoke. "Cherry pie was my daughter's favorite."

Past tense. *Was* her daughter's favorite. The tart sweetness turned to chalk in his mouth.

"Apple, though. My younger daughter and my husband both preferred apple."

Lars had to force himself to finish chewing, then to swallow, his throat suddenly dry and uncooperative.

He wiped his mouth on a napkin, no longer interested in finishing the pie.

For a moment, their eyes met, and he caught a glimpse of an abyss.

He was relieved when she broke away, turning again to the window and the snowy sidewalk and street outside.

In a voice so low he could barely make it out, she spoke again.

"My son preferred cake."

Lars said nothing. Words had never been a talent of his. People talked too much anyway.

Jenna Shaw was lost in whatever memories had hold of her. So still she was. Like Midas had brushed against her and turned her to a cold golden statue.

He could get up and walk away right then, and she wouldn't bat an eye, wouldn't even register his absence.

He fought an urge to do just that. To walk away and leave her there with her half-eaten pie and her past tense.

Lars pulled his wallet from his back pocket, fished several bills from its worn leather confines, and tossed them on the table.

"Come with me." He slid out of the booth and stood.

He thought maybe she hadn't heard him, until she mumbled, "Thanks, but I'll pass."

"Yeah?" he asked sharply, pushing down the sympathy that was one step below useless. "You got a pressing engagement somewhere?"

She whipped her head around, and he took a mean gratification in the fire that flared in her eyes.

"It wasn't a request. You don't think you're going to bunk at my place rent free, do you? Time to earn your keep, missy."

"Do you have to practice being such an asshole, or is it a God-given talent?"

His lips twitched, but he managed to bite back the laugh. "I could say the same for you, lady. Now come on. Maybe you'll learn something."

Lars nodded to the waitress as he walked toward the exit. He held the door open and looked over his shoulder.

She had stood, at least, though she hadn't moved from the booth. He could read her hesitation, even from a distance. Lars raised one eyebrow at her and tilted his head. A challenge.

Her face clouded with resentment. A step in the right direction. He watched as she snatched Owen's coat from the seat and shrugged it on.

He managed not to crow with victory as she huffed past him out the door, but he couldn't stop the smirk from spreading once her back was turned.

11

"You finally find yourself a girlfriend, Pops?"

The boy, who looked about ten years old, was sitting on the steps of a squat brick building that butted up against the church on the west end of town. He wore a ragged coat and a grin full of mischief.

"Isn't she a little young for you?"

"Why aren't you in school?" Lars demanded. Jenna ignored the way the child waggled his brows in her direction. "Don't you have a test today?"

"Mama's sick again," the boy said with a shrug.

Lars fumbled with a set of keys and unlocked the heavy door.

"Well, get in here, then. You can help set up for lunch, then take a plate home to your mom." He held the door open to a large, dimly lit room. "After that, you get your rear end to school."

"What are we having today, Pops?"

"Filet mignon and poached salmon hors d'oeuvres." The old man flipped a set of switches along the wall, illuminating an institutional room with eight or ten tables lined up like battered soldiers.

"What's that mean?" the boy asked.

"Soup, Terrence. We're having soup. It's a soup kitchen, not five-star gourmet on the Riviera."

"Why you got to be that way? You forget to take your fiber this morning or something?" the boy asked.

"Why don't you shut your gob and go put the plates and bowls out on the line already? Unless you want me to call the principal, get her down here to drag you back by the ear."

"All right, all right. No need to get your shorts in a bunch," the boy said with a grin. He ran off to what was presumably the kitchen portion of the soup kitchen like he'd done this routine before.

Lars followed at a slower pace.

Jenna stood motionless.

Lars stopped at the doorway to the kitchen and looked back at her. "Well?" he asked.

She had nothing to say. Even Cassie was silent.

"Look, lady. The way I see it, unless you're planning to do yourself in today, right now—in which case, I'd ask that you take that mess outside so you don't traumatize the boy—you get in here and put yourself to use. I got lunch to make."

"I . . ."

Jenna had never felt so much of nothing.

"I'm no cook," she managed. Inane words that said nothing of the struggle inside of her. The struggle to move, to care. To be.

The old man's sharp eyes studied her.

"Did I ask if you were a cook? You've got ears, don't you? You can take directions." Lars shifted his weight and raised one of those damnable eyebrows. "Unless you're too good to peel potatoes."

She straightened her spine and sent him a black look, unsure whether to be grateful for the distraction or give in to resentment that he'd recognized how badly she needed it.

She brushed past him, head held high, and decided she could do both.

"That's what I thought," he mumbled as she passed.

"Careful, old man," she said in a hoarse voice. "*Murder-suicide* has a nice ring to it."

But the bastard was laughing at her again.

12

Lars Jorgensen wasn't an easy taskmaster, and Jenna hardly a model student, but she peeled as he demanded. Then she chopped and she stirred and she ladled into bowls.

His gruff instructions flowed over her all the while, peppered with irrelevant information about the people who began to file into the church building in search of a hot meal.

"Not a lot of homeless in Raven," Lars said. "Not like over in Minneapolis or Saint Paul."

Jenna hoped he wasn't expecting a reply. The fog had begun to settle back upon her, and she struggled to get through the tasks at hand.

Lars didn't seem to notice.

"Minnesota in the winter's a hard place to be without a roof over your head," he continued as he handed trays to the people who came by the pass-through window that separated the kitchen from the larger room.

"We have a few folks around, but the town council tries to make sure arrangements are made for the rough months."

Jenna slid a vegetable peeler down a carrot, cutting away the outer layer to reveal bright orange beneath. Turn, repeat, with as much precision as she could muster. Lars's words were background noise.

"Mostly we've got working poor. Families who've fallen on hard times for whatever reason."

Turn, peel, repeat.

"Terrence's mother, she's a drinker." The cheeky-faced boy had taken a sandwich and bowl of soup home. "He takes care of himself and his little sister best he can."

Jenna gathered the peeled carrots and moved them to the oversized chopping block. The stock pot full of the soup Lars was dishing out had come directly from the refrigerator, then gone onto the stovetop to heat. Jenna was prepping a different soup for a different day, apparently. She didn't question him.

Chop, add to the pot, repeat.

"How are you today, Mr. Jorgensen?" asked a young woman with dark smudges beneath her eyes as she made her way through the line that filed in front of Lars.

"I'm well, Tess." The gentleness in the words momentarily pulled Jenna from her stupor. "How's Jamie doing?"

The woman smiled. "He's picked up some work over in Mankato."

"That's good news." Lars handed her a tray and another to the little boy who stood clinging to her leg.

The boy, too young to be in school, had his face partially hidden from Jenna. Shy eyes peeked around his mother, seeking out the stranger in his midst, and battered her already defeated senses. Sarah, her lovely, sweet Sarah, had been the same.

Jenna gasped, pulling her gaze from the reticent child with the hurtful eyes to the cutting board in front of her.

Is that my blood?

"Good Lord, woman," Lars barked, the tenderness gone like a puff of smoke in the wind. Jenna found herself relieved to see it go.

Lars dug around in a drawer, then moved Jenna toward a sink, where he turned on the faucet so she could hold her hand beneath it. The cut was deep and long, and she watched the red dilute and run in rivulets down her hand, then disappear down the drain.

Lars was waiting with a bandage, which he applied with quick efficiency.

"You can serve," he said, brusque now. "You're cutting those carrots wrong anyway."

He took her by the arm and moved her back to the pass-through window, where there was still a small line of people waiting on their meal.

"Tray, bowl, ladle, next." As if she were an imbecile.

She managed to do as he'd instructed, avoiding eye contact with the blurred faces moving past while he grumbled behind her back.

"Uniform pieces," she heard him mutter with disgust. Then something garbled that might have included the words *suicidal woman* and *knife*.

"Stir," Lars told her when she'd finished serving the people waiting. He placed a long-handled spoon in her hand.

This time she made no move to do as he demanded.

"What are you doing?" she asked, the spoon dangling from her fingers.

"What does it look like I'm doing? I'm cutting potatoes into uniform pieces. Cut them in different sizes, they cook at different times. It's not rocket science."

"Not that. *This.*" She gestured around the room with the spoon. "Why did you bring me here?"

He glanced up, then wiped his hands on a rag. If she'd thought he might prevaricate, make up some line about how he needed help making lunch, she was wrong.

He walked toward her, took her by the arm, and slowly turned her to face the small crowd of people who'd gathered at the tables.

"What do you see when you look at them?"

"People. Just more people." People who weren't Matt or Cassie or Sarah or Ethan. Jenna had nothing left for strangers.

Lars gave her a hard stare. "Look closer, lady."

"What? What do you want me to say?" she demanded. "Do you want me to feel sorry for them?"

"Sorry? Do they look like they need your pity? Look at them!"

"I'm looking!"

"You're not seeing. Do you see tears? Sadness?"

Unwillingly, Jenna looked to the shy boy who'd hidden behind his mother's leg. He was giggling as an older man played a game with a coin and his nose.

"What is your point?" she whispered.

"My point?" Lars shook his head. "My point is, whatever hell you've been through, chances are someone in this room has been there too."

Rage—complete and all-encompassing—flared inside of her.

"You don't know me. You don't have any idea what I've *been through*," she whispered, the jagged words sawing through his presumptions.

Most people would have backed away from the violence in Jenna's tone. But Lars Jorgensen didn't know when to quit.

"No. I don't know you, and I don't know your story. And you don't know them." He pointed a gnarled, age-spotted finger toward the small crowd. "Tess over there? She nursed her mother through cancer last year. A long, slow, lingering death."

Lars gestured again. "Bill, the man sitting with them? He served nearly ten years for manslaughter after he and his buddy wrecked a car when they were teenagers. They were drunk, and his best friend died. Bill was behind the wheel. He's never been the same."

His words were angry bees buzzing around her.

"Carolyn, the woman in the corner? She has dementia. Her son and his new wife sold the house she's lived in her entire life from underneath her, but she keeps trying to go back home anyway."

"Stop. Stop it." Jenna fought off the images he was throwing at her.

He didn't stop. "My *point* is that these people, they get up every day. Every single day. They get up and they fight back the urge to give in. They go through the motions, and they laugh and they talk and they eat and they sleep, and they *live*."

Jenna shook her head, her eyes squeezed tight. It wasn't the same. It wasn't.

"This isn't living."

Lars dropped his hand from her arm and took a step backward. His eyes shuttered. Instruction time was over.

She'd failed his test, without realizing it was being administered.

"That's a pompous thing to say." Lars went back to throwing potatoes in his soup. "A slap in the face to every person who fights their way through the day."

The vegetables splashed hot liquid onto the stovetop with a hiss.

"May as well tell them they should all just chuck it in too." He set the cutting board back onto the counter with a bang.

"Well, maybe they should!" The savage finality in the statement shocked even Jenna.

She didn't know where the words had come from. She didn't recognize herself anymore. Her chest was heaving, her knuckles white and tense.

The old man grew still. His back was to her, but she saw him take a deep breath, knew he was going to turn and hurl more meaningless words in her direction. She was done being lectured. Words wouldn't change what had happened to her family. They wouldn't change anything at all.

Jenna fled before he had the chance to try, running for a door in the back of the kitchen. She didn't know where it led. Anywhere was better than here, with this man and his accusing eyes.

The blazing sunlight, coupled with the cold, stole what little breath she had left, and Jenna drew in a frantic gasp.

She glanced feverishly around. Nothing was familiar in this hard, strange place. She longed for the wooden box she'd left behind at Lars's cabin. She wanted, *needed*, to touch it, hold it tight to her hollow middle. To place her forehead against the cool, polished grain.

She folded into herself and sank to the concrete steps at her feet. On the stoop that led to the back door of a place where others came to find warmth and sustenance, she rocked back and forth with her head tucked between her knees.

She had no sense of time passing, only the edge she was teetering on.

Jenna didn't hear the crunch of feet in the snow, nor see the girl who stood in front of her, watching with a judgmental intensity.

When the girl spoke, Jenna gave a startled shriek.

"You're the lost one."

Jenna blinked, her mind valiantly attempting to catch up to what she was seeing, this apparition of a woman-child who'd materialized in front of her.

Not an apparition. She pushed the notion away as the girl slowly blew a bubble with her pink gum. Jenna struggled to focus. She could almost forgive herself the slip. The girl was a cobbled-together bundle of contradictions.

Her hair was a dark auburn, done up in the double victory-roll style of the nineteen forties. Her pale-green eyes were thickly lined, coming to points as sharp as her gaze. She wore black-and-white striped leggings and pink snow boots that coordinated with her bubble gum.

The girl's cosmetics couldn't conceal her youth. She was fourteen at most.

Jenna shook her head. "I'm sorry . . . what?"

"The lost one," the girl said again. "The one with nowhere to go."

"How . . . how do you . . . ?"

The girl blew another slow bubble with her gum and gave Jenna an appraising look. The pink sphere expanded, its edges thinning. Jenna knew it was coming, yet the inevitable pop as it burst still made her flinch.

The teen pulled the gum back into her mouth, showing a slight gap between her two front teeth. "You're not crazy, are you?" she asked with a suspicious candor.

"Um . . ." Jenna closed her eyes, shaking her head again. Such a bald question from this strange child.

"I mean, I don't care if you are. Crazy, that is. Different strokes for different folks and all that."

"That's open-minded of you," Jenna said, managing to string together a coherent response at last.

"But the thing is," the girl continued as if Jenna hadn't spoken. "My granddad has had enough crazy in his life. He doesn't need any more from some weird, lost woman."

"Your granddad?"

The teen's eyebrows lifted slowly, a mocking salute. Stupid question. Those brows might be plucked and neat, as opposed to bushy and gray, but there was no possibility this girl wasn't related to Lars Jorgensen.

"Lars is your grandfather," Jenna said tiredly.

"Which is why it matters if you're crazy."

Jenna rubbed one hand along the back of her neck, then took a deep breath and blew it out slowly. "I guess *crazy* is a relative term, isn't it?"

The girl didn't smile, merely continued to point her assessing stare in Jenna's direction. "This isn't a joke," she said.

Jenna looked up and met her eyes. "Who said I was joking?"

The girl's eyes narrowed, and she shifted the weight of the backpack she had slung over one shoulder. "I don't believe you appreciate the gravity of the situation."

"Nice," Cassie whispered, and with a sudden clarity Jenna recognized something in this girl. Not her face—she'd certainly never met the child before—but the essence of her was achingly familiar.

"I have a feeling you're about to elucidate me."

The girl did a double take, then tilted her head in recognition of a rare adult who wasn't going to patronize her.

But she didn't mince her words.

"My grandmother was crazy," she said. "She ran off with their two youngest kids a long time ago."

Jenna sat back and stared, her mouth dropping open against her will.

"They're dead. Everyone knows it," the girl continued, fully aware of the shock her words had caused. She walked up the steps, brushing past Jenna as she went. With one hand on the door leading into the church kitchen, she fired a final volley over her shoulder.

"He's had to live with that . . . well, forever. So, no offense, but if you're going to bring some extra crazy into his life, he's had more than his share already."

"I'm just passing through," Jenna whispered without looking at her.

"That's good. That's very good to hear."

Lars hadn't just been preaching when he spoke of people living in their own hell.

He had firsthand experience.

Jenna heard the heavy door open at her back. Muted sounds escaped—chairs scraping, voices mingling. When the door shut, silence surrounded her once again, but somehow it was heavier than it had been only moments before.

13

Jenna sat for a while longer, fighting the immobility trying to take hold of her limbs and her mind. With effort, she forced herself to rise.

She'd taken control when she'd driven away from everything she knew, and she wouldn't give in again. No matter the detours, she knew her destination.

For now, she had an apology to make.

Jenna turned as the door opened and Lars and his granddaughter emerged.

"You can't be skipping school like this, Hannah," the old man was saying with a scowl.

"You worry too much." The girl planted a kiss on his cheek. "Thanks for the twenty."

"Go on with you. Consider it a bribe. Your time bought and paid for, and I don't want to see you outside that school for the rest of the week."

The girl winked and gave him a grin that showed off her youth, despite the makeup. She skipped down the steps, passing Jenna without a word.

Jenna and Lars watched her go. The spell she'd unknowingly woven held them until she was around the corner and out of sight.

"That girl's going to be the death of me," Lars said. "Too smart for her own good, and full to the brim with trouble."

He shook his head and turned his attention back to Jenna.

"Glad to see you're still here." His blunt exterior was firmly back in place. "Got plenty of dishes to do. If you think you can handle that without drowning yourself in the dishwater."

Jenna clamped her jaw on the retort that sprang up and reminded herself she owed this man an apology.

Eventually, perhaps, she'd be able to force one past her lips. For the moment, the best she could manage was to glare at him in silence as she made her way back into the soup kitchen to help him clear up.

While Jenna stacked and collected trays, she thought about her options.

"I don't suppose I could pay you to give me a ride to a town where I could rent a car?" she asked as she set the dirty trays next to the industrial stainless-steel sink.

There was a pause. Lars didn't answer.

"I know you want me gone. It would solve both our problems."

"You think so?" The old man gave a bark of laughter. "All our problems, poof. Just like that?"

"Look, if you don't want to, just say so. It's fine. I'll ask around at the diner. Somebody will want the extra cash. Or I'll call a taxi to come and pick me up."

She twisted the faucet handle at the sink, letting the basin fill with warm, soapy water. She didn't see the way his brow furrowed as he leaned back against the counter and crossed his arms.

"Nearest cab company comes from fifty miles away."

She focused on the dishes in her hands as she scrubbed. "It's not like I'm saving money for a family vacation."

"And just where are you gonna go?"

"Why do you care?" She tossed the sponge into the soapy water and turned on him.

They stared at each other, neither willing to give in.

"No need to run off like a scared rabbit. I'm not the big bad wolf," he finally said.

"Scared?" she scoffed. "You think I'm scared of you?"

"I think you're scared of everything, Jenna Shaw," he said. "I think you're scared of living, or you wouldn't be in such a big damn hurry to stop doing it."

Suds dripped from the tips of her fingers, where her bandage was coming loose, and puddled on the tiles at her feet.

"More than that, you're scared to take the time to heal from your hurt. Because then you just might realize what a fool you are."

He was wrong. He had to be wrong.

"Give Owen a chance to get your van running. If you're so sure you're right, a few days shouldn't make a difference."

"I'm not going to change my mind," Jenna whispered.

He stared at her like he knew exactly who she was trying to convince.

"A few days. If Owen doesn't get you on the road again in a few days, I'll take you. If you're in that big of a hurry."

She searched his eyes. She searched her parched heart.

"Of course," he continued, turning away to wipe down the counter, "if you can't handle spending another night in the spare room, I completely understand. I have that effect on women."

"What effect?" Jenna asked in a tired voice. "Fear?"

"Yup," he said. "Too much time in my company and women start throwing themselves at my feet, declaring their undying affection. It's a burden I've borne all my life."

A dry choke of laughter fell from her lips. "I think my affections are safe."

"Okay." He shrugged. "But that's what they all say, just so you know."

Jenna went back to the waiting dishes. She hadn't agreed to his request, had she?

"You didn't disagree," Cassie pointed out.

Jenna's brow creased. Cassie's words did nothing to quiet her troubled thoughts.

14

Jenna closed the dresser drawer after running her hand across the smooth surface of the box. Familiar melancholy clouds gathered. She stood and forced herself to walk out of Lars's spare room.

She quickened her steps past the bed she longed to crawl into and hide from the world.

The cabin was sparse. Efficient, she supposed, for an old man living alone. The furnishings, though clean, were worn, their style dating them to many decades before.

Her fingers trailed down the kitchen counter as she listened to the hum of the aged refrigerator, the only sound in the place other than that of her own soft steps. Lars had disappeared somewhere upon their return. To the garage maybe, or the woods for a walk by the lake. Jenna doubted he'd gone far.

"Can I trust you alone?" he'd asked before stepping out the front door.

"I guess we'll find out," she replied.

She was drawn to the bookshelf on the far side of the living room, past the overstuffed recliner.

"You can't judge a book by its cover," Cassie said.

"But you can judge a person by their books," Jenna continued, finishing her daughter's thought.

One of the few things she and Cass agreed on.

Jenna remembered the night Cassie had come home from a first date with a boy she'd had a crush on for months. Jenna went on alert at the way Cassie tossed her purse on the floor and flopped onto the couch where she and Matt were watching a movie, pretending they hadn't been waiting up.

"You're home early," Matt said. He sounded disinterested, but Jenna knew better.

Cass had only sighed and rolled her eyes.

Jenna and Matt shared a look over the bowl of popcorn. She gave him a small shake of her head.

By the time the credits rolled, Cassie had fallen asleep on the couch. At sixteen, she was long past the days when Jenna could have scooped her into her arms and carried her up the stairs to her bed, so she pulled a throw over her daughter's body and lifted her head ever so slightly to place a pillow beneath it.

Cassie's eyes had fluttered open, and Jenna knelt beside her, brushing the hair back from her daughter's face. She was struck by how little time she had left with her.

"You okay?"

"Mm-hmm," Cass murmured, giving her mother a sleepy smile and closing her eyes again.

That would have to do. Jenna lightly kissed her daughter's cheek and rose to go to bed herself.

"Mom?"

Jenna, her hand on the doorjamb, turned back. "Hmm?"

"He doesn't read. I mean, he knows *how*, but he said he doesn't see the point."

"Ah." Understanding and an overwhelming surge of love washed over her. She struggled to hold back a smile. "That's too bad."

"Too bad for him," Cassie mumbled, rolling over.

Yes. Jenna studied her child's silhouette, a girl growing into a woman in front of her eyes. *Too bad for him.*

The boy had been at the memorial service, looking ill at ease in a suit and tie as he stood awkwardly next to his mother.

Jenna set the memories aside but made no attempt to stop herself from snooping around Lars's bookshelves.

There were a fair number of thrillers, and a few classics sprinkled among the latest chart-toppers. Children's books, well thumbed, sat shoulder to shoulder with nonfiction texts sharing a common theme. Mental illness.

The last gave her pause.

Set in various places along the bookshelves, with no apparent rhyme or reason to their pattern, the books gave way to recesses where framed photographs were propped.

Jenna scanned the images. She stalled on a photograph of three children together, then purposefully moved on, refusing the urge to look more closely at the faces of Lars Jorgensen's dead children.

Her gaze fell on a final image. A wedding portrait.

She reached out and lifted the frame from its resting place. A much younger Lars looked into the eyes of a woman in a flowing white dress and lace veil.

Even with many years separating Jenna from this woman, she felt the happiness radiating from her. The corners of Jenna's mouth lifted in a sad salute. To the hope. To the unknown future that waited, unfurled, before this ill-fated couple.

With a shake of her head, Jenna came back to the present. Whatever had derailed this life, it had nothing to do with her.

She set the photograph firmly back in place and tipped out the spine of a recent best seller, one she'd never read.

Jenna didn't hold much hope that the novel would quiet her mind for long, but somehow, with the comforting softness of the recliner welcoming her as an old friend, the rhythm of her heart smoothed, at least for a little while. The minutes slipped through her fingers like water.

When the rattle of the doorknob pulled her from the story, she glanced up, bewildered by the changing light streaming from the windows.

As he closed the door behind him, Lars lifted a brow in her direction.

"Make yourself at home," he said as he walked toward the kitchen.

Jenna placed the book upon the side table next to the armchair, rose, and walked across the room. She wiped her palms against the legs of her jeans and stood on the opposite side of the counter from him. He was pulling ingredients from the cupboards.

"Can I give you a hand?" she asked.

He glanced up at her. "Look in that drawer and get a big pot out to start some water boiling for the pasta."

Jenna, fighting awkwardness, did as he asked.

The two of them fell into a stilted rhythm as they dodged each other in the small space, performing an ungainly dance in near silence.

When they were done, it was a simple meal. Salad, spaghetti, and pull-apart bread from the old gas oven. A simple meal shared by two strangers with little in common, save an intimate understanding of loss.

"I, um . . ." She sounded weak, even to her own ears. Lars met her eyes over the kitchen table. She cleared her throat and started again.

"I owe you an apology. I shouldn't have said what I did, at the church."

Lars was silent for a beat, studying her.

"I don't believe in debts," he said finally. "You said what you said. Landed on no ears but my own, and I've heard worse. You don't owe me a thing."

Lars turned his attention back to his meal.

"Hannah told me about your family," she blurted out. Heat started to climb up her neck. It was too late to reel the words back. "About your wife and your two youngest kids."

Lars's expression didn't change, but there was a slight hitch, a tightening around his eyes.

"I'm sorry," she went on, even as she willed herself to stop speaking. "I know how pointless those words are. Believe me. And I know it's none of my business. I just wanted to tell you I'm sorry. Sorry about the assumptions I made, about the things I said. I . . . I'm sorry that your wife and children died."

Lars set down his fork and leaned back in his chair. The heat at Jenna's neck had spread upward and rested on her cheeks. She looked down at her plate.

"Well, you got two out of three, Jenna Shaw." His words were quiet, measured. "Saying sorry never did anybody a bit of good, so far as I can see. But I don't suppose it ever did any harm either."

Jenna raised her head. There was pain in the old man's features. But she saw it was a pain that no longer crushed him, the way her own did. This man's pain had grown old with him.

"And you're right," he went on. "It's none of your business."

The wooden legs of his chair scraped across the floor as he pushed it back and rose. He gathered their plates.

"As for my wife, you're mistaken." He carried their dishes to the sink. His back was to her, but she heard him perfectly well when he spoke again.

"Audrey's very much alive."

15

When Jenna woke the next morning, Lars was gone.

It was Owen she found seated at the kitchen table, reading a newspaper and sipping coffee. Her steps faltered when he raised his brows at the pajamas she was wearing. They belonged to Lars, old-man pajamas that lacked only a pair of worn slippers and a nightcap to complete the look Cassie had called "Ebenezer-chic" the previous night.

Jenna had fallen asleep with thoughts of her own ghosts—past, present, and future.

"It's not what it looks like," she told Owen.

The shrug of his shoulders only embarrassed her more.

"Dad asked me to drop by, see if you wanted a ride into town this morning." He folded the paper and picked up his cup.

An overwhelming urge to leave this place and these too-familiar men washed over her anew.

What was she doing here?

"Come on," Owen said. "You don't want to hang around the house all day, do you? Get dressed and you can enjoy all the excitement of Raven, Minnesota, while I check on the part for your van. Might be I can get you back on the road today after all."

Jenna sighed, but the thought raised her mood some, and she drank her coffee quickly while she retrieved her wrinkled clothing from the small laundry room Lars had suggested she make use of the night before.

"You're starting to get ripe, missy." He'd deposited the clean, folded pajamas and a bar of soap into her arms. "Take a shower. Wash your clothes."

She had, all the while feeling like she'd tumbled down Alice's rabbit hole.

"Only to find the Mad Hatter's retired and living off a pension while hair grows in his ears," Cassie added.

But the muted, satisfying sensation of being clean again had felt as good as anything had since the day she'd received the call. It was little enough, but it was something.

"I hear you met Hannah yesterday," Owen said during the drive back into Raven.

Jenna nodded.

"You'll have to forgive her," he said. "She's walking a line right now between who she is and who she wants to be, and it's exhausting. At least for me."

Jenna recognized a father's worry, and her throat tightened.

At one time, she might have tried to minimize his fears. Now she knew the truth. He was right to be afraid.

"She seems like a great kid," Jenna said.

He gave her a small smile. "Her mother, Valerie, she's not around much. For the best, probably." His words held no malice. "But Hannah and Dad are close. He spoils her. We both do, I guess, in different ways."

"She's very protective of him," Jenna said. "She told me about your mother. About your younger siblings."

Owen turned his face to her, his astonishment evident.

"Not specifics," Jenna hastened to add. "Just enough for me to put my foot in it with Lars."

"Dad talked to you about that?"

Jenna shook her head. "No, not really. I'm sorry, I shouldn't have brought it up. I just . . . I think I might have upset him."

Owen's features were inscrutable as he looked back at the road.

"You don't have to talk about it," Jenna said. "I don't want to pry." She turned away.

It was a hollow truth to accept. Jenna had been a journalist not so long ago, in another life, but she'd found a different perspective after being on the other side of tragedy.

The remainder of the drive passed in silence. When Owen parked the truck at the garage, Jenna reached for the door handle and turned to thank him for the lift, but Owen made no move to exit the vehicle.

"It was hard on Dad," he said suddenly. "Hard on both of us, but especially him."

"Owen," Jenna began. "You don't have to—"

He continued as if she hadn't spoken. "All the newspapers, scrambling to cover the story. People everywhere, so many people." He was lost in his memories. "And then, after so much fuss, no resolution. No answers. Eventually, all those people began to fade away. Until the only ones left were Dad and me. Alone, trying to figure out how to live with it."

Jenna's mouth opened, and she heard herself asking the question she'd told herself she didn't want to know. Too late, it hung there between them, floating like a soap bubble about to burst.

"And your mother?"

Owen took a deep breath and met her gaze. "My mother," he said with a sigh. "My mother is in the same place she's been for the last twenty-nine years. The Minnesota State Secure Psychiatric Hospital."

16

The secondhand coat was puffy and garish, a bright hunter's orange.

"That is one ugly coat," Cassie said as Jenna crossed the street to Owen's garage.

"Ugly and warm," Jenna replied under her breath.

She carried her purchases from the secondhand shop, along with the small bag from the general store where she'd bought a toothbrush and a few other basics.

Owen was busy with a customer but spotted her coming through the doorway.

She held up the coat he'd loaned her with a questioning look. His smile was distracted as he tilted his chin toward a coatrack next to the entrance.

"Yes, Mrs. Harvey," he said to the white-haired woman in front of him. "We can change the oil and give it a look-see while it's here for new tires."

"I only want you to use that specific brand." The elderly woman spoke in the overloud voice people sometimes use when they can't hear themselves well.

Jenna waved in Owen's direction without meeting his eyes and made her way back onto the street.

She sucked in what she hoped would be a cleansing breath and pulled up the zipper of the traffic-cone-orange coat.

With the few items on her to-do list crossed off, Jenna forced one foot in front of the other with the halfhearted idea she'd explore the town.

The silence at least gave her a chance to sort through and unravel the threads crisscrossing her mind, tangling together to form a jumbled knot of confusion.

Jenna's feet carried her places her mind paid no attention to while she found and worried at a new thread in the mix.

College. A long time ago. She'd had a roommate who was a good person. Not someone who did things only to put on a résumé, like so many others—like Jenna herself, if she was honest—but a genuinely good person.

Iris was her name.

Iris had talked Jenna into lending a hand at the campus crisis center where she volunteered three nights a week.

"I don't think I'll be good at that," Jenna had demurred. "What do I say?"

"You don't have to fix anything. You just have to be willing to connect," Iris had said. "It's the connection that makes the difference."

Jenna had left the crisis center after her one and only shift knowing she was out of her depth. She'd made excuses when Iris asked if she'd like to volunteer again. At some point, the girl had stopped asking. The next semester, Jenna quietly applied for a change of dorm rooms and a new roommate.

Now, though, Jenna thought she understood what Iris had been trying to tell her. Connections were what kept people tied to the world. Without connections, there was nothing left to stop them from simply floating away.

Something as simple as a stranger on the other end of the line willing to listen. Or a crotchety old man who believed he knew best.

Connections.

That was what she was forming here. And that was exactly what she didn't want to do.

The only connections that mattered were gone, severed completely and irrevocably. If she was going to find the strength to do what she was planning, Jenna needed to ensure it remained that way.

"Force your protagonist to make a choice," Cassie said. "Then follow through on it, see where it leads. A passive protagonist is the worst."

"I've made my choice," Jenna said.

"Then what are you doing here?"

A ripple of shock coursed through her at Cassie's admonishment that she hadn't yet managed to kill herself.

"Not here in the metaphysical sense, dummy," Cassie said. "*Here,* here. Open your eyes."

Jenna focused on the world around her.

She couldn't have known where the Raven Public Library was located. And yet, there she was, standing on the sidewalk just outside the entrance.

"A coincidence," Jenna said.

"Mm-hmm." Her daughter sounded unconvinced.

17

Research, for Jenna, was second nature.

What she hadn't expected was to be stonewalled by a pleasant-faced librarian as soon as she'd mentioned what she was looking for.

"You a reporter, hon?" The woman's voice dripped with honeyed sweetness but couldn't hide the underlying mistrust.

"I was, once upon a time," Jenna answered truthfully. "Not anymore."

"A writer, then?" the woman prodded. "One of those true-crime authors looking to cash in on an old story?"

"No." Jenna tried to swallow her defensiveness.

"That's good." The librarian gave her a cold stare.

"I'm just passing the time," Jenna said.

The woman's lips pursed. The set of her hand upon her hip told Jenna she didn't believe her.

"I'm not a reporter," Jenna said. "I'm not a true-crime writer. I'd simply like to read about the case."

She should have stopped there.

"If that's okay with you," she couldn't help adding.

"You need to work on your people skills," Cassie said after the librarian grudgingly led Jenna to an ancient microfiche machine, delivered two boxes of film, then walked stiffly away without saying a word.

"These are the wrong ones," Jenna said under her breath as she examined the labels on the film boxes.

"Guess you shouldn't have pissed her off."

"Language," Jenna admonished. She rose and walked back to the checkout counter.

"The years you requested have been misplaced, dear," the librarian told her. "The year prior and the year after are the best I can do."

The woman's shoulders were squared and she had a dare in her eyes.

"What did I tell you?" Cassie said.

Jenna wouldn't be put off so easily. "The computers?" she asked, gesturing to the bank of three monitors lined up along the wall. "I assume they're open to the public?"

The librarian gave a chilly nod.

"Thank you," Jenna replied.

She'd taken two steps in that direction when the woman spoke again.

"I should mention, though . . . the internet is down today."

Jenna stopped and turned back to the woman, who'd crossed her arms, waiting for Jenna's next move.

Of course it is.

Jenna returned to the counter, placed her hands flat upon the sides of the boxes of film she'd left there, and pulled them toward her. "Thank you for your *help*," she said, leaning on the last word.

She received nothing but a thin smile in return.

Out of sheer stubbornness, Jenna loaded the film from the later year into the microfiche.

"Well, that was fun," Cassie said. "What exactly are you hoping to find?"

"Shush," Jenna murmured. She didn't have an answer for that.

Hours passed, unmarked and unnoticed. She paid no more attention to the minutes ticking past than she did to the librarian who sent irritated glances in her direction from time to time, even as she whispered into a telephone from the glass-walled office behind the desk.

Jenna prodded and pushed at the scant information available. She began looking for rocks to peer beneath that had remained undisturbed for a very long time.

She found what she was searching for buried behind local sports team victories and bake sale advertisements. A single follow-up article.

Jenna leaned forward in the uncomfortably hard plastic chair and scanned the article. It was light on facts, leaving behind as many questions as it answered. The faces of two children who'd vanished from the surface of the earth stared back at her.

This is a mistake. What are you playing at?

With a growing sense of dread, Jenna reminded herself she couldn't drown in the flood of someone else's disaster.

Not unless she allowed herself to be swept away.

"You've never been a good liar," Cassie said.

Jenna's hand shot out, flicking the switch on the side of the machine. The ghost children vanished, and she could breathe again.

If only she could erase the image from her mind as easily.

18

Lars was parked along the street waiting for her when Jenna came out the door of the library. She did a double take at the sight of his truck, then turned in his direction, her head down against the wind, which had started to pick up.

When she opened the passenger door and climbed in, her face was guarded. Troubled.

He knew what she'd been doing. Eleanor Lutz, the librarian, had called him straightaway.

"She says she used to be a reporter, but claims she's not working on a story. I don't know, Lars," Eleanor had said. He could picture her face on the other end of the call, full of typical nervous worry. "There's something about her. I can't put my finger on it, but I don't like her."

"You didn't like me much the first time we met either," Lars had reminded her.

"You were six years old, and you were a jerk," Eleanor said. Lars couldn't deny that. At six, he hadn't cared about anything except hockey, fishing, and baseball. Impressing a girl who always had her nose in a book hadn't been on his list of priorities.

"It's fine, Eleanor. I know who she is. She's staying at my place. Temporarily," he added, trying to set the woman's mind at ease.

"Then what is she doing sneaking around behind your back, digging up all this old stuff again?" Eleanor demanded.

But Lars understood why Jenna didn't ask her questions directly, though he'd never be able to explain it to Eleanor.

With enough time and distance, even the worst wounds could appear healed, but Lars knew better. It seemed Jenna Shaw did too.

"Owen says he might have made some progress tracking down the part for your van," Lars said to Jenna as the truck trundled down the road.

She didn't reply.

"Forecast is calling for more snow." He turned the truck toward home.

She didn't ask where they were going. She didn't ask how he'd known he could find her at the library, nor mention what she might have learned.

The air around them bristled with unspoken things.

When he pulled into his driveway and turned off the truck, Jenna made no move to get out.

She opened her mouth to speak, then closed it again, looking away.

He waited.

The two of them stared out at the ice he'd pulled her back from, and Lars wondered if he was destined to do it again.

Finally, she turned and spoke.

"My family . . ." She stopped, but he didn't interrupt. He could give her little except his silence while she gathered her thoughts.

"A plane crash." Her gaze was drawn again toward the frozen lake. "A plane crash took them all."

She was rubbing the palm of one hand with the thumb of the other, massaging the hollow there.

"They were coming back from Alaska. It was a small plane, one that was supposed to take them to the airport in Anchorage. A mechanical malfunction. No one knows why. My husband, my two amazing daughters, so different from each other. And my son. My baby."

One corner of her mouth lifted sadly. Her voice trembled as it navigated the high wire she was forcing it across.

"Matt used to tease me that Ethan was my favorite."

Lars braced himself for tears, but he underestimated her.

"In some ways, maybe he was right. Ethan was six. He loved me in a way the girls didn't. Not better or worse, just his own way. No one on earth would ever love me that way again. He was my last. He made us whole. I thought we were unbreakable."

The harsh, haunted sound that came from her throat made the hair on the back of his neck stand up.

She turned to look at him, and the nearness of her, the raw, unvarnished pain that radiated from her, pinned him to his seat. He couldn't have spoken nor moved a muscle even if he'd wanted to.

"But nothing's unbreakable, is it?" Jenna whispered.

Lars had no words to give her.

She reached for the handle on the passenger door and stepped out into the cold, hunching against the wind in her bright-orange coat as she made her way toward his home. He let out a pent-up breath as he watched her go.

He was a fool.

Only a fool would believe himself capable of helping this woman.

19

The previous summer had steamrolled by, never hinting it would be their last. School was scheduled to start in a few weeks, bringing back the sense that the chaos was controlled, scheduled, delineated by report cards and holiday breaks, if only they could make it through summer.

The days had gone blindingly quick, leaving Jenna, once night had fallen, to search for her own pulse. Was she still in there, somewhere? A real and whole person, with needs and dreams and an identity that didn't begin and end with the word *mom*?

She was, always. But sometimes the pulse was faint. On those nights, she'd be the first to reach for Matt in the dark, a gentle hand on his. With his touch he would help her remember.

When John had called, insisting they were long overdue for a visit, Matt read the resignation in his wife's face.

"We don't have to go," he said.

"It's his fortieth birthday, and the kids haven't seen their cousins in such a long time. He's your brother. We should go."

"But you hate the cold."

She tried to smile. The cold didn't matter so much as the *effort* of it all.

Effort was in short supply by the end of the summer.

She dug down and found the resolve to give Matt a genuine smile, if not a large one.

"It's okay." She took a deep breath at Matt's dubious expression and exhaled slowly from her mouth. "The kids will love Alaska, and we haven't seen them since they moved. It'll be fun."

He hugged her tightly, recognizing the feat of determination for what it was.

"I love you," he whispered.

"Love you back."

Two days later, they met for a rare lunch alone.

"I've been thinking. Why don't I take the kids to Alaska on my own? You could stay and have a break. Get a head start on that book before school starts?"

"What? No. I couldn't do that." She shook her head. "What would your family think? Besides, traveling with three kids? Alone? That sounds awful."

She dismissed the idea. It was a sweet offer, but she couldn't do that to him.

"I'm serious, Jen. They're not babies anymore, and Cassie can help."

He was sincere. He'd do this, give her this, and not think twice about it.

"What about John and Melanie?"

"What about them? They have five kids, Jenna. John went on a whiskey tour of Scotland a few months ago with some old college friends, and Melanie takes a vacation every summer with her sister, religiously. If anyone will understand the need for a break, they will."

A flicker of hope flared. An entire week. Alone. Nothing to worry about but the dog and the blinking cursor in front of her.

"No." She stamped at the little fire before it could catch and burn. "I can't do that. It's his fortieth birthday. And the kids. I can't just . . ."

Matt raised an eyebrow at her. "What? Leave them in the bumbling care of their father?"

"That's not what I mean."

He smiled and wiped his mouth on a napkin, then sat back and looked at his watch. "Listen, you don't have to decide right now. Sleep on it a few days. I'll hold off buying the plane tickets, but think about it. Okay?"

She tugged her earlobe but didn't say no. He winked and gave her a kiss on the cheek.

Jenna did think about it. It was hard not to. Over the next week, the embers of that little flame smoldered, never quite catching nor completely burning out.

It was the doll that sent the flames shooting up. The doll Sarah didn't even play with anymore. Ethan conscripted the little thing with her blonde curls and empty smile to sacrifice to the velociraptors.

"That's mine!" shrieked her normally levelheaded middle child, tromping through her brother's menagerie of dinosaurs and army men to rescue her doll. "You can't take my stuff!"

"No!" Ethan cried. "The raptors aren't really gonna eat her, Sarah! It's just pretend!"

The two of them tugged on either end of the poor doll, screaming at each other.

"Stop it already! I'm on the phone!" Cassie shouted before slamming her bedroom door.

With a final, great tug, Sarah yanked her kidnapped possession from her brother's grasp, and he fell backward onto the plastic *Tyrannosaurus rex* he'd gotten for his fifth birthday.

With an ominous crunch, the cries escalated from mad to hurt.

The final casualties included one ripped doll's dress, a tyrannosaurus leg that needed to be reattached, and a purpling bruise on a little boy's back.

"Did you really mean it? About taking the kids to Alaska," Jenna asked Matt that night. She knew the answer but needed the reassurance.

He smiled. "I mean everything I say."

Shutting the door that final day, after her family was packed and prepared and hugged and kissed and loved and on their way, was a moment she savored.

The relief was a real, physical thing. A palpable sensation of muscles relaxing in ripples and waves, beginning at her fingertips and rolling down her body.

She smiled at Beckett as the golden retriever watched her. She bent down and hugged him, rubbing her hands up and down his soft coat.

"Beckett, do you hear that?" she whispered.

He licked her cheek.

"That's silence, Beck. How do you like that, huh? It's been a while, buddy."

He padded off to ease himself into his favorite spot at the corner of the couch with a sigh that was strangely human.

Jenna stood and stretched. She took a deep breath, pulling the peace around her into her lungs like incense. Serenity smoothed her features, leaving a Madonna's faint smile on her face.

One week later, the call came. She would never take a breath as full and weightless again.

20

Lars went through the motions of putting together a patchwork meal. The house, which had held only himself since Owen had moved out so many years back, was quiet. For once, too quiet.

Jenna had gone to the spare room and shut the door. There was no crying, no wailing at the fate that had fallen on her shoulders, no tossing breakable things at the walls.

He almost wished she would.

Instead, he prepared food she wouldn't feel like eating. He didn't much either.

He knocked on her door.

"Dinner. If you want some," he mumbled from the hallway.

There was no reply. He stood there for a moment, worry niggling at him. Should he check on her, or give her some privacy? *Woman's earned a bit of privacy.* He remembered the sound of her laughter just moments before she reached the thinnest part of the ice.

He raised his hand to knock again, when he heard her muffled reply.

"Thank you, but I'm not very hungry."

Lars stared at the closed door for a beat, then placed his hands into his pockets and shuffled back to the kitchen.

For a while, he pushed cold pasta salad around on his plate before he sat back and set his fork down, giving up.

Alone in the room, he gave in to the memories tugging at him. An indulgence he rarely allowed these days.

It was Owen who'd pulled him back from the brink of losing himself for good. Only Owen, and nothing more.

He picked his head up one day and looked, really looked, at his son. The son Audrey left behind.

Owen was as lost as his sister and baby brother. He needed his father.

So he did the only thing left to do. He gave in to time. He began to pack the past away, to accept there were things beyond his control, things he might never know. He forced himself to be present for his son.

It was the most difficult thing he'd ever done.

He'd never shaken the guilt of the choices he'd made. He still begged his missing children for forgiveness each and every night before he closed his eyes.

Now he was an old man. Owen was grown, with a daughter of his own. Time had done its work. Not without pain. But Lars had learned to carry the pain in his heart instead of walking in its footsteps.

Now the doctor said his heart was diseased. That it was only a matter of time.

He wasn't surprised. The weight of that kind of pain shoved into such a small space was destined to take a toll.

It was a payment long overdue.

Lars stared out the windows at one more winter coming in, whether they were ready for it or not.

Jenna had no Owen. She had no one at all. There was only him.

An old man with a broken heart.

21

When Jenna woke the following morning, she was alone in the tiny house. But her host had left a note. No opening salutation, only Lars Jorgensen getting straight to the point.

> *If you want to know what happened to my wife and kids, you'll find more in these boxes than you'll ever find at the public library. I should warn you, there are no answers here, only more questions.*

Jenna stared at the man's scratchy handwriting, then glanced at the two battered file boxes sitting on the kitchen table, their lids fitted poorly over the bulging contents.

No answers, he'd written. *Only more questions.*

But did she care enough to find out what those questions were?

Whatever interest she'd briefly found in the history of the Jorgensen family yesterday had been a fleeting impulse. Inconsequential. And Lars's dusty, faded tragedy was inconsequential too. Or so she told herself.

Jenna didn't have emotions to spare for other people's pain.

"So losing us has somehow transformed you into a different person entirely?" Cassie asked, but Jenna refused to be baited.

The note slipped from her fingers and wafted to the tabletop. She rose and walked toward the phone, doing her best to ignore the boxes at her back.

"Jorgensen's Garage," said the voice on the end of the line.

"Owen, this is Jenna Shaw."

"Jenna, I'm glad you called, but I'm afraid I don't have good news."

Jenna let out a sigh.

"Owen, I could really use some right now."

"I know, I know. But the weather's causing shipping delays. It's really coming down out there. I just don't see how that part's going to make it in today."

She glanced behind her at the windows. In another time, another life, she might have appreciated the glory of the white washing down upon the world outside.

"Okay, Owen. Thank you." She hung up before he could apologize again.

Jenna's arms fell to her sides and she slowly pivoted, taking in the empty house around her.

It was warm, secure, safe. Empty, but safe. And all she wanted to do was get out. She wanted to run from this place, from both the abrupt, unexpected kindness, and the ancient hurt she'd stumbled upon here.

"Oh, stop being dramatic," Cassie said. "Go read your book or make a cup of tea or make some snow angels or something. You don't have to look in the boxes. No one's forcing you if you don't want to."

Jenna took a deep breath. With determined steps, she walked past the boxes on the table without a glance in their direction.

Settling into Lars's recliner, Jenna folded her legs beneath her and opened the book she'd left on the side table. She found the place she'd bookmarked and tried to lose herself again in the thriller as it unfolded.

She managed to get several paragraphs in before Cassie whispered, "But you know you want to."

Jenna forced herself to focus on the page in front of her.

She angled her back to the boxes, blocking them from view, as if doing so would somehow block them from her thoughts. She persisted even as the character of the girl in the novel took on the image of the dark-haired daughter of Lars and Audrey Jorgensen.

Jenna lost her place and traced back to the beginning of the page she'd reread twice already. Finally, her eyes fluttered closed and she hung her head with a sigh.

"As impressive as your massive bout of denial has been," Cassie said, "are you ready to face it now?"

"What do you want from me, Cassie?" Jenna asked the empty house.

There was no answer at first. Jenna's gaze landed on the boxes lined up side by side, waiting patiently.

"Nothing you can't afford to give," came the reply at last.

22

The bones of the story Jenna had glimpsed at the library were laid out in front of her. The boxes contained brittle yellowed clippings of articles she'd been hoping to find the previous day.

Twenty-nine years before, in the summer of 1988, Audrey Jorgensen, wife and mother of three, disappeared one sunny afternoon. Also missing were her two youngest children, Francine and William Jorgensen. Francie, as she was called by her parents, was four years old. Her baby brother, Will, only eighteen months.

It was presumed Audrey had taken the children. A natural assumption. Yet, three days later, a woman who turned out to be Audrey was found wandering along a street in a small town in Iowa. She was dirty and disheveled. She had no shoes on her feet.

She had no children with her.

Reports from eyewitnesses claimed Audrey was incoherent, that she rambled and spoke nonsense. But when questioned about the whereabouts of her children, she had nothing to say.

Nothing at all.

Reporters fed upon the sensationalist story until they'd wrung from it every drop of blood to be had. Neighbors were interviewed, old acquaintances, any and all witnesses in the Iowa town where Audrey was found.

In the end, though there were plenty of words printed, the ink beneath the various bylines contained nothing more than speculation, each scenario as unlikely as the next.

Could there have been an accident that affected Audrey Jorgensen's memory? Reporters dug into her marriage to Lars. Was she perhaps running from him, secreting her children away from an abusive husband?

There was no indication that was the case.

Some intrepid soul suggested the most damning of possibilities. Had Audrey Jorgensen done the unthinkable?

The authorities and the family were at a loss. Leads were followed that went nowhere. Tips were run down and eliminated. There was no map, no signpost to show which way to look next. There was nothing except an unstable woman who either couldn't or wouldn't say.

Everyone had a theory, and the public waited with bated breath to see which would prove right.

They were in for a very long wait.

The press circled the Jorgensen family, what was left of it, feeding off the catastrophe. But when no additional facts came to light, they inevitably moved on to other calamities.

Interest revived, for a time, a few months later when Audrey was charged with child endangerment, but hope that answers—or at the very least, an interesting spectacle—would be provided in court was soon dampened.

Audrey Jorgensen was found incompetent to stand trial. She was remanded to the Minnesota State Secure Psychiatric Hospital until such a time as she was deemed of reasonably sound mind to do so. A day which never came.

And that, as they say, was that.

Only it wasn't. Not for Lars.

The bulging boxes were a testament to his unwillingness to let it go. They were filled with every scrap of information Jenna imagined he'd ever collected regarding what had happened to fracture his family.

There were maps marking places witnesses had come forward claiming they'd seen either Audrey or the children during those missing three days. There were transcripts from court hearings, notes written in Lars's hand about possible routes Audrey could have taken, logs of conversations with people he'd spoken to directly.

There were bus schedules with certain departures circled in red. Photographs of people leaving small tokens and flowers at a makeshift memorial site Jenna recognized as the driveway to this very house. Close-ups of individuals, mostly men. Notes on Lars's search to discover the identity of any he didn't recognize, a desperate attempt to link any of them to his wife.

Lars had spoken with Audrey's friends, with her extended family. As far as Jenna could tell, he'd spoken with every person who had even the vaguest, most tangential link to what might have happened that day.

Lars was a meticulous record keeper. Each note was dated in his scrawling penmanship. His search went on for years. It was thorough, comprehensive, fully documented, and well organized. In the end, it was useless.

Then the monthly reports from a private investigative firm began.

But throwing money at the problem yielded nothing more. In time, the monthly reports gave way to quarterly ones, then yearly.

No additional facts or leads have been found to pursue, came the typed reports, destined to be filed away, one behind the other.

The most recent was dated less than a year ago.

Jenna could hardly comprehend what he must have been going through.

What he must still be going through.

She sat back and rubbed the heels of her palms against her eyes.

The small part of her that had once been a reporter clamored for more. It was a hell of a story. The rest of her knew this wasn't a story at all. It was just hell.

Unable to help herself, yet dreading what she'd find, Jenna opened the lid to the second box. She'd been right to hesitate. Instead of pages filled with hand- and typewritten notes and reports, she found a different sort of record.

The second box held photo albums Jenna dared not touch. She couldn't bear to look at the faces of the children who were destined to disappear into the fog of the unknown. Her fingers moved past those, where she found mementos, keepsakes. A baby-blue rattle with marks along the edge where it had been chewed. A Christmas ornament with a footprint pressed into clay, dried and tied with a red ribbon. A christening gown, the white lace faded to yellow but wrapped in tissue all the same. A tiny pair of leather baby shoes, stiff with age.

Jenna lifted a small tin, no larger than a half dollar. There was a tiny picture of a mallard duck on it. She removed the lid and caught her breath when she saw what was inside.

A fine, silky lock of hair curled around the edges, twisting and turning back upon itself.

Jenna's hands trembled as she put the lid back on and placed the tin carefully into the box with the other scraps of memory.

She was reaching for the cardboard covering to shut the box and its heartbreaking contents away when she noticed something she'd overlooked. Tucked between the photo albums was a spiral-bound notebook.

Her hand stalled over the notebook, but it was too late for second thoughts.

Jenna pulled it from the box and thumbed through the pages, by now familiar with Lars's handwriting. The book was thick and heavy, its pages dog-eared from use. It appeared to be some sort of journal or diary, each entry dated and separated by a single blank line.

Jenna opened the notebook to one of the middle pages and began to read.

November 16, 1990
 Audrey recognized me today. A miracle, considering the amount of drugs they have her on. Spoke with Nurse Bennington about reducing the dosage, but without the Thorazine she gets agitated, and they're afraid she'll try to hurt herself again. Asked her about Francie and Will. I got the same blank stare.

Jenna flipped the pages, skimming the contents as she went. Many of the entries were short, merely a date followed by the words, *Audrey silent today. Asked her about Francie and Will. Nothing.*

Years upon years, Lars had visited his wife, logging each visit in his own hand. Years upon years, he asked the same question. Always, it seemed, he got the same answer. None at all.

Jenna pushed the chair back from the table. The legs scraped the floor, echoing through the cocoon-like state she found herself in, breaking it apart at the seams. She stood and moved to the kitchen, grasping for the mundane to pull her back from the mess in her mind.

Coffee. A shower. A change of clothes. Jenna deliberately laid out a list, hoping to separate from a past that wasn't hers. A past that felt like a groping hand grasping her about the ankle all the same.

"That's it, then?" Cassie asked.

"Well, what do you want me to do about it, Cass?" Jenna measured grounds into the filter for the coffee pot that was as old as everything else in the house.

Had Audrey Jorgensen chosen the appliance herself? Jenna turned back from that line of thinking. It didn't matter. A coffee pot didn't hold Audrey's secrets.

"But something does," Cassie said. "Something, somewhere is the key. And you're not even going to bother to look for it?"

Jenna took an empty cup from the cupboard and set it on the counter harder than she meant to. The emotions she had brushed against while sifting through the contents of those boxes had left her raw and aching.

"Why, Cass? Why would I do that? I've got nothing to give this man! He's a stranger with a sad story, and I'm full up with sad stories."

Jenna put her hands over her eyes and turned her back to the counter. It made no difference. Cassie wasn't standing in front of her, a living, breathing person she could turn her back on. Cassie was her constant, her only, the one thing she couldn't turn off or turn down or turn away from.

And she was relentless.

"You're wallowing. You're so full of guilt and self-pity that you're using us as an excuse to give up and die!"

"So what if I am?" Jenna demanded. "I *am* guilty! I should have been on that plane, but I was relieved, Cass! I was *glad* you were gone! *I should have been with you!*"

Tears were boiling just beneath the surface, struggling to break through and have their way. Her breath was coming faster, her heart beating an erratic, staccato rhythm.

"And what would that have changed?" Cassie asked softly.

Jenna covered her mouth with one hand, struggling to hold back the sobs.

Nothing, she thought. *Nothing. And everything. Because then I wouldn't be left here with holes in my soul, carrying the weight of your love. It's too heavy, Cassie. It's too heavy.*

23

A kind of sickness had taken hold of Jenna. This place, with its cold, false serenity, was getting to her. Chipping away her resolve. Pulling her deeper into its mire.

Mostly, she was sick of herself.

"I've been sick of you for months," Cassie said. "You turn everyone's sympathy away because you don't need it. No one feels sorrier for you than you do."

A key rattled in the door, breaking the chain of spinning thoughts cloaked in Cassie's disgusted voice.

Diane Downey pushed her way inside the cabin, bringing remnants of winter weather with her. She stomped her boots on the mat at the door and removed her heavy coat. Bits of snow fell to the ground, where they puddled and died.

Jenna took a deep breath to calm herself and said quietly, "Hello again."

The older woman spun in Jenna's direction with a hand on her heart.

"Oh my goodness, that's the second time you've scared me," Diane said, catching her breath. "I didn't expect anyone to be here."

Jenna forced her expression into bland pleasantry. "You must be dedicated to brave that snow."

"Dedicated? To Lars Jorgensen?" Diane laughed and shook her head. "Not exactly. I clean at another house a few miles down the road and realized I left my music behind."

She walked over and picked up the small white device and attached headphones sitting on top of the microwave and held them up for Jenna to see.

Jenna managed a weak smile, but Diane didn't notice. She'd caught sight of the boxes on the table.

Jenna hadn't replaced the lid, and the housekeeper had a clear view of the contents of the second box.

"What's this?" she asked. With no attempt to hide her curiosity, Diane walked to the table and picked up the baby rattle that was resting in the box. She turned it slowly in her hand. It made a soft sound, like captured rain.

But if Lars had wanted his cleaning lady to have access to these personal things, she surely would have seen them before now.

"I'm not sure if—"

"These belonged to the little ones," Diane said, her voice as quiet as a prayer. She placed the rattle back in the box and ran a hand over the other keepsakes.

"Yes," Jenna said.

Diane pulled out one of the two photo albums Jenna had avoided and slowly cracked it open. The pages, made from stiff cardboard covered with transparent film, gave a sticky, peeling sound as Diane forced them apart.

Jenna stayed where she was, not daring to take a closer look at the images that held the older woman transfixed.

"A terrible, terrible shame, this was." Diane flipped the pages. "Those poor babies."

The older woman blinked several times, holding back tears.

"Did you know the family, then?" Jenna asked.

Diane turned another page and ran a thumb along one of the photos.

"No," she replied with a sniff. "By the time I came along, the little mites had been gone for years, Mrs. Jorgensen locked away in the psychiatric hospital."

Jenna watched her face, then found the words to ask a question that had been nagging at her. "You don't like him, do you? Lars?"

Diane looked up in surprise. She opened her mouth to respond, but whatever she intended to say, perhaps a denial of the obvious, she bit back.

"No," she said. "I can't say I do."

Jenna remained silent. After a beat, Diane continued, urged on by an innate desire to fill the gap.

"He hasn't always been the way he is now, you know." She glanced up to meet Jenna's eyes. "When I first started coming here? Well . . . let's just say, Lars didn't have as good a handle on his demons as he does now. I've dealt with my fair share of worthless men. My husband, for one. But I needed the work."

"It was just Lars and Owen then?" Jenna probed.

Diane nodded. "Poor sweet boy. Everybody looking through him, past him, forgetting him. Even his own father."

Jenna tried to imagine what life must have been like for the boy who'd become the man with the tired face, left behind by everyone he loved.

In a flash, Jenna's mind turned against her with a speed so vicious she didn't have time to brace herself. Owen's young face became Ethan's. What would her son have looked like once his cheeks had lost their sweetness? Would he also one day have had a daughter who was too smart for her own good, who wore too much makeup?

She would never know. Instead, her mind tortured her with a vision of what her angelic son's face must have looked like after the crash.

Her baby. Her baby boy. Were they together, Ethan, Matt, and the girls? Did they have time to cling to one another, to comfort and to soothe, or was there only frantic, screaming death?

Too slow to mount a defense, Jenna caught her breath and folded her arms tightly across her middle, struggling to hold herself together.

"Excuse me," she managed to mumble. "I . . . I've got to . . ."

Jenna didn't finish the sentence, trailing off as she turned and searched for any escape at hand.

The cabin wasn't large, and within a few steps, she was standing at the bank of windows. The snowfall was so thick she could barely make out the shape of the lake. Jenna leaned her forehead against the cold glass, then turned her cheek to the pane, trying to cool the burning panic that threatened to consume her.

"Calm down," Cassie said.

"Don't tell me to calm down."

"Are you all right?" Diane asked from a muffled distance that could have been miles.

"Get it together," Cassie said in a harder tone.

"Yes," Jenna managed. "Just need some air."

"You're sure? Because I need to get going."

Oh God, please do, Jenna thought. *Go. Just go away.*

"I'm fine," she said, willing her voice to an even pitch. "Thank you, though."

"Okay. If you're sure," Diane called. "If I don't see you again, it was nice to meet you, Ms. Shaw."

"You, too, Diane," she called with false cheer.

Jenna fumbled with the latch on the window while Diane made her exit. Once the door closed behind the housekeeper, Jenna managed at last to get the window unlocked. She pulled the pane up, and the glacial air slapped her in the face.

Jenna knelt in front of the window and took long, deep breaths, willing her heartbeat to a steadier rhythm. She counted backward from one hundred, slowly, patiently. Her pulse began to slow.

It almost worked.

Then came the distant sound of laughter. Children's laughter. Her eyes widened and she searched for the source of the sound, but saw little except white falling downward. She had no idea where it was coming from. Worse, she couldn't be sure it was real and not some figment of her overstressed mind.

Jenna lurched to her feet and slammed the window closed, shutting out the world again.

"I have to get out of here," she said under her breath. "A cab. I'll call a cab."

She stumbled toward the kitchen, toward the phone on the wall.

"A cab to where?" Cassie asked.

"To anywhere," Jenna said. "The next town, the next state. To the other side of the damn world."

"You're being irrational." Cassie mimicked the words Jenna had often spoken to her daughter.

"Fuck off, Cassie!" Jenna cried.

"Language. Real classy, Mom."

"I'm not your mom!" Jenna yelled, turning in a quick, tight circle and hiding her face in her hands. "I'm no one's mom anymore! Don't you *get* that?"

Jenna stumbled toward the spare bedroom, practically running. From her daughter's voice. From the image of her baby boy, his face broken and lifeless.

Her body bumped along the wall. She burst through the doorway, her eyes open now and searching.

Scanning the room, her gaze landed on her leather bag, lying on the floor next to the bed.

She lunged toward it, crumpling to her knees as she did. Her hands were frantic as she dumped the contents onto the rug, too impatient to dig through the dark interior to find what she sought.

Jenna swept through the leftover remnants of her life. For a moment, she thought it wasn't there. Her hands grew frenzied. With a distinctive rattle, the pill bottle rolled across the hardwood floor, spinning away from her. She scrabbled after it on her hands and knees as it came to a stop against the wall.

She grabbed the bottle with both hands, her breathing quick and short. Her fingers wouldn't cooperate. She fumbled, and a whimper escaped her lips. "No," she cried.

With a final, desperate gasp, she managed to twist the childproof cap off the bottle, but her hands were trembling and the pills fell, spilling across the floor.

Jenna dived after them, reaching for as many as she could gather and raking them back toward her. Nothing existed except the little white saviors.

I can't do this anymore was her one clear and coherent thought, and it played on a loop. *I can't do this anymore. Not anymore.* Her mantra. Her prayer.

Boots came into view in the doorway as she gripped the hard, bitter pills in the palms of her hands.

Lars stood looking down on her.

"It's bad manners to kill yourself while you're a guest in someone's home."

24

Lars was shaking as he reached into the back of the cupboard and pulled out the dusty bottle of bourbon. He unscrewed the cap and splashed just enough of the dark-amber liquid into a glass. Just enough to smooth his rattled nerves.

By some small miracle, Lars had managed to avoid a drinking problem after the disappearance of his children. He couldn't take any credit for that.

If Francie and Will had been found straightaway, if he'd been able to bury them, to visit their graves and mourn for them in the natural order of things, he would have given his heart and his soul over to drink.

Most likely, he'd never have come back from it.

But the not knowing—it had fueled a burning obsession to discover where his children were. It had consumed him, filling his days and nights, his every waking thought, with how he could make things right.

Too little, too late, as his mother used to say.

But he'd hoped. For a long time, he'd parceled out that hope, rationing it in trickles and drops to quench his parched heart.

For far too long.

If Lars was grateful for a single thing in his pathetic, wasted life, it was that Owen had been strong enough to weather the worst time of both their lives alone. Lars had been no comfort to the boy; he'd barely registered his existence.

But when Lars had reached the bottom of hope, and the well had finally run dry, Owen was there to pull him up.

Standing before Jenna on her hands and knees, clutching those pills, he saw a woman at the bottom of her own well, one that was bone dry.

He threw back the glass, gulping at the fiery burn.

The look on her face when he'd knelt in front of her and carefully pried her fingers open, taking the last of her hope away . . . it gutted him.

She'd stared back at him from an empty, cavernous space. He knew that space.

To be left behind was a terrible burden to bear.

She'd sat, immobile, her empty hands hanging at her sides, as he collected the pills she'd spilled across the floor.

A glass of water from the faucet, and he'd given her two of the sleeping pills. He had to place them in her mouth, put the cup to her lips.

He'd guided her to the bed, knowing sleep would be the only peace she'd find that day.

He wasn't a spiritual man. The idea of a higher power controlling things from some amorphous place in the sky would have only given him another target for blame and loathing. He was content to direct that where he knew it belonged.

Yet as he stood in his empty kitchen with a devastated stranger sleeping though her pain in another room, he couldn't help but wonder if Jenna had ended up here for a reason.

With a faulty ticker pointing him toward his finish line, Lars had accepted he'd go to his grave without answers. Without that acceptance, he might as well have booked himself into the room next door to his wife.

But Jenna Shaw might just be his last chance for a thin slice of redemption. If he could somehow manage to pull her up from the depths, maybe—just maybe—his long, empty years wouldn't have been for nothing.

Maybe he was where he was supposed to be. He'd never left this place, refusing to sell the cabin where his children had lived, with some unformed idea he owed it to Audrey, and to Francie and Will, to keep the lights burning.

He knew they weren't coming back. He'd known it for years. Even Audrey. She'd die in that place, without any sense of time passing or chances wasted.

But maybe he could still do some good.

Lars finished off the bourbon with a final gulp.

Or maybe, he thought, setting the empty glass on the counter, *I'm nothing more than a foolish old man looking for forgiveness at the bottom of the ninth inning, and in the wrong place, at that.* More likely, Jenna Shaw had washed up on the shores of his life by chance, and the best thing he could do for her was let her be.

The woman had clearly made her choice. Who was he to stand in her way?

25

"Get up."

The words cut through the cloud of sleep. Jenna groaned and rolled over.

"Get up," Lars said again.

The quilt she was buried beneath was stripped away, and Jenna sat up in the bed with a gasp.

"Wha—"

Reality crashed in as she remembered where she was, remembered the day before with a hated clarity.

"I've been waiting on you to wake up for an hour." Lars tossed the quilt across the foot of the bed. "Get dressed. The roads are clear. It's time to go."

Jenna's heart beat heavily in her chest as Lars walked out of the room.

She shook her head to dissipate the remaining fog of drug-induced sleep and rose to meet whatever came next.

This was what she wanted.

Wasn't it?

Shoving away the whisper of doubt, Jenna pushed her hair out of her face and took a deep breath.

Half an hour later, showered and dressed, she made her way to the truck, where Lars was waiting with the engine running.

Snow sparkled in the midmorning sun.

She placed her large leather bag, where she'd stowed everything she owned, including the box containing her family's ashes, on the floor mat between her feet.

Lars glanced at it but made no comment.

When the truck came to the top of the hill, Lars turned the wheel to the right, away from Raven.

"Owen can keep the van." It was the first time she'd spoken that morning. "He can sell it, get some sort of return on his time and trouble."

Lars wasn't in a talkative mood. He merely raised a brow in her direction and sent her an inscrutable look.

She took the hint, and they drove in silence for ten more minutes before she spoke again.

"I feel like I should thank you for your help, Mr. Jorgensen. Even if I didn't ask for it, and frankly didn't want it."

"That might be the worst thank you I've ever heard," Cassie said.

Jenna shook her head and tried again. "What I mean is, I'm sorry. I'm sorry for bringing my mess to your door. You're a good man. A good man to try and help, even if I am a lost cause."

She couldn't meet his eyes. Another moment of silence passed before Lars spoke.

"I was fresh out of the navy when I met Audrey," he said, surprising her with the abrupt change of subject. "I'd spent two years at sea, give or take, most of it in the galley, cooking minced beef or griddle eggs for a crew of almost two hundred. Audrey was . . . she was dazzling."

Jenna turned and watched his profile, drawn in by the words that seemed so out of character. But then, she didn't know him, Jenna reminded herself.

"She had something. Something I'd never seen up close. An energy. It lit up everything around her, made it all brighter, including me." His smile was slow, bittersweet.

He spoke like a man in a confessional, and a chill traveled up Jenna's spine, despite the orange jacket that held her body heat close.

"I guess it was what you'd call a whirlwind romance. Do people still say that?"

He glanced over, but Jenna shrugged, unsure what her role was supposed to be in this story. His story.

"We were married within a month," he said. "I met her mother for the first time on our wedding day." Lars shook his head. "That should have been my first clue. Mrs. Soderholm—Beverly—I thought she didn't like me. But her worries didn't have anything to do with me being a sailor who barely had his land legs back."

Jenna was falling under the spell of his words.

"She tried to warn me," Lars said, his brows drawn low over his gray eyes. "Sometimes I wonder what might have changed if I'd listened . . . but that kind of regret is a waste of time. By then, it was too late. I was head over heels."

Jenna remembered the look on the faces of the young couple in their wedding portrait.

"When the judge said, 'For better or worse,' I agreed quick enough." Lars pinned her with his piercing gaze. "Nobody tells you how bad the worse can get."

"No," Jenna whispered, thinking of the phone call that had shattered her happily ever after. "No, they don't."

26

"Told you she was great, didn't I?" the half-drunk groom said.

Lars grinned. "Never shut up about it."

The men turned together and leaned their backs against the bar while Steve's eyes searched out his blushing bride. When she saw him watching, Maggie gave a sweet smile that showed off her overbite.

"When you find the one, you just know," Steve said at Lars's side.

"I'm happy for you. Really."

Maggie Shipman might not have been the great beauty Steve had described during their deployment, but there was no denying the look in their eyes when the couple smiled at each other.

Lars didn't regret coming to the wedding, exactly, but he wondered if it was too soon to make his excuses and head home. He'd socialized with enough strangers to last him a good long while.

He opened his mouth to tell his friend congratulations again and good night, but his attention was pulled across the room.

It was her laugh that caught him first. He searched out the sound, following the full-throated music back to its source. The woman's smile was wide, unencumbered by modesty or restraint, her head thrown back in a pure embrace of the moment.

Lars lost track of his thoughts, and his plans to call it an early night became scrambled with other, more basic ideas as the woman threw her hands in the air and twirled with an abandonment he'd rarely witnessed.

She stopped suddenly, halting her impromptu pirouette midspin. Strands of long dark hair, still moving, wrapped around the bottom half of her face and clung like a veil. For a moment, only her eyes were visible. A frisson of excitement coursed through Lars. From across the crowded room, the woman's gaze was leveled on him.

A cheer went up from the crowd around her, and Lars felt he'd lost something when her eyes broke away from his. She turned back to the people nearest her and dropped into a bow with a quick flourish.

"Who is that?"

"Who?" Steve asked.

Who else was in the room?

"The woman in the dress," Lars said.

He missed the odd look his friend sent his way. Lars watched her as she laughed again and shook her head at a man standing nearby.

Steve must have followed his line of sight.

"The brunette?" he asked, and Lars could only nod, struck by the plain sound of the word. *Brunette.* There was nothing plain about this woman.

"Came with Bob, Maggie's brother."

"What's her name?"

"Something with an A, I think. Amanda? Angela? Only met her tonight."

"Are they serious?" Lars asked.

"Serious?" Steve laughed. "Shouldn't think so. Never seen Bob serious about anything, much less a girl."

Lars's pulse quickened.

"Why don't you ask her yourself? Looks like she's headed this way."

When his friend spoke again, Lars barely heard him.

"Think I'll go check on my new wife," Steve said, then clapped Lars on the shoulder and faded into the crowd.

Lars couldn't take his eyes off the woman.

The way she moved, with a confident intensity that drew a man's attention. His weren't the only set of eyes that followed her.

But it was toward him she came.

He watched, transfixed, as she stopped. There were at least ten feet still between them. She tilted her head a bit to one side and smiled, studying him. He fought the urge to stand up straighter, to run a hand through his hair, which was only just beginning to grow out from his military cut.

Those seconds were heavy with anticipation, fraught with meaning he didn't fully comprehend. All he knew was he wanted, more than he'd ever wanted anything, for this woman to draw closer. To come to him. To choose him.

The music of the band and the murmur of the crowd grew faint in his ears. Everything else fell away from that moment, those seconds that would define the rest of his life.

With a grin of acceptance, she turned sideways to him and began a soft shoe shuffle that closed the final distance between them.

Lars laughed, her irreverence contagious. When she stopped just in front of him, he studied her face, unable to keep the smile off his own.

It wasn't her features that held him. It was the light that shone through, brightening her smile, making her eyes sparkle like the stars over the ocean he'd stared up at so many nights on the open sea.

"Want to dance, sailor?" She held out her hand.

Her date was left passed out and forgotten in a chair along the edge of the room.

They danced, and one day Lars would share with their children the story of how their mother had tap-danced her way into his life.

27

Lars drove on.

Jenna knew there was more to this story than Lars had shared. An iceberg, massive in scope and lurking beneath still waters, that he and Owen had run against, shipwrecked with only each other to cling to.

The deserted roads Jenna had grown used to since wandering off the interstate, lined with snow-covered fields and dotted with barns and silos in the distance, contributed to a sense of isolation that fit her state of mind.

Yet without her noticing, the roads had begun to widen. Other vehicles passed, reminding her there was a town up ahead, somewhere in the distance. A town where she could get an overpriced cup of coffee. Where she would rent a car to take her away from this place.

Forever.

"Are you sure that's what you want?" Cassie asked.

Jenna frowned. Her daughter was far more troublesome in death than she'd ever been in her lifetime.

As if reading her thoughts, Lars slowed the truck without a word and pulled along the shoulder of the road.

He put the vehicle in park and looked across the cab, meeting her questioning glance.

"Don't go," he said. "At least, not yet," he hastened to add at her look of confusion.

Jenna shook her head. "I don't . . . But why?" she asked.

If she didn't know better, she could have sworn there was a look of embarrassment about him. Embarrassment, tinged with something else. Was it hope?

"Come with me."

"Come with you where?" Jenna asked. He wasn't making any sense. "If you're hoping to run off to the Bahamas together and sip mai tais, my schedule's pretty full for the foreseeable future."

"Liar," Cassie said.

The old man didn't bat an eyelash at her lame humor. He just stared at her with an intensity Jenna didn't care to acknowledge.

"It's your decision," he said. "But the rental cars aren't going anywhere."

Actually, she thought, *they are. By design, in fact, rental cars are going lots of places. Lots of places that aren't here.*

"What harm will it do, Mom?" Cassie nudged.

"I'm asking you to do this for me," he said.

Jenna shook her head, not meeting his eyes.

"I'd hazard a guess this man hasn't asked anyone for anything in a long, long time. Are you really going to sit there and tell him no?" her daughter prodded. "Don't you owe him more than that?"

"I don't owe you anything," Jenna told him.

"That's debatable," Cassie said. "Not to mention rude."

"No, you don't," Lars agreed. "I'm asking all the same. I'll bring you back tomorrow, if that's what you want."

Jenna opened her mouth, but the words she had every intention of putting out there died on her lips. She sighed.

"One more day is all I'm asking."

"One day, Mom. If you're so determined, one day isn't going to change anything."

No, it's not, Cassie. And I can see through your attempts to manipulate me. Stop it.

"Then it shouldn't matter," Cassie replied.

"Okay, fine," Jenna said, capitulating with no attempt at grace. "One day," she added.

Lars didn't gloat. He simply put the truck into drive and steered them back onto the road without a word.

But Jenna couldn't shake the sensation she was being pulled into a whirlpool, down and down, and her chances for escape were getting slimmer by the second.

28

The warren of squat brick buildings sat apart from the rest of the world, separated by chain fencing topped with rolls of barbed wire.

The Minnesota State Secure Psychiatric Hospital. The word *hospital* was there, but there was no mistaking the security portion of the program.

This was a prison.

The guard at the gatehouse allowed them entry only after examining their identification and recording the information in his log.

Jenna looked around as Lars maneuvered the truck through the campus and found a parking spot in the visitor's lot. If she'd expected menacing Gothic architecture and patients wandering the grounds in bathrobes mumbling to themselves, she'd have been disappointed.

"You have no room to be judgmental about people hearing voices," Cassie reminded her.

The buildings were old, built for function rather than atmosphere. The impression left was cold institutionalism. Impersonal and efficient. In its way, just as chilling.

Lars obviously knew the routine by heart.

"Leave your things. Everything but your ID. You can't bring anything into the unit anyway." He emptied his pockets of everything except his keys and wallet.

She did as he asked, and they exited the truck together and walked toward the glass doors leading inside.

They were met by more guards, more questions, and more places to sign their names and state their business. Jenna followed Lars's lead.

After what seemed an eternity, they were directed to an empty waiting room that could have graced any other hospital in the country, except for a few subtle differences.

The chairs and tables were bolted to the floor. There were windows spilling light into the room, but they were narrow and high on the walls, leaving no view to the grounds outside. The room was stifled and still, and Jenna felt sure it was by design.

"This unit is an improvement over the last," Lars said by her side. "When Audrey first got here she was in B unit, where most of the inmates are taken. More guards, more locks, more dangerous patients. I had to speak to her through glass."

"And now?"

He shrugged. "Audrey's not a danger to anyone. Not even herself anymore. And we got old, didn't we? Me, out there. Her, in here, behind walls." He glanced up to a security camera mounted near the ceiling. "She's spent more of her life in this place than out."

Jenna considered him. "She's never . . . ?" She trailed off. The enormity of everything Audrey Jorgensen had never said was hard to wrap her mind around.

Lars met her gaze. He knew what she was getting at.

"Nearly twenty years I asked her. Nothing. Then one day, she looked at me and said, 'Where are my babies, Lars?'" He sighed, a sound full of regret and despair. "She got so wound up, they had to sedate her. I never asked again. There was no point. She doesn't have any answers to give."

Jenna looked down at her hands, picked at the cuticle on her thumb, and wondered if that could possibly be true.

The rattle of locks being turned drew her attention to a doorway leading into a white tile-lined hallway. Jenna sat up straighter, suddenly nervous.

Lars rose as a guard entered the room, and Jenna followed suit. The guard was joined by an orderly in scrubs. The orderly was leading a woman in loose gray sweatpants and a matching shirt.

Audrey Jorgensen shuffled into the room on feet encased in scuffed canvas shoes. Her hands hung limply by her sides. A shock of silver hair fell down her back. Jenna did a quick mental calculation. She couldn't be more than sixty years old.

This woman would have passed for eighty.

It wasn't just age to blame for her slow and painful gait.

There was a blankness in Audrey as she stared at the ground, her body moving automatically, if slowly, where she was told to go.

"Mr. Jorgensen." The orderly led his charge to a chair across from Jenna and Lars. "Good to see you today, sir."

"You too, James. How is she?"

"Oh, not too bad. Finally kicked the cold that had her feeling so poorly."

Lars sat and took his wife's thin, pale hands into his own.

James took a seat across the room on a bench, giving them some space and a modicum of privacy. The guard stood armed by the door they'd entered, reminding Jenna that even if the patient had no shackles or handcuffs on her wrists, this was a correctional facility.

"Audrey, love," Lars said. "Can you look at me?"

It was a request, not a demand. For a moment, Jenna thought Audrey hadn't heard his question.

But after a pause, she raised her eyes and looked in her husband's direction. Jenna had doubts she was focused on him, but Audrey spoke.

"Lars?" Her voice was a high, birdlike whisper.

"Yes." He gave her a small smile. His gentleness shouldn't have been a shock to Jenna. She glanced at him all the same, trying to untangle her thoughts about him treating his wife with such care, as if she were a fine piece of china.

Frailty and age aside, and regardless of how charmed Lars had been by Audrey as a young woman, this was still the person responsible for his lost children.

How could he look at her with such love? How could he look at her at all?

"Audrey," Lars said, unaware of the uneasy turn of Jenna's thoughts. "I brought someone to see you. Her name is Jenna."

A bit late, it occurred to Jenna to wonder why Lars had brought her here.

Audrey turned slowly in Jenna's direction. Despite her discomfort, Jenna raised her eyes to meet those of the older woman.

For the briefest of moments, Audrey's gaze remained vague and unfocused, just as Jenna had suspected it would.

"Mrs. Jorgensen, I'm pleased to meet you," Jenna said woodenly, the words ringing false in her ears. Politeness alone pried the sentiment from her lips. She needn't have bothered. Audrey wasn't interested in her words, polite or otherwise.

Yet seconds later, Jenna's senses went on alert when the skin around Audrey's face tightened, the muscles constricting and pulling her eyes wide. A spark ignited within the depth of the older woman's gaze, and she pulled back suddenly.

Instinctively, Jenna did the same.

Audrey's mouth opened and shut, and she struggled to form words. Her head swiveled to her husband.

"Who . . . Lars . . . ?" She sounded strained, higher pitched than even before.

She was frightened, Jenna realized with a start.

"Audrey, it's okay, she's a friend," Lars said, trying to soothe his wife, even as confusion showed on his features. "Her name is Jenna."

Audrey leaned farther away from them. Her head was turned downward, facing the table, her chin on her chest, but her eyes flicked up to look at Jenna again, then skittered away. She was unable to meet the younger woman's gaze for more than a few seconds.

"Audrey, honey. It's okay," Lars tried again.

His wife shook her head back and forth and began to mumble. Jenna couldn't make out the words, but it was clear her presence had upset Audrey. Jenna simply didn't understand why.

"Audrey, what is it? What's wrong?" Lars started to rise from the table. He glanced toward the orderly, whose attention was on a magazine. He seated himself again.

"I can't hear you, love." He reached across the table that separated them.

The jumble of sounds tumbling from Audrey's lips made no sense, partly because the woman's head was hung low and she seemed to be speaking to the hands she was wringing in her lap, but also because Jenna had begun to back even farther away.

A new comprehension washed over her. This wasn't research, from a safe and impersonal distance. This was real.

Audrey Jorgensen was an inmate at a mental hospital, and she was there for a reason.

The walls were too close, the air too warm, and suddenly Jenna wanted nothing more than to be far away from this room, with its armed guard and its bolted chairs, and especially this stranger who looked at her with such irrational fear.

"What? No, Audrey, no," Lars was saying, having apparently made some sense of his wife's mad ramblings.

He glanced over his shoulder at Jenna, an unspoken apology in his face.

"No," he said, more firmly. "Look at her again, Audrey. Look closer."

The woman shrank away from him, but slowly she lifted her head, and the sheets of silver hair parted to reveal fearful, hopeful eyes that locked on Jenna.

Her jaw worked, silently at first. Jenna couldn't turn away.

"Francie?" Audrey whispered. "My Francie?"

Horror dawned. Jenna shook her head, desperate to disabuse this woman with the needful eyes of her mistake.

"No," Jenna said, more forcefully than she intended. "No," she said again, quieter, with a glance at the orderly, who'd looked up from his magazine.

She leaned closer to Audrey, speaking distinctly.

"My name is Jenna Shaw. I am *not* your daughter."

Audrey's entire countenance stayed trained on Jenna. Her words had no perceivable effect.

"Jenna, I'm sorry. I didn't expect this," Lars said.

"Francie," Audrey pleaded. "Francie, do you hate me?"

Jenna shook her head again, powerless to stop this delusion that had taken hold like a fever.

"I'm sorry, Francie, I'm so sorry," she cried.

"I'm not Francie!" Jenna hissed.

"Francie, can you forgive me? It was all my fault, Francie, all my fault." Audrey was reaching for Jenna across the table, though she wasn't, not really. She was reaching for the daughter she'd lost.

Jenna hugged her arms tightly across her middle and backed away from the woman.

Lars was losing control of the situation, if he'd had any to begin with. He tried to reach his wife while Jenna stood silently and watched from a safer distance.

"Audrey, look at me. Look at me, love. This isn't Francie. This is Jenna Shaw."

But an old pain had Audrey in its grip. No words from Lars would ease the pressure.

"It's all my fault, Lars," she said to her husband. There were tears forming in her eyes, as she stared first at him, then back at Jenna. They began to roll down her cheeks in silent rivers. "All my fault."

"No, love." Lars rubbed his hands across hers. "No, it's not your fault."

A poisonous fog began to cloud Jenna's vision. Each time Lars said those words, the fog began to swirl, faster and more chaotic.

"It's not your fault," he repeated, over and over.

They were the same words Cassie whispered to Jenna each night, in that space just before sleep claimed her, when she had no defense, when she was incapable of screaming back at her daughter, "That's a lie!"

The words drilled into her. She wasn't sleeping now.

Jenna moved back to the chair and leaned close to Audrey again, stared until Audrey met her gaze. Jenna looked the other woman in the eye and spoke the words as if she were speaking into a mirror.

"Of course it is." Her voice was discordant, alien to her own ears.

Lars turned and gaped at her, but Jenna had no time for him. No time for his lies.

"You lost them. It was *your* job, the only job that mattered. You were their mother."

Jenna saw the pain blossom in Audrey's dim eyes, expanding to fill the whole of her existence. Jenna didn't care.

"Do you think you're off the hook, blameless somehow, because you were *unhappy*? Because you had your own issues to deal with?" Jenna gave a harsh laugh. "It doesn't work that way, and none of the meaningless platitudes in the world can change that."

"Jenna," Lars said, stern and shocked. She didn't look at him. In that moment, he didn't exist.

"You *failed*," she said, drilling the word home. "You failed in a million different ways leading up to that point, and then you failed one last time, on a scale so massive and irreparable it can never be fixed."

"Jenna, that's enough," Lars said, no longer keeping his voice low.

"Maybe you tell yourself you didn't mean for it to happen. Maybe you'd do anything in your power to change it. But you know what? It doesn't *fucking* matter. Because you can't."

"Jenna!" Lars shouted.

The guard stood straighter at the door. The orderly was halfway across the room, his magazine tossed aside.

It was too late. The damage was done. Audrey Jorgensen, already a broken woman, crumpled into a pile of guilt and regret as sobs shook her frail body.

Jenna said nothing as they gathered Audrey to take her away. She watched, her jaw tight and her body trembling.

She didn't hear what Lars said to the orderly, or to Audrey before the door opened and she was shuffled into the unknown.

But Jenna saw Lars standing with his hands hanging at his sides, helpless as they took his wife away. She heard, even after the heavy door closed behind them, the hollow cries of a mother who couldn't find her children.

They echoed inside of Jenna, joining a chorus of her own.

29

Lars and Jenna rode back to the cabin in stony silence. Jenna, aware of the line she'd stepped across, couldn't bring herself to apologize. She'd been needlessly cruel, but nothing she'd said was untrue.

She didn't know who she was more upset with, Lars, Audrey, or herself.

When they arrived at his home, Lars stepped out of the vehicle without a word. Unsure what to do now, Jenna watched him walk up the driveway to his front door. He opened it wide, then turned to look at her. She was still seated on the passenger side of his truck. He lifted his brows and made a gesture toward the interior of the house with his head.

Are you coming in or not?

Jenna sighed.

She opened the car door and trudged up the driveway, her bag slung across her shoulder, to where he waited.

Jenna spent the next hour staring at a crack in the ceiling above the bed in the spare bedroom, where she stretched out, fully clothed. The carved box lay on the bed beside her.

Cassie was blessedly silent. *She's not speaking to me either.*

When Lars knocked on the doorframe, Jenna sat up and swung her legs over the side of the bed. She half expected him to throw her out now, though if he were going to do that, why had he brought her back in the first place?

"I could use a hand with dinner. If you're not too busy," he said drily.

Jenna recognized an olive branch when she saw one.

"Sure," she mumbled, rising from the bed.

Lars had turned on a radio in the kitchen, which was playing low in the background. The routine of being ordered about by the old man had become familiar.

"No wine, but there's beer, if you'd like one."

He handed her a mallet and two packets of dried egg noodles to pound on while he threw some unrecognizable things together in a large bowl.

Eyeing the goopy mess as he poured it into a casserole dish, she decided a beer might be just the thing.

"What are you making?" Jenna ventured to ask as she popped the top on a can.

He reached past her and took the packages of pounded noodles, then sprinkled the contents over the lumpy concoction.

"Hot dish."

He didn't see the look of confusion pass over her face.

"And what, exactly, is involved in hot dish?" she couldn't stop herself from asking.

He shrugged his shoulders as he lifted the glass dish and transferred it to the waiting oven.

"It's hot," he said. "It's in a dish. What else is there to know?"

Jenna's brows lifted as she sipped the beer.

"I guess that's the basics covered, then," she muttered.

He handed her a stack of plates. "Set the table."

Lars had apparently put aside his ire.

She took the plates and began placing them around the kitchen table, wondering if there was a subtle way to ask what was on her mind.

There wasn't.

"Why don't you hate her?"

Lars looked over from where he was pulling glasses from the cupboard and remained silent for a beat.

"How much experience do you have with forgiveness, Jenna?" he finally asked.

Her hands stilled, and she studied his back as he went about his business.

"Is it really that simple for you?"

"Simple?" He glanced over his shoulder with a look that showed her what he thought of that question.

"No," he said, shaking his head. "Forgiveness is hard. It's painful. It's giving when you've nothing left to give, from places you can't afford to lose anything else." He turned and studied her, crossing his arms as he leaned back against the counter. "But it's never simple."

Jenna struggled to wrap her mind around that.

"But how?" she finally asked. "*How* can you forgive her?"

He shook his head. "Forgiving Audrey was the easy part. Forgiving myself? That was a tough mountain to climb."

"I don't understand."

He sighed. "I know you don't."

Lars moved to the refrigerator and pulled out a beer for himself. He popped the top and took a great swig before he looked her in the eye.

"There was a reason Audrey left that day and took the kids," he finally said. "Everyone assumed it was because she was unstable, and that was true. She had a long history of being unpredictable, was prone to mood swings, bouts of mania. No one—not me, not her mother, none of us—expected her to come so dangerously undone. But we should have."

"You couldn't—"

Lars shook his head. "Yes. We could have. We should have. We didn't want to see it. *I* didn't want to see it. And I've had to find a way to live with that."

"That doesn't mean you're to blame," Jenna insisted.

"Blame." Lars huffed. "What the hell good does blame do? Blaming Audrey doesn't bring my kids back. It doesn't heal my wife's shattered mind. Blame is about as useless as a glass hammer." He ran a hand through his hair. "And I pounded myself with that glass hammer until I was cut and nearly bleeding to death."

"But why?" she pressed.

"Because I was leaving her, Jenna," he said. "I was leaving, and I was taking the kids."

Jenna rocked back on her heels. Lars took another drink of the beer and set it on the counter.

"What?" she asked. "But that wasn't . . ."

"It wasn't in the newspapers? No, it wasn't. That bit of information managed to slip by the press."

"But you . . . you loved her. You *still* love her! It's all over your face when you look at her."

"Yes," he sighed. "I do. I did, even then. And wouldn't the world be a fine place if everything were so simple?"

30

"You can't do this!" Audrey screamed from another room. There was a crash as something broke against the wall, then the sound of hysterical sobs.

His hands stalled, but Lars forced himself to continue packing the bag open on the bed.

They'd been at it for hours. First came the disbelief, then tears, which had become screams, then more tears.

He'd sent the children outside. It wasn't the first time they'd heard their parents argue. The thought brought him low.

Lars could tell Owen had some inkling this time was different. Bigger.

"Take them to play, son. Don't bring them back in until I come to get you, okay," he'd said as he shuffled his children out the door.

"But Mom, is she . . . ?" Owen had glanced around his father to where his mother was sobbing into her hands, curled up on the sofa.

"She'll be all right. It's going to be all right, I promise," he'd said.

That was exactly what he was trying to do, God help him. Make it all right.

"Audrey, it's for the best," Lars said when his wife's figure appeared in the doorway to their bedroom.

Her breathing was heavy, her face ravaged by redness and tears.

"Please, Lars, please don't do this. Not like this," she begged, motioning to the mess he'd made trying to pack what he thought she might need. "Don't send me away like something you're ashamed of. Don't let the kids see it happen this way."

Tears were coursing down her cheeks, but her words were quieter. She was struggling to stay calm.

"Audrey, honey, there's no good way to do this. It's not . . . it's not good for the kids. The mood swings, the days you can't get out of bed, the screaming fits . . . And the up days, Audrey, they're almost worse. It scares them. Don't you see that? It scares *me*. It's not—"

"I'll do better." She spoke in a rush, moving toward him and gripping him around the middle in a fierce hug. "I can do better. Please, Lars."

She laid her head against his chest and held him like a drowning woman clinging to a buoy on a storm-tossed sea. His hands hung loosely at his sides, filled with nightgowns and undergarments. He forced them to stay there, though they trembled to hold her. To protect her from this. From herself.

"Don't send me away," she pleaded. "I'll prove it to you." She pulled her head back and searched his face while he stared at a spot on the wall above her head.

"It's too late, Audrey," he said, exhausted from the effort to stay the course. "Your mother is already on her way."

"Lars," she begged. "Think of the kids. They need their mother."

"Yes, they do," he replied with a heat he'd believed was all used up. "They need their mother to be here! All of you. But you're not, Audrey. Half the time, you're lost in someplace I can't reach you. The other half, you get these grandiose ideas, then drain the bank account. Either way, you leave and we can't get you back, and they deserve better than that. *I* deserve better than that!"

His wife of eleven years stepped back. She dropped her arms and stared hard at him as her quicksilver moods shifted.

"This is about her, isn't it?"

Lars sighed and turned to the bag. He stuffed the clothing inside.

"I don't know what you're talking about. This is about us. About you. It doesn't have to be permanent, Audrey. Just until you get some help. Your mother made plans for you to see a doctor while you're home and—"

"*This* is my home," she cried. "These are *my* kids, not hers! You're *my* husband, not hers!"

"Audrey, stop it!" he yelled. He turned to face her, saw the way she stepped back from him. He never raised his voice, and the look in her eyes when he did twisted his guts.

"Audrey." He placed his palms on her cheeks. The wetness of her tears lay between their skin. "Audrey, I love you. I've loved you from the moment I met you, and I've never stopped."

She met his gaze, and the devastation there tore him apart.

"Then please, Lars. Please, I'm begging you, if you've ever loved me, give me one more chance. I can do it," she said. "I can do better. You have to believe me. One more chance."

"Audrey." Her name was a sigh, a wish, a final touchstone of wasted hope.

"One week," she said, sensing his regret. His weakness. Using it against him. "Give me a week, and I'll prove it to you. I will. This time will be different."

He gave in and held her against him, a fellow survivor in the rough seas swirling around them.

It wouldn't be different.

Not this time. Not ever.

But he was going to drown right alongside her.

31

"It was too much. Just too much. She was getting worse month by month, and I . . ."

He raised his hands and let them fall. "I gave up on her."

Jenna was saved from responding by a knock on the door. Lars took a deep breath and stood straighter, a man recovering from a daze.

"Come in," he shouted and busied himself with moving dishes to the sink.

Owen opened the door, and he and his daughter came into the cabin on a flurry of crisp wind.

"Hey, Grandpa." Hannah rushed over and gave Lars a peck on the cheek. She was all smiles and brought a sparkle of energy into the place that only youth can.

"Hi, sweetheart," Lars said, his whole being focused now on this conundrum of a girl. "Don't you look pretty."

She rolled her eyes. "Gramps, you're not supposed to call a girl pretty."

He raised his gaze to Owen over Hannah's head, but his son just shrugged.

"And why's that, hon?" Lars asked.

"Because beauty is arbitrary." She twirled to the refrigerator. "It's a subjective social construct designed to pit women against one another in pursuit of male attention." She cracked open a can of soda.

"Pop," Cassie whispered, amused. "They call it pop around here."

Hannah took a deep drink and smiled at her grandfather. "Which in turn, distracts women from their own self-actualization."

"Heaven forbid," Lars said in all seriousness. "Am I allowed to say you look brilliant today, or will that distract you from actualizing yourself?"

Hannah thought it over. "I can live with that."

The girl grabbed an apple from the bowl on the counter and headed out of the kitchen. "Homework," she threw over her shoulder.

The two men watched her go with similar looks of bemused affection.

Hannah skidded to a stop when she saw Jenna. "You're still here."

Jenna gave her a small smile. "Looks that way."

The girl tilted her head and asked, "Why?"

"Hannah," Owen said sharply, but neither Jenna nor Hannah acknowledged the rebuke.

"A fair question," Jenna said. "Would you believe me if I told you I'm still trying to figure that out?"

Hannah lifted a single sardonic brow. "It's not the best answer I've ever heard."

Jenna conceded the point with a shrug. "But it's truthful," she said.

Hannah studied her for a moment. "All right, but maybe you should put a little more effort into it."

"Hannah June, that's enough." Lars was quiet, but stern. "Jenna's my guest, and that's all you need to know to keep a civil tongue."

Hannah kept silent at her grandfather's words, but she never broke eye contact, and Jenna got the clear sense Hannah was reserving judgment, despite the instruction.

"You've got to have a certain level of respect for that," Cassie said.

"Duly noted," Jenna told the girl.

Hannah crunched into the apple and inclined her head as she sauntered past Jenna. Just so they understood each other.

"Jenna, I'm sorry," Owen began once his daughter had settled herself on the sofa with her homework and her headphones.

"No need to apologize," Jenna said. *I have a teenager of my own,* she almost said.

Had. I had a teenager of my own.

"Are you expecting someone else?" Jenna asked Lars, steering the subject to safer topics. His story had distracted her, and she'd realized a bit late she'd set the table with more than two places. Now, she noticed there was still one unaccounted for.

"Can't slip anything past you," came Lars's deadpan reply.

He didn't volunteer anything else, and she refrained from asking more.

With a raised brow at his father's conversational skills, Owen turned to Jenna.

"I at least owe you an apology for the holdup on the part for your van, Jenna. I promise you, I'm doing my best to get it here."

She waved off his apology. It wasn't like Owen had any motive to purposely delay Jenna's departure. At least, she didn't think he did.

Lars, on the other hand . . . Jenna had begun to realize he was laboring under the misconception that he would change her plans—both immediate and long term—if he managed to toss enough distractions into her path.

"But you're determined not to let anything get in your way, aren't you? And you always accused me of being stubborn."

Jenna pushed Cassie's words away. One opinionated teenage girl was enough to deal with at the moment.

"Dinner should be ready in thirty," Lars said, placing the salad he'd thrown together in the fridge to stay fresh until then.

He plunked a bowl of baby carrots and a prepackaged container of vegetable dip on the table and pulled up a chair with Owen and Jenna.

Owen studied his dad's version of appetizers. Judging by the look on his face, this wasn't normal behavior.

Lars had called his family here for a reason.

"Dad, what's this about?"

"Patience, boyo." Lars didn't seem inclined to say more, but Owen stared him down.

"Fine," the old man said after a moment when no one filled the silence. He rose from his chair and shoved his hands deep in his pockets as he began to pace the kitchen.

Jenna glanced at Owen, but he gave nothing away.

Lars stopped, then turned to the two of them. "I've got a proposition for you," he said.

Owen remained silent, but his brow dipped lower over his eyes.

"For . . . whom, exactly?" Jenna asked, her gaze moving back and forth between the Jorgensen men.

"For both of you." Lars locked his eyes onto something behind them and over their heads.

Jenna and Owen exchanged a glance.

"What kind of proposition?" Owen asked.

"Well, now, that's the thing. I need you to hear me out," Lars began.

"I don't like the sound of this," Jenna murmured.

"That's exactly what I mean, missy. Passing judgment before you even hear what I have to say, that's the sort of thing I'm talking—"

There was a light rap on the door, and Lars practically leapt in that direction, seizing the interruption as if it could save him from a conversation he himself had initiated.

"Come in, come in." He welcomed a small bundle of a woman with bright eyes beneath a stocking cap of cherry red.

"Oh, Lars, why you still insist on living out in the back of beyond year-round is a mystery to me," the tiny woman said as she unwound from her winter gear.

"Can't imagine being anywhere else, Beverly."

The visitor had already drawn past the old man, dismissing him once she spied Owen.

"There's my boy!" she crowed, holding her arms wide. Owen rose with a smile lighting his face and engulfed the tiny woman in a hug that lifted her off her feet.

"Dad didn't tell me you were coming," Owen said, clearly pleased.

"Where's that girl of yours—"

"Nana!" Hannah cried, having looked up from her homework at the commotion.

The child hurtled across the room and was welcomed with an enthusiasm equal to her own.

Jenna's throat tightened. If she scratched below the surface, she'd find a deep envy for this family who still had one another to cling to, but the moment was too touching to mar with her own loss, and she purposefully took a deep breath and basked in their glow instead.

A soft smile played across her lips when the woman turned in her direction.

"And who do we have here?" the newcomer asked, her head tilted to one side.

"Beverly, this is Jenna Shaw," Lars said.

The woman glanced from Lars to Jenna to Owen, trying to work out what role Jenna played in their little tableau.

Their visitor was older than Jenna had assumed. Though at first glance she seemed near Lars's age, there was a fragility that gave her away.

A memory clicked into place.

Beverly Soderholm, Lars had called her.

The woman who'd joined them wasn't Hannah's grandmother, as the name Nana implied. Not directly. She was Owen's.

Beverly Soderholm was Audrey Jorgensen's mother.

32

Dinner passed in a series of sometimes awkward but mostly pleasant moments that Jenna found a bittersweet pill to swallow. She struggled not to weigh the evening down any more than her presence, as a virtual stranger in their home, already did.

Luckily, Ms. Soderholm picked up on the way Jenna redirected the questions put to her, and the older woman didn't push the conversation into uncomfortable territory.

Instead, she was lively and engaging, as effusive in her gestures and conversation as she was in her affection for her family.

Listening to her, Jenna thought she saw hints of the kind of electricity Lars claimed had first pulled him to Audrey.

An image of the broken Audrey's fearful face passed across Jenna's mind, and her smile grew stiff.

In spite of these moments, dinner was remarkably and notably . . . normal.

Right up until Lars said the words that dropped a ticking grenade into their midst.

"I had a reason for asking you all here tonight," he began on a prophetic note. "I know I said years ago that it was time to shut the door on the past, to live for the family we still have . . ."

Owen placed his glass on the table and sat back in his chair, watching his father closely.

"And I believe it was the right decision at the time."

"It was the only decision, Lars," Beverly interjected in the most somber voice Jenna had heard her use since she'd arrived.

"Maybe," said Lars.

"Not maybe, Dad. It was. You were drowning in it," Owen said softly.

A look passed over Lars's face as he watched his son run a finger through the ring of condensation his glass had left on the table. There was sorrow in the old man's expression. Sorrow and regret.

Lars cleared his throat.

"Be that as it may, it's time to open that door again," he announced. "I'd like Jenna to look into the facts of the case. From beginning to end, if she's willing. And I expect cooperation from all of you."

Hannah was the first to speak into the stunned silence that fell.

"Jenna? This Jenna? The lost lady?"

Lars shot his granddaughter a chastising look.

Jenna shook her head, pushing back from the table and this man and his ridiculous announcements. No one was paying her any mind, least of all Lars.

"Dad, why? Why now, why her? You're not making any sense."

"Jenna's a reporter."

"What?" the other three people around the table asked in unison as they turned to stare at her accusingly.

Jenna backed away from the combined heat.

"Former," she clarified. "Former reporter. Not anymore, not for a long time."

"And you're what? Digging into all this to put yourself on the map, make a name?" Ms. Soderholm asked.

"No!" Jenna interjected. "No, I'm not!"

"She's not," Lars tried to reassure them. "She has nothing to do with this."

The family appeared only slightly mollified.

"But I'd like her to," Lars added, throwing Jenna straight back into the hot seat. "Maybe there needs to be a book written about all this after all."

"What?" Jenna exclaimed as the table exploded with noise, everyone clamoring to be heard at once.

"Dad, I don't understand why—"

"Lars, you know how I feel about—"

"Grandpa, you don't even know this—"

"This is crazy. The last thing I need is—"

Lars put his pinkie fingers to the corners of his mouth and let out an ear-shattering whistle capable of cracking the ice on the lake.

"That's enough. If you'd all kindly allow me to finish . . ."

Mutiny was evident in their faces, but, miraculously, each of them held their tongues.

"As I was saying . . . Jenna is a reporter."

Jenna opened her mouth to correct him again, but he held up a finger in her direction.

"*Was* a reporter," he adjusted.

She wanted to ask how he knew that, but Lars continued, saving her the trouble.

"Eleanor Lutz, the librarian, mentioned it, and I did a little research on my own."

"You googled me?" Jenna asked. Like she had any right to be offended.

"Of course I did," he said. "You're not a bad writer."

Jenna couldn't help the small spark of satisfaction at his words. She shook it off, but there'd once been a time she'd taken pride in the work she did.

"What exactly are you asking, Lars?" she said.

"I want you to go through it all. To investigate. To dig. I know it's asking a lot, but—"

"I've never done investigative work. I wrote news reports and I did freelance features. This isn't really . . ." She trailed off. Now hardly seemed the time to mention how much the idea would have once appealed to her.

"Dad, we've been down this road, and it only ends in heartbreak. Do we really need—"

"Yes," Lars said. "Yes, we do." He turned away from his son's tortured face. "Jenna, will you help me? Will you help me try to find my children?"

She didn't know what to say, and she heard herself begin to stumble over a response.

"Please, Jenna," Lars said.

"I don't . . . Lars, I've seen your notes and the reports from the private investigators. I think it's really unlikely that I . . . of all people . . ."

"She's right," Beverly chimed in. "I want to know what happened as badly as you do. You know that. But this girl, she's a stranger. What do you think she'll be able to bring to the table that no one else could?"

Lars shrugged. "Nothing."

The answer was so unexpected that conversation ceased.

"Jenna could probably comb through everything available about the case and still come away empty handed."

"Then why?" Owen said, the words a desperate plea. "Why do this to yourself again?"

"Because I have to try. One last time, I have to try."

"But, Dad, there's always going to be one more last time. It's the same thing all addicts say."

Lars rose from his chair, looking away from them out the kitchen window. He stared at the gathering dusk over the snow-covered landscape.

"Lars, this won't bring back those babies." Beverly rose and placed an aged, bony hand on her son-in-law's arm. "You know if it would, I'd open a vein right here and let this woman write an entire book in my own blood."

Lars raised a hand and patted Beverly's, but the troubled look never left his face.

"No," Owen said fiercely into the silence. "I'm not doing this. Not again."

His face was shadowed, unreadable, but there was a leashed anger in his words.

"Hannah, get your things."

His daughter's eyes were large as she stared at her father.

"Come on," he said.

She scrambled to her feet, searching for her stuff.

"Son, I know it's not fair to ask—"

"No, it's not. Hannah, get a move on." Owen made an impatient gesture toward his daughter, who quickened her step.

He fished a set of keys from his pocket and pressed them into Hannah's hands.

"Go start the truck. I'll be right behind you."

She opened her mouth to argue but must have thought better of it when she caught sight of her father's face.

"Night, Grandpa. Bye, Nana." She ran to give her great-grandmother a quick hug, then left without any fuss.

"Dad, I can't stop you from doing this, but I won't have any part in it," Owen said to his father once the door had shut behind Hannah. "It almost killed you before, and I won't stand around and watch it happen again."

Owen was shrugging into his coat when Lars spoke again, pulling the pin from the grenade that had been sitting among them, waiting for this moment.

"I'd like you to reconsider, Owen," Lars said quietly. "Think of it as an old man's dying request."

With those words, the explosion came, silent and deadly, sending smoke and shrapnel around the room.

33

The lamplight was burning low and casting shadows when Ms. Soderholm padded through the room on quiet feet.

Jenna had taken a blanket and pillow to the sofa and left the spare room to the older woman. Sleep had proven elusive anyway.

Beverly Soderholm was quiet as she rummaged around the kitchen. "Join me for a nightcap?" she asked Jenna.

"Of course." Jenna folded her legs beneath her to make room for the small woman at the other end of the couch.

"Can't sleep," Ms. Soderholm said, though she looked done in. She passed Jenna a glass with an inch of dark liquid sloshing around the bottom and took the offered seat.

"Lars told me a bit about you, Mrs. Shaw." A hush hung over the cabin that seemed to amplify every creaking sound the old house made. The two women kept their voices low.

"I apologize if we were out of line. Accusatory," she went on.

Jenna waved her hand. "Not necessary," she replied, swirling the liquid in the glass.

She was strangely comfortable with this woman she'd only just met.

"I suppose you've all had your fill of reporters," Jenna said.

"Vultures, the lot of them," Ms. Soderholm agreed unapologetically. "Are you going to go through with this? Do as Lars asked?"

She peered at Jenna closely, measuring, judging.

Jenna sighed. "I've been sitting here trying to figure out a way to say no and still be able to face myself in the mirror."

Not to mention how to deal with her daughter, who had a decided opinion on the matter.

Ms. Soderholm had no answer for that, and the two women sat in an almost companionable silence, each lost in their thoughts.

"Audrey was a beautiful baby," Ms. Soderholm said suddenly with a wry twist of her lips. "Not easy—Lord, never that—but beautiful."

Jenna studied the woman's profile as she stared into the embers of the fire that burned low behind the grate.

"I was a single mother," she went on. "Told everyone I was a widow. It wasn't true. He was married. To someone else."

"Ms. Soderholm—"

"Beverly, please. Call me Beverly."

"Beverly. You don't have to—"

"I'm not ashamed," the older woman broke in. "He, on the other hand. He should have been. I was just a kid, drunk on the attention of an older man." She took a sip of her drink. "I've paid for my sins."

"Somehow, I doubt he ever did," Jenna ventured to guess.

Beverly gave a short stab of laughter. "Oh, he paid plenty. Through the nose he paid, like clockwork." She raised her glass in salute. "All I had to do was forget I knew him, which wasn't nearly as hard as it should have been. Audrey never wanted for a thing. Neither did I, come to that. A situation I won't apologize for."

"It couldn't have been easy, though," Jenna said, with a new respect for the woman sitting next to her.

"Not easy, no," Beverly agreed, shaking her head. "But looking back, perhaps it was *right* that it was just the two of us. Audrey . . ."

The woman's face clouded.

"She was seven years old when I realized there was something about her. Something not . . . right. Up until then, I told myself she

was just difficult. Some kids are, you know. I used words like *creative.
Temperamental, high-strung.* Told myself she took after me."

Beverly ran a hand across her eyes, and Jenna wondered what time
it was. Though, she supposed, these kinds of conversations were best
suited to whispers after midnight.

"Winters were bad. Her mood shifted, and she seemed lost in some
dark place no amount of persuasion could pull her from. When the
first signs of spring showed up, I used to breathe a sigh of relief. Soon
enough, that was full of worry too. Because summers . . . Summers
could be so much worse."

Ms. Soderholm—Beverly, Jenna reminded herself—pushed farther
back into the couch cushions, perhaps trying to find some distance from
the memories.

"There's a name for everything now, isn't there? Some official label
doctors cook up with a dismissive little acronym to go along with it.
Seasonal affective disorder, they call it. SAD." She turned her head with
her cheek still lying against the cushion and gave Jenna a look that was
difficult to decipher.

"I can recite Audrey's recipe card by heart. Stir together a strong
helping of disorders, equal parts bipolar and manic depressive. Add a
dash of SAD and a pinch of oppositional defiance, then top it all off
with a sprinkle of postpartum depression. Mix and bake."

Jenna's brow creased at the litany of phrases.

Beverly took another deep drink. "My apologies if I sound flippant."

"No," Jenna whispered.

"I'm not." Beverly studied her glass as if answers might be found
there. "Far from it. I haven't been flippant about anything concerning
Audrey since she was a child and climbed onto the roof of the house
one day with the neighbor girl and jumped off."

Jenna stiffened.

"The other little girl thankfully had enough sense not to jump,
though Audrey tried her best to convince her to."

"Oh my God," Jenna murmured. "Was she . . . ?"

"Hurt?" Beverly asked. "Of course she was. She broke her leg."

Jenna raised a hand to her mouth.

"To this day, I couldn't tell you what her intentions were. It was spring and she was on a terrible upswing. The other child—Pamela, her name was—told us Audrey was convinced she could fly. That she'd tried to convince Pammy she could too. But when I asked Audrey, she told me she thought it would be a good way to die."

Beverly threw back her head and drained the last of the amber fire, then set the empty glass on the coffee table. She rose, their midnight heart-to-heart apparently at an end.

"Knowing my daughter as I do, Mrs. Shaw, my money is on a little bit of both."

The older woman showed every bit of her age as she walked out of the room.

Jenna set her own untouched drink next to Beverly's empty glass.

Sleep was farther away than ever.

34

Jenna had finally dropped into a deep and haunted darkness where her dreams were nothing but unformed sensations. A creeping sense of cold, of time stretching infinitely outward.

A touch of chill snaked its way across her cheek and she shivered in her sleep, struggling to find warmth in the desolate landscape of her mind.

"Francie," came a whisper, floating through the black.

Jenna shook her head, denying the sound and the emotions that came with it.

"No," she mumbled. "No."

More whispers, unintelligible, yet pressing their need on her.

"Francie."

"No!" Jenna broke through the surface of her dreams with a strangled start, gasping for breath, for safety, for sanity.

Her eyes and her mind struggled to adjust, to hold on to anything real, but the fingers of cold continued to stroke her cheek.

"Francie." A whisper in the night. Close. So close.

The face, pale and desperate, that leaned over her was no dream.

Jenna's scream ripped through the silence as she scrambled up and away from the ghostly mirage hovering over her.

"Shh, sweetheart," the figure said, moving toward her in a failed attempt to soothe Jenna's panic. "Shh, it's Mommy. Mommy's here, honey."

Jenna could only scream again, until feet pounded down the hallway and out of the bedrooms, feet that brought help, that brought reality back with a crash and a bang of slamming doors.

"Audrey?" came Lars's sleep-addled voice. "My God, Jenna, are you all right?"

He made his way to her as Beverly skidded to a halt at the scene that greeted her in the living room.

"Audrey," she said when she saw her daughter standing like a lost specter in the middle of the room. "Oh, Audrey."

Lars wrapped a blanket around Jenna's shoulders and looked her in the eye.

"Did she hurt you?" he asked slowly. "Are you hurt?"

Jenna shook her head, words still impossible to form. Her heart slammed an erratic rhythm in her chest, and she tried to drink in deep, calming breaths.

Looking around, Lars saw the front door had been left swinging wide, and the warmth had leached out of the room as winter made itself an uninvited visitor.

"Christ," he muttered, moving to shut the door, his face pale and shaken.

He shut the cold and the falling snow outside where it belonged. He turned, opened his mouth to speak, but the warbling ring of the telephone cut him off. Jenna gave another strangled scream, though she managed to shut it down with a hand to her mouth before it ran wild.

Each of them stared at the phone with anxious expectation, as if God himself were calling.

Visibly shaking off his disquiet, Lars reached for the phone before it could intrude with another persistent ring.

"Hello?" His voice was rough with the dregs of sleep and an edge of shock.

His eyes flitted up to lock onto his wife, who was standing mute and forlorn next to her mother.

Audrey may have been flesh and bone rather than the ghost of Jenna's nightmares, but with the woman's gray hair flowing madly around her face and a deep, searching confusion in her eyes, Jenna could forgive herself the temporary lapse. Beverly rubbed one hand up and down her daughter's back. She'd laced her fingers through Audrey's with the other, her knuckles white.

The skin on the back of Jenna's neck prickled at Audrey's eyes watching her.

"I'm just going to stop you there," Lars said into the phone, pulling Jenna's attention back in his direction. "I'm fully aware my wife is not in your facility, Dr. Taylor, because I'm looking at her."

There was a pause.

"No, there's no situation. Everyone is safe, and Audrey is calm," he said with brisk efficiency.

"Yes, that'll be fine. Of course."

He hung up the phone and ran a hand through his thick, sleep-tousled hair.

"We're about to have company," he told the trio of women. "Audrey, love," he said with a shake of his head. "You still know how to cause a stir, don't you?"

He walked toward his wife and placed a hand upon her cheek. Her eyes met his, this man who'd stood by her side through it all. A stable port in a storm of her own making.

He pulled her to him in a reverent hug. The melancholy air that had settled upon the cabin was full of regret, of loss, and, undeniably, of love.

"I'll put the coffee on," Beverly said with a sigh.

35

Instead of the sun breaking over the horizon, the red and blue flashing lights of police cruisers marked the coming of the day.

There was a myriad of questions, each group looking to fill in the gaps of what had happened and who was responsible.

"Mr. Jorgensen, did you have any hand in helping your wife escape from the psychiatric facility? Were you aware of her intentions in advance?" This from the police lieutenant who had led an unresisting Audrey to the back of his official vehicle to transport her where the courts had deemed she belonged.

There were representatives of the hospital who had their own questions to ask and answer. Dr. Taylor, the director, arrived with hospital security as well as a nurse who was familiar with Audrey and would ride with her on her return trip.

"We're reviewing events of the night, and obviously, our priority is to keep both the members of the community and the patients in our charge safe," he said. "That directive broke down somewhere tonight, and we'll be vigilant in searching out exactly when and where that breakdown took place. I want to assure you, Mr. Jorgensen . . ."

On and on it went.

Lars answered their questions, to the extent he was able, with a resigned directness Jenna couldn't help but admire, given the circumstances.

Owen arrived. Whether Lars had found the time to call him or he'd been contacted in some other way, Jenna couldn't know. He inclined his head in her direction and spoke quietly to his father while his mother was driven away.

After the crowd dispersed, all with a low-key composure Jenna had come to associate with Midwesterners, she found herself at a loss, left with an antsy need to be *doing* something. Anything.

She gathered coffee cups, their contents gone cold, and ran a sink of warm, soapy water. She could have placed them in the dishwasher and been done with it, but then what would she do with her hands?

Beverly found a dish towel and took a clean cup from Jenna's hands to dry. The older woman had a few questions of her own.

"I spoke with the nurse. She told me Audrey was stirred up yesterday evening. I wasn't aware Lars had taken you to meet her."

Jenna glanced over, but Beverly had a guarded look that was impossible to read.

"I asked her to go," Lars said from behind the pair. He was standing with his back against the counter, arms crossed, contemplating the cracked tile floor.

"Dad, I don't understand you," Owen said from the opposite side of the counter, where he was leaning with his head in his hands.

Jenna didn't understand him either, but kept her opinions to herself. This wasn't her family. Thoughts of the ashes packed away in the spare room were never far from her mind, if she needed a chilling reminder.

Ignoring his son's frustration, Lars went on.

"It's hard to imagine. They said she was uncooperative. Disruptive, even. There was some sort of upset in the dining hall. Several patients ended up in the infirmary."

"Mom *hurt* someone?" Owen raised his head and leaned back slightly.

"No, no," Lars said. "But she may have been the spark that set the others off. And in the chaos, they lost track of her."

"So how did she get out?" Owen asked, voicing the question they were all wondering.

Lars shrugged. "Your guess is as good as mine, son. Apparently the orderlies and the guards on the unit thought she was in the infirmary with the others, and vice versa, so it was late before they realized she was gone."

"Sounds like someone is going to be begging to hold on to their job," Beverly added.

"She must have hitchhiked," Lars went on. "There's no way she could have made it all this way on her own. Not in this weather."

"It's good she came here, then," Jenna added mildly. "At least she's safe now."

"What I still don't understand is *why*," Beverly said with surprising force. "Why now? After all these years of nothing?"

A pit formed in the base of Jenna's stomach, and she swallowed a heavy lump in her throat.

"Jenna, I don't know if you understand the significance of what's happened," Lars said.

She was beginning to.

"Mom's never agitated," Owen continued. "Never. The Thorazine used to make her jittery, but since her medications were changed years ago, she's been as placid as the lake on a windless day."

"Looks like the winds have started blowing," Beverly said, meeting Lars's gaze over the cup she was drying in her hand.

"They said she was talking. None of it makes any sense, but she's saying things, Bev. Things she's never said before." There was a kind of wonder in his tone.

"What was she saying?" Beverly asked.

Lars shook his head. "I didn't understand it. Something about, 'He wouldn't come. Why wouldn't he come?' Or something like that. Nurse Bennington told me Audrey repeated it over and over, asking the nursing staff, the orderlies, the other patients. No one had an answer."

Owen went pale and dropped down on the edge of the couch. Lars moved to sit next to him.

"It's a shock," he said. He looked toward Jenna and Beverly and said the words no one else could bring themselves to hope, much less say.

"What if . . . Bev, what if she's starting to remember?"

Beverly put a hand to her throat and leaned her back against the counter for support.

"Twenty-nine years," she whispered. "She's never spoken of those missing days. Not once." She shook her head. When she finally looked up, her eyes bored into Jenna's, the stranger in the room. "Until you, Mrs. Shaw."

Jenna squirmed under the scrutiny.

"You visited her yesterday, and within hours she's saying things she's never said, not to her doctors, not to her family, not to the courts."

"I didn't . . . I didn't mean . . ."

"Audrey's confused Jenna with Francie," Lars said. "You heard her."

Beverly was looking at Jenna when she spoke again. "I did, and I can see that, I suppose. The dark hair. But I showed Audrey pictures of Francie and Will every time I visited her for years. I never got any response at all."

Jenna looked to Lars for help. His face was troubled. All their faces were.

"What are you trying to say, Beverly?" Lars asked.

"I think a better question would be, what are you two not saying? Clearly, something happened yesterday to set Audrey off. Maybe that's all for the good, and maybe not, but I think it's time somebody tells us the truth."

Beverly crossed her arms and waited.

"She was upset when we left," Lars admitted. "That's true."

"Upset how?" Owen asked. "Mom doesn't get *upset*."

Lars blew out a breath. "I don't know, just—"

"It was me," Jenna interrupted. "I did it."

They might as well know. Jenna had always tried to teach her children to fess up to what they'd done.

All eyes turned toward her. There was compassion and empathy in Lars's face. The others reserved judgment.

Shame washed over Jenna as she remembered the aggressive, unrelenting words she'd hurled at a woman who was clearly mentally ill. A woman who had no defense, even in her own mind.

"What exactly did you do, Ms. Shaw?" Beverly prompted.

"I . . . I told her . . ." Jenna took a deep breath and straightened her spine. "She thought I was her daughter, and instead of comforting her, I told her I couldn't be Francie, could I? That her daughter was gone, and she had no one to blame but herself."

Jenna heard Beverly's sharp intake of breath.

"I told her that her kids were never coming back, and it was all her fault."

36

An uneasy sense of foreboding had overtaken the cabin.

Owen left to get Hannah to school and open the garage. Beverly was gathering her things, readying to make the drive back to her home, a condominium an hour west of Raven.

"Ever shoveled snow?" Lars asked Jenna with a quirk of an eyebrow.

"Can't say I have, but I'm a fast learner."

She dressed quickly and pulled on the warm clothing needed to protect her from the elements, grateful for the mundane task.

They labored side by side until Jenna's arms burned. She shed one of her layers and went back to work.

By the time they were done, the driveway along with the steps down to the lake were clear.

"You do this every time it snows?" Jenna asked, leaning her weight against the dented snow shovel she'd buried in a drift.

"Unless you want to climb through it to get to your car, you do."

She marveled at his matter-of-factness. Was it an innate part of him, or was this what years and the grinding sands of loss did to a person? Shaped them into something smooth and hard and polished.

With enough time, would he be polished away to nothing? Thoughts of his heart and the conversation he'd shared last night, which included phrases like *mini-stroke* and *matter of time*, came back to her. She supposed, yes, he'd one day be polished away to nothing. Nothing but memories.

They all would, wouldn't they?

Then even the memories would fade.

"Lars, I can't help you find out what happened to your family."

He glanced up and met her eyes, then went back to removing the last of the snow covering the walkway.

"Because you don't want to? Or because you don't think it'll make a difference?"

She turned to stare out across the lake that had drawn her here in the first place. "Both, maybe."

There was a crunch as Lars pushed his shovel into the snow behind her, then he was by her side, staring at the same view that held her.

Did he see what she saw? Or did the magnificence lessen with familiarity?

"If you don't want to, there's not a lot I can say to that," he said. "But don't fool yourself into thinking it won't make a difference."

She shook her head. "You said yourself, you don't think I'll find anything."

"There's more than one way to make a difference, Jenna Shaw."

Like pieces to a puzzle she wasn't aware she'd been searching for, his words clicked into place. Her breath caught at the image forming.

"You didn't ask me to do this for you, or your wife and son, or even your missing kids." She jerked around to face him. "You asked me to do this so I'd have a reason to stay."

She didn't mean stay in Minnesota, and he knew it.

Lars shoved his hands into the pockets of his coat and continued to stare across the expanse of frozen water.

He didn't deny it.

"It's your decision, Jenna. But it *would* make a difference. It would make a difference to me."

He said nothing more before he walked away to gather the snow shovels and stow them in the garage.

She watched him go, horrified at the swell of emotion that came over her.

At least he wasn't there to see the tears pooling in her eyes. Jenna didn't know if she could handle that humiliation on top of everything else threatening to surface.

She swiped at her eyes, hiding the evidence of how much the old man's words had affected her.

"I think he's gone and fallen in love with you," Cassie said.

"Hush," she mumbled.

Jenna could tell the difference between romantic love and a different sort of attachment. Lars's heart belonged to Audrey, for better or worse, and it always would.

"You can't deny he's come to care for you, Mom," Cassie said.

"God knows why," Jenna murmured, avoiding the natural next step—an honest examination of whether she'd come to care about the old bastard in return.

"Regardless of his reasons, there's one question you can't avoid."

Jenna didn't have to wait long for her daughter to put into words what she didn't want to face.

"What's it going to do to him when you decide to leave? For good?"

Jenna's forehead creased as she stared at the ice that had crept farther across the lake, meeting in the middle to form what looked to be an impenetrable barrier.

"Don't you think he's been through enough?"

Jenna had no answer for that.

37

The ride was just as bumpy as ever when Lars drove the two of them into Raven.

They'd said goodbye to Beverly. Jenna had expected an icy farewell, given the woman's reaction to what Jenna had done to her daughter, so the hug Beverly pulled her into had taken her off guard. Jenna's arms hung stiffly at her sides until she managed to bring them up to pat the woman gingerly on the back.

"Whatever the reason, Jenna," Beverly said into her ear, "this might be a good thing."

There were calls to make and return to both the hospital and the police station. Audrey had made it safely back into the custody of the psychiatric facility, but Lars frowned at the news that she was still distressed and acting strange. The hospital staff had sedated her.

"There are bound to be repercussions for this business," he mused as he drove.

"What can they do?" Jenna asked. "She's already locked away."

"Maybe," he said. "But there are units like the one she's in, and then there are others. I hope they don't try and say she's dangerous now."

He had plenty on his mind, and Jenna didn't want to add to his burdens, but an idea was floating around she couldn't put to rest.

"I know you see the similarities. You can't hide from me, remember," Cassie said.

Jenna didn't respond, but Cass was right. The Thacker case had been tugging at her consciousness, begging for acknowledgment for days.

But to speak would constitute involvement.

"Lars," Jenna finally said.

"Hmm?" he asked.

She cleared her throat.

"Just ask!" Cassie exclaimed.

She silently shushed her, but gave in.

"Lars, has anyone ever tried helping Audrey retrace her steps?"

Jenna received only silence in reply. After a moment, she saw he wasn't intentionally ignoring her; he simply wasn't listening.

"Lars?" she asked again.

"I'm sorry, what?"

"I asked if anyone has ever tried to help Audrey retrace her steps from those missing days?"

"Retrace her steps?" he repeated, as if he didn't understand her language.

"Yeah," she said. "You know, like, walk her through the day she left, beginning with what they know."

"Well, no." He frowned. "Not exactly. I don't know how to describe the state Audrey was in, Jenna." He raised his shoulders, then let them drop. "She was as close to catatonic as a person can be and still be moving around."

He glanced at her, tried to explain. "She wasn't mute, but she was completely incoherent. When questions were put to her—and there were plenty—it was like she didn't even hear them."

The memories were obviously hard for him to relive, but she couldn't squash the idea that had begun to take root.

"Audrey wasn't on this plane of existence anymore," he went on. "We tried everything. Believe me, if retracing her steps had been possible, we would have done it. She's never given any indication she remembers what happened during those three days." He shook his head again. "Eventually, we stopped asking."

Jenna let that sink in.

Let it go, her inner voice told her. Not Cassie's voice, her own. *Let it be.*

"I used to have this . . . I don't know if you'd call it a fantasy, or what. This *hope,* I guess. That Audrey and the kids had been kidnapped. That someone, somewhere, had held her against her will. Stupid, right?"

He glanced at her with the tortured face of a prisoner of war.

"I wanted so badly for someone else to be responsible. I always knew, deep down, that was bullshit."

His voice was bleak, his eyes locked onto the road in front of them.

"To believe that, you'd have to ignore Audrey's history, her instability. She always was a runner. Even when she was young. Beverly can tell you about the times she'd disappear as a teenager. Days on end, then she'd reappear, dirty and bruised, needing to be deloused."

Jenna's face tightened. She tried to push away the image, but it wouldn't go.

"She always struggled. With marriage. With the kids. Hell, with life."

He spoke with an exhausted resignation, and she was drawn in by his pain. His regret.

"Whatever happened during those days, it was a culmination of Audrey's illness and my lack of understanding of it. No one else was responsible. Just she and I. Only a fool would believe otherwise."

He pulled the truck into the church parking lot and let it idle.

"So to answer your question, no, we never managed to retrace her steps. The police tried but never had any success. Neither did the investigators I hired. It was like she and the kids just up and vanished."

His fingers beat an anxious rhythm on the steering wheel as he stared at the brick building where they'd soon work to bring some semblance of hope to a group of people who had little left to hope for.

"And then she reappeared. From nowhere. But Francie and Will . . ." He turned the key to shut off the ignition. "They never did."

38

Lars was particularly quiet while they prepared and served lunch, giving a distracted smile now and then to one of the small crowd. Jenna couldn't shut out the nagging sense there was more that could be done.

When Owen appeared at the back door of the church as they were cleaning up, Jenna was relieved.

"Thought I'd grab a bite over at the diner." He picked up a wooden spoon Jenna had just washed, then set it down again. "Anyone want to join me?"

Jenna looked over at Lars, but he was somber, stacking dishes.

"I'll pass, son, if you don't mind. Not much of an appetite. You two go ahead."

A kernel of hesitation lingered at leaving Lars when he was in such a low mood. *He's come through worse than this,* Jenna reminded herself.

"I'll join you," she told Owen. "If you don't need me anymore, Lars."

A few days prior, the old man would have made a dry remark about having gotten along perfectly well without her help for sixty-odd years, but he just sent them a dismissive wave.

Jenna gathered her things and joined Owen, hoping the privacy would give Lars some space to sort through his thoughts.

The crowd in the diner could have been the same people there on her previous visit. Many of them probably were, but they barely cast a glance in her direction as she entered ahead of Owen.

The lull in conversation was less noticeable, at least.

"Can I ask you something, Jenna?" Owen said once their orders had been placed.

"Sure," she replied, though she couldn't hide her reservations. His mood had been affected by the events of the early morning as well. Father and son were strikingly similar.

"Why are you helping us?" he asked, getting straight to the point.

She thought for a moment about how to answer.

"I wouldn't say I *am* helping you. I told your dad I don't think I can add anything to the investigation that's already been done. I've read through the notes. It was all very thorough."

The answer was disingenuous and she knew it. Her urge to leave, to get out before she'd gotten too deep, was still there. It had never gone away. But she had a suspicion, one she wasn't ready to recognize, that it was too late for that.

"I had plans," Jenna said, not meeting his eyes. "I still have plans."

"Dad told me about your plans."

Jenna held her breath, waiting for his judgment to flow over her.

When it didn't come, she asked, "Are you going to try and talk me out of it? Tell me how selfish I'm being?"

His head tilted to the side. "Would that work?"

"No."

"Then no, I won't."

Jenna studied him, this man she'd paid little attention to before now.

"I could, I suppose." He fiddled with a napkin in his large, calloused hands. "Probably I should. But even if I say all the things I'm supposed to, you seem like a smart woman. I'm guessing you've thought of those things already."

"Many times."

He sighed heavily and sat back in the vinyl-covered booth, balling the napkin into a knot and tossing it onto the table in front of them.

"Then who am I to try and gloss over what you've been through? For what? To ease my own discomfort?"

A powerful sense of relief washed over Jenna.

"I don't like it," he continued. "I don't know you. Not really. But I don't like the idea of waking up in a world you've chosen to leave."

Jenna opened her mouth, but no words came out.

"The world would always be less for that choice. But I guess the world deserves that, after what it's done to you. Whether I like it or not doesn't make me qualified to judge."

Jenna took a deep breath before she trusted herself to speak.

"Thank you," she whispered.

Owen's mouth twisted and he shook his head.

"Don't thank me. I haven't done anything. A specialty of mine, doing nothing."

There was a bitter resignation in him today. His demeanor had shifted, somehow.

"Owen," Jenna said, leaning in. "Are you all right?"

A silent chuckle that had nothing to do with amusement contorted his features.

"Do you consider yourself an honest person, Jenna?"

She sat back.

"Yes," she finally answered. The word sounded too much like a question.

"But you kept secrets of your own, didn't you?" came her daughter's faint whisper. An accusation Jenna couldn't deny.

"As honest as the next person, I suppose," she went on, relegating thoughts of her secrets to the farthest corner of her mind.

"And if the next person isn't as honest as you'd think?" he asked.

"What are you trying to say?"

"I've always thought I was an honest person," he said. "But people have an infinite capacity to lie. To other people. Even—maybe especially—to themselves."

The conversation had taken a turn Jenna hadn't anticipated, and her body went still, waiting for a glimpse of the destination Owen was leading them to.

"There are so many unanswered questions," he said. "But only a few that matter, and those consumed my dad. Where did Mom go? What happened to Francie and Will?"

He shook his head, shackled by memories that wouldn't let him go.

"The other, smaller questions got shoved aside. And it was easy to convince myself . . ." He trailed off.

Jenna stiffened slightly.

"Everyone gossiping, whispering behind their hands. Why did she take two kids, and leave the other one behind? They were too polite to say it to my face, but I heard them anyway. Felt their stares, all of them wondering what was wrong with me that my own mother didn't bother to take me with her."

She studied his face and caught a glimpse of an old hurt.

He smiled a dark smile, full of regret.

"They didn't know, and I didn't tell them. I lied to everyone, then managed to convince myself my lie was true."

"Owen," Jenna said. She didn't know what to ask. He answered her anyway.

"My mother didn't want to leave me, Jenna," he said. "She begged me to come with her. I can still see her face, red with tears. Begging. And I refused to go."

Jenna flipped through her mental notes, scrolling backward through the facts Lars had recorded so diligently over the years, then packed away into a file box.

Owen had been at a friend's house down the street from their home when his mother had fled with his little brother and sister.

"I refused to go, and I ran off. I wanted to play with my friend. For one day, I just wanted to be a normal kid, doing normal kid things. I didn't want to get caught up in the chaos of Mom's moods. Not again."

"Owen." Jenna reached across the table to place her hand on his. "You were a child. No one will blame you. You know that, right?" He continued as if she hadn't spoken.

"'Why wouldn't he come?' That's what she's asking, Jenna," Owen said. "She's starting to remember, after all this time. And her memories are more clear than my own, even after three decades in a psych ward."

He shook his head, carrying the weight of his private burden.

"So which of us is the crazy one?"

39

It was Cassie's relentless nagging that prodded Jenna on.

"Every scene needs to move the plot forward, remember."

Jenna tried to ignore her.

"Otherwise, what's the point?" She refused to be shunted aside.

Her subconscious daughter wasn't going to let it go.

"Lars, I think you should consider hypnosis."

Jenna spoke the words in a rush, knowing they came out of left field. But the idea had been spinning in her head, slowly at first, then with increased speed.

She held her breath, waiting for the inevitable dismissal most people had when a word like *hypnosis* was thrown into regular conversation.

When it didn't come, only a silent, assessing glance in her direction, she plunged on.

"Some people call it a scam or pseudoscience—and I'll admit, there's not a lot of verifiable medical evidence—but if you can get past the preconceived ideas, what's left is basically a deep, guided meditation."

"You sound like you have experience with this?" He narrowed his eyes in her direction.

He hadn't shut her down. Not yet anyway.

"Some," she said. "I did some research on hypnotherapy for an article. It's still controversial, what with the allegations of abuse by unlicensed therapists, but there are a lot more people out there that have been helped than hurt."

She didn't mention it was mostly people who needed help to quit smoking, or overcome a fear of flying. No need to give him a reason to be dismissive.

She also didn't mention the Thacker case.

Lars was quiet, his eyes on the road.

"It's something to consider," she continued. "If Audrey is beginning to remember, then hypnosis—or guided meditation, if you're more comfortable calling it that—could be a tool to help her put everything back in place."

He pulled the truck into the driveway of the cabin, but said nothing.

"Just something to think about," Jenna added in a mumble as she opened the passenger door. She grabbed the bag of groceries sitting on the seat between them.

She'd volunteered to take care of dinner, insisting she could cook even without his hovering instructions.

He was still sitting, showing no signs of movement, when she shut the truck door carefully behind her and made her way inside.

Jenna was seasoning steaks for dinner when she caught sight of Lars through the window. He was standing at the top of the steps that led down to the lake.

She had no idea if she'd made things better or worse. It would be up to Lars to decide if he wanted to pursue the idea, but at least Cassie would leave her alone about it.

"You should have told him," Cassie said, proving her wrong almost immediately.

Jenna sighed.

Crystal Thacker, a single mother of two, was thirty-two years old when she was murdered in her bed, a shotgun blast to the head. Crystal's younger daughter had been traumatized by the horror she'd witnessed that night and couldn't speak about it. The hypnotherapist Jenna interviewed for the magazine article considered the recovery of her memories of the event one of his professional successes. With his help, the little girl, only eight years old, had recalled watching numbly as her older sister and her sister's boyfriend had attempted to cover up the crime.

Upon questioning, the pair had confessed to the murder.

But a criminal investigation resolved with the aid of hypnosis was a rare bird indeed.

"I can't, Cass," Jenna murmured. "It probably won't work, and I can't bring myself to give him that much hope."

Hope was a frightening thing to rekindle. As impossible to control as a wildfire on a dry plain.

Dinner was quiet, each of them lost in their thoughts.

Lars sat back and wiped his mouth with a napkin.

"Turns out you're not a bad cook either."

She gave him a small smile. "High praise."

"I don't know if anything will come of it, but I'll call around tomorrow. It can't hurt to try."

No, Jenna thought. *It never hurts to try . . . It's not until you fail that it hurts.*

But she couldn't say that. It had been her suggestion.

Wheels were beginning to turn in places other than the Jorgensen cabin as well. Like the electric current Dr. Frankenstein put to his monstrous creation, Audrey's escape had breathed life and renewed interest into an investigation that had long been pronounced dead.

Before Lars had a chance to make those calls, he received one of his own. A new detective had been assigned to the case. Though the file had never been officially closed, it had been years since any resources had been put into an active investigation of Francie and Will Jorgensen's whereabouts.

Jenna tried to curb her curiosity, but she couldn't help but overhear parts of the conversation.

The words "Could call it guided meditation, if you're more comfortable with that" caught her attention.

"No, I haven't spoken with the hospital administration or Audrey's doctors yet. Not sure whose permission would need to be gotten first in a situation like this . . . Maybe so, maybe so. But if a judge is willing to sign off on it, I don't see why . . ."

Jenna waited with as much patience as she could muster for news. Days passed. More calls. There was a visit from Sergeant Allred, the detective in charge of the cold case, who interviewed Lars and Owen again. He took Lars's file box of notes with him when he left.

Jenna didn't push for answers. She helped Lars shovel snow when it was needed, assisted on the days it was his turn to serve lunch at the church kitchen, and cooked dinner every other night.

Lars was visiting his wife on the day Diane came to clean again.

The housekeeper chatted while she tidied the kitchen and dusted Lars's shelves. Jenna found herself glad for the company.

Owen stopped by just as Diane was finishing up.

"Well, now, if you aren't a sight for sore eyes," the older woman cried as the big man smiled and landed a kiss on her cheek.

"I managed to get out of there for a while and thought I'd bring lunch to my favorite lady."

"Oh, go on with you." Diane swatted at his shoulder, but her cheeks flushed with pleasure.

"Join us, Jenna?" Owen asked, holding up takeout bags from the Raven Café. "I have plenty."

Diane brought out a side of Owen that Jenna hadn't seen before. He was playful, teasing. The older woman preened under his attention.

Jenna sat back and smiled at the two of them.

"Mmm," Owen said suddenly, wiping his mouth on a napkin. "I forgot to tell you. Mrs. Johnson's Yorkie just had a litter of puppies."

"Really?" Diane's head tilted with interest.

"Took all I had not to bring you one, but if Hannah had seen it, I'd have been stuck with it."

"Well, I don't know if I'm ready for a new dog, not so soon after Fitz passed on—Fitz was my little sidekick for a lot of years," she added to Jenna. "Do you care for dogs?"

"Not enough," Cassie said, pushing in the knife.

A vision of Beckett's face the last time she'd seen him rose in Jenna's mind.

"I love dogs," she told Diane truthfully.

"Really?" Cassie asked. "I wonder what Beck would say to that?"

"I . . . I had a golden retriever. His name was Beckett." She didn't want to talk about Beckett, but Cassie would never leave her be if she didn't acknowledge him.

"Oh dear," Diane said. "I know how hard it is when a pet passes."

"Don't you dare lie, Mom," Cassie warned.

Jenna exhaled a long breath.

"He's not dead," she admitted. "When I came here, things for me were a little . . . up in the air. My neighbors took him in. I didn't know when I'd be back home and, well . . ."

Cassie was listening to every word, judging it for truth and finding it lacking.

"I miss him," Jenna confessed. *There, Cass. I admit it.* "I miss him terribly. He's a good dog. The best."

With Owen studying her so astutely and Cassie implanted in her head, pressure pushed in from every direction.

Jenna stood and took her plate to the sink.

"Well, if Mrs. Johnson has a litter, I don't see why you can't get one for Hannah, too, Owen," she heard Diane say at her back.

Jenna closed her eyes, thankful the housekeeper had turned the subject away from Beckett.

She couldn't erase the image of those soulful brown eyes watching her go.

She'd read somewhere that dogs don't have any real sense of the future. That every time you leave them, to go to work, or run to the grocery store, or just walk around the block, all they know is now. They believe, each time you leave, that it's forever.

Beckett, sweet, trusting Beckett, straining at the leash to go with her. *Sometimes, it is forever.*

"If you'll excuse me," she said quietly, "Owen, thank you for lunch. It was lovely."

Grabbing her coat, Jenna decided to take a walk. The winter was still bruising for someone used to warmer places, but the cold had an impressive ability to cleanse.

So she walked. And in the days after, she walked and she read borrowed novels and she played solitaire, with actual cards instead of an electronic device.

What Jenna didn't do, though she couldn't bring herself to examine her reasons, was check on the state of her minivan.

"Good news," Lars said a few days later as he hung up the phone. "The judge who presided over the original case is still on the bench, believe it or not. The man must be eighty if he's a day."

Jenna didn't care how old he was, only what he had to say.

"Given the change in Audrey's state, he agreed to allow the police to take an . . . *unconventional* approach in the new investigation."

"What does that mean, exactly?" She barely dared to hope.

"It means as long as Audrey remains under police supervision, the judge will allow her to be put under hypnosis in an attempt to retrace her steps."

His eyes were large, unblinking. He wasn't smiling. Jenna felt a *but* coming.

"*If* the hospital administrator is willing to sign off on it."

And there it was.

One more hurdle to cross.

40

Dr. Reid Taylor's office could have been lifted from a movie set, with its warm wood and deep, expensive chairs upholstered in hunter green, its bookcases lined with leather-bound texts, and its walls filled with framed diplomas polished to a shine. Jenna wondered if the fancy degrees were forgeries.

Dr. Taylor was trying very hard to look like a psychiatrist should.

Jenna chided herself for judging the man based on his decor, then the doctor leaned back in his office chair and touched the tips of his fingers together to form a steeple while he contemplated his response.

She bit her lip in an effort not to roll her eyes.

Next to her sat Lars, looking more like the aging sailor he was than someone comfortable in a psychiatrist's office.

"Believe me, Doctor, I know how irregular this is, but I think it's important to explore any memories Audrey may have coming to the surface," Lars said.

Dr. Taylor pursed his lips and turned his chair to face them.

"Mr. Jorgensen, I appreciate your desire to delve further, but I must admit I have some serious reservations. I can't help but feel, considering the patient's recent history, it would be safer for all involved if these issues were explored within the confines of the hospital."

Lars met Jenna's eyes for the briefest of moments, and she saw him struggle to hold on to his temper.

"So you've said, Doctor."

"I'm thinking of the patient's well-being. It seems an unnecessary risk, in my professional opinion."

Lars pulled in a deep breath and opened his mouth to speak, but whatever words he'd been about to spill out he managed to pull back, visibly wrestling for control.

"Dr. Taylor," Jenna broke in, before Lars said something he'd regret. "In all the time Audrey Jorgensen's been confined in your facility, has there ever been any indication she was regaining her memories?"

The doctor flipped open the manila file on his desk, presumably containing information about Audrey. She was certain the man had already read what was in there cover to cover. It was a nice prop to have.

"No, Ms. Shaw," he said. "There doesn't appear to be any indication of that, but—"

"And she's been a patient here for how long?" Jenna continued.

"Twenty-nine years, as I'm sure you're aware."

"So for nearly thirty years, your staff has had unlimited access to Mrs. Jorgensen, and she's presumably seen numerous doctors and undergone a battery of traditional types of therapy."

"Ms. Shaw, I can see the point you're getting to, but my decision is made. I simply cannot see the advantage to—"

"Do you have children?" Lars asked in a deceptively even voice.

A cloud passed over Dr. Taylor's face before he managed to school his expression back into a professional guise.

"I do," he said, "but that's hardly—"

"Do you know where they are?" Lars continued. "Right now, at this very minute?"

"Well, no, obviously, not at this moment."

"Do you know where they'll lay their heads down to sleep tonight?"

Dr. Taylor shifted uncomfortably in his impressive leather chair.

"Mr. Jorgensen, I appreciate what you're—"

"Do you know, right now, at this very minute, if your children are alive or dead?"

The doctor's hands stilled and he slowly closed his mouth.

"I know, in my heart, Dr. Taylor, my two youngest children are dead."

Jenna turned to stare at Lars.

"I've known it for a long time," he continued in his low, resonant way. "What I don't know, what I haven't known for over three decades, is where they lie when the sun goes out at night. I don't know if it's cold where they are. If it's safe, if the darkness is too deep for light to shine in."

Lars rose from his chair.

"Please consider that while you deliberate on the . . . *appropriateness* of your decision."

He turned and walked out of the psychiatrist's perfect office. Jenna hurried to catch up, leaving the doctor alone with Lars's words.

41

Jenna gathered her clothing to once again drop into the ancient washing machine.

"You could just buy a change of clothes, you know," Cass said. Jenna refused to take the bait. The days she'd spent at this out-of-the-way cabin, with nothing but a surly old man for company, were piling up, one thin layer on top of the next.

It doesn't matter, she thought. *A strong gust of wind and it will all scatter and blow away.*

She pressed "Start" on the washer and hoped Cassie would leave it alone. The time was coming when she'd have to face leaving this place. This was nothing more than an unexpected detour.

Jenna heard the front door open and close.

"Next time you're in town, I should catch a ride. I've used nearly the last of your laundry detergent and—"

She broke off when she rounded the corner and saw not Lars, but Owen.

"Your dad's not here," she told him. "He's driven over to the hospital again, I think."

"That's all right. It's you I've come to talk to."

"Still here, then, living a life of leisure, I see."

Jenna turned to find Hannah sitting in judgment on the couch. She glanced down at her pajamas and squelched the urge to explain she'd put them on to wash her single set of clothing.

"The only rule when dealing with negative reviews: do not engage," Cassie said. Jenna was heartened that, for once, Cassie was on her side.

"Hannah," Owen said with a warning.

The girl opened her eyes wide in mock innocence and placed a pair of headphones over her ears.

Owen looked like he was about to apologize for her, but Jenna waved it off.

If he spent all his time apologizing for his daughter being a teenager, he'd have time for nothing else.

"What's up?" she asked.

"This." He held up a ring of keys.

For a split second, she didn't recognize them. Then, after a pause like the one that comes between seeing lightning flash and hearing the boom of thunder trailing behind, Jenna's old life and current life came together with a crash.

She felt blindly for a chair and dropped down at the kitchen table.

"The van is fixed," she said in a hushed voice.

Owen's face was serious as he studied hers.

"Yes." He pulled out a chair and sat down across from her.

"I have a confession." He set the ring of keys on the table between them. "It's been fixed for a while."

"What?" she asked. "But why . . . ?"

"Dad asked me to stall."

She didn't know what to say. Jenna slowly picked up the keys, their weight cold and metallic in her hand.

"I don't understand," she murmured, though she did.

"He said it was for your sake. That you were in no state to be . . . Well, it doesn't matter what he said. Regardless of his motives, the decision needs to be yours. It's parked at the garage, when . . . and if . . . you need it."

Owen gave her a sad smile.

"For the record, Jenna, it's been a long time since Dad had a friend."

Her brow furrowed at the word. "Is that what I am?"

The notion simultaneously warmed her heart and chilled her bones. "I'm afraid so."

"Is he this high-handed with all his friends?"

The question had less heat than it might if Jenna weren't so keenly aware of how many days had passed since she'd bothered to ask after the state of the van.

"Mostly, yes." Owen squeezed her hand, then rose and called to his daughter.

When they'd left, Jenna was alone with nothing but her thoughts, her keys, and her box of ashes.

42

"Jenna," Lars called. "Come give me a hand."

She was staring at the crack in the ceiling again, but her thoughts had started to feel like a prison, so she rose and walked toward the kitchen.

There was a spring in Lars's step as he unloaded the groceries from the brown paper bag.

"I need a sous chef." He placed something green and leafy into the sink to rinse.

"Crispy roasted duck and fingerling potatoes," he told her, pulling two bottles of red wine from the bag. "Open that and pour us a glass, will you?"

"You're not planning to get me drunk and take advantage of me, are you?"

He snorted.

"We're celebrating," he said as he placed potatoes in the sink to rinse as well.

Her head came up, and she watched his back until he glanced over his shoulder.

"Dr. Taylor's agreed," he said. "He had some stipulations. He wants a police presence and Audrey's current psychotherapist there at all times—just to cover his own ass in case something goes wrong, if you ask me—but he's agreed."

"Lars, that's . . ." Jenna's misgivings about her eventual departure could wait. "That's fantastic!"

"I've been telling myself not to go and get my hopes up." He shook his head and turned to stare out the window at the lake, the one constant that had witnessed it all from the beginning. "It's hard not to wonder, though. Maybe this time."

"All you can do is try," she said.

"And celebrate the small steps along the way. Which is why I need you to dry those potatoes and pour us both a glass of that fancy nine-dollar wine."

Her keys were in the dresser drawer, next to the carved box. They'd be there when she needed them. It wouldn't do any harm to raise a glass . . . with a friend.

She didn't notice then that these thoughts were wholly her own, not wrapped in her daughter's persistent voice.

And her subconscious wisely refrained from pointing that out.

A bottle and a half of Pinot Noir and one stellar meal later, Jenna's thoughts were pleasantly fuzzy and she found herself chuckling at stories of Lars's navy escapades.

He'd pulled the well-worn deck of cards from the cabinet and given her a few quick lessons on how to play poker.

"How does any self-respecting thirtysomething not know how to play poker, Jenna Shaw?"

She shrugged as he dealt her another two cards.

"Not a high priority between soccer practices and dance recitals."

He glanced at her and took another drink from the bourbon glass filled with red wine.

"No, I suppose not."

She tilted her head. "It's okay," she said, surprising herself. "I don't talk about them, but it makes no difference. They're always there anyway."

He said nothing. The language of grief was one he was familiar with.

"I'm sorry, I don't want to bring you down." Jenna stood to fill her glass with water from the faucet.

"I've been down here for thirty years," Lars said. "You had nothing to do with it."

The enormity of his words hit her. A lifetime he'd spent, subject to the whims of his memories. The good, the bad, and everything in between.

The sound of Ethan crying filled her.

"Mama, you're not coming?"

His little voice trembled, and she knelt to hug him tightly, selfishly, to her, this little person who loved her best of all.

"Not this time, bud." She wiped his tears tenderly away with the base of her thumb. "You're going to have an amazing time, though. You've got your dad, and your sisters, and the cousins. It'll be so much fun, Ethan. An adventure for the ages!"

The girls had already piled into the car for the drive to the airport. There'd been hugs from Sarah, and a grudging "See ya" from Cass, who was still mad at her. Only Ethan was having trouble saying goodbye.

Another sniffle, and his big eyes blinked up at her.

"Promise?" he asked.

Jenna met Matt's eyes. He was patiently leaning against the side of the car. He sent her an indulgent wink.

"Pinkie promise." She held out her smallest finger for her son to hook with his own.

"Okay, if you say so," he whispered.

She hugged him to her, hard and fierce, so she didn't have to see the look of abandonment on his face while he tried so hard to be brave.

Even that she wasn't spared. She could still picture him through the window of the car, and the look in his eyes when he placed his hand on the glass, watching her watching him as they drove away.

"Thank you for dinner, Lars," Jenna murmured. "I think I'll call it a night."

She didn't see his face as he watched her go, shuffling the deck of cards in his hands over and over.

43

Given the heightened emotions of the small crowd gathered in Lars Jorgensen's kitchen, an observer who knew only that one of the people in the room was under psychiatric treatment would be hard pressed to say which one of them it was.

Audrey was seated on the sofa next to her mother. Her eyes were angled downward, though she occasionally raised them to glance around before dropping them to the worn rug at her feet. She didn't speak and had no interest in the hushed argument taking place across the room.

"Dr. Nordquist, regardless of how you personally feel about hypnosis as an accepted form of therapy, I can assure you I am a board-certified clinical psychologist with years of expertise in its application. I'm not some quack standing on the side of the road in a sandwich board, and I resent your implication," hissed Dr. Nancy Young.

"Hosting a therapy session outside the confines of the hospital is absolutely unprecedented, not to mention dangerous," Dr. Nordquist replied.

"We've been over this. I strongly feel the inclusion of a relevant environment in Mrs. Jorgensen's hypnotherapy could be beneficial in triggering the memories she's repressed, which, if I might remind you, is the entire reason we're here."

"I have only the best interests of my patient in mind, madam. I assure *you* that if I feel you're—"

"Can we get on with this please?" interrupted the police sergeant.

Lars broke away from the group to stand beside Jenna and Owen. "I'm a hair's breadth from tossing them all out on their ears," he muttered.

Jenna frowned. She couldn't blame him. The dueling doctors, as she'd come to think of them, had been at each other's throats from the moment Dr. Nordquist, the psychiatrist sent by the Minnesota State Secure Psychiatric Hospital, had made a denigrating remark about "so-called doctors hawking snake oil as therapy."

Dr. Young had bristled—understandably, Jenna felt—but the time for sniping was over. Apparently, Sergeant Allred had reached the same conclusion.

With a hand on both of their shoulders, he took a moment to give the two doctors a piece of his mind. Jenna couldn't hear what was said, but when the trio raised their heads, Dr. Young grabbed the hem of her suit jacket and pulled it taut as Dr. Nordquist straightened his tie.

The two of them turned to face the room.

"Please forgive me." Dr. Young pushed her hair from her face and took charge of the situation. "Mr. Jorgensen, if I could have you, your son, and Ms. Shaw remain here at the kitchen table, that would be best. We don't want to crowd Mrs. Jorgensen."

She sent the briefest of glances at her fellow doctor, then moved on.

"Sergeant," she said with a questioning glance in the policeman's direction.

"I'll stay by the door. You've made it perfectly clear my presence will make it harder for the patient to relax, and I heard you, but I will not leave her unsupervised."

Dr. Young nodded. "Per the judge's instructions, the session will be recorded and provided to you."

"That's fine," said the sergeant, all business. He'd already set a camera on a tripod that was directed at Audrey Jorgensen as they spoke.

He took up his post at the front door.

"Finally," Lars said.

Dr. Young pulled a chair from the kitchen and placed it next to Audrey and Beverly on the couch.

"May I stay?" Audrey's mother asked.

Dr. Young nodded again. "Yes, but I'll ask you not to speak or interrupt, as it will only cause confusion for your daughter."

Dr. Nordquist took the only seat left, which happened to be Lars's worn and faded recliner. The doctor tried to maintain some professional dignity, but it was difficult as the cushion was well used, and he sank into the chair with a harrumph.

"Now, Audrey." Dr. Young leaned forward slightly. Her demeanor transformed before their eyes. "My name is Nancy, and I'm a doctor. I'm here to help you, if I can."

Her voice was warm, with a gentle cadence that made it clear her focus was solely on Audrey Jorgensen and no one else.

The door rattled behind Sergeant Allred, and everyone in the room, save Audrey, turned to see Diane Downey enter and run directly into the policeman's back.

"Oh my goodness," she said, looking around at the tableau arranged before her. "Oh my."

She placed a hand to her chest.

"Who, exactly, are you, ma'am, and what is your business here?" the sergeant said rather loudly into the housekeeper's stunned face.

"I . . ." Diane looked frantically around the room.

Jenna understood Sergeant Allred's frustration, but judging from the way Diane's shoulders drooped and she shrank back into herself, she clearly wasn't comfortable in the face of such harsh words.

"Diane. I'm the housekeeper," she said meekly.

"There'll be no housecleaning today," the sergeant said. "You can go now."

"I . . . Of course." She stepped hurriedly backward and out of the house.

Jenna and Owen rose at the same time.

183

"You stay," she told him. "I'll go."

Jenna hurried out the door behind her.

"Diane, wait," she called.

The housekeeper was practically running to get back to her car.

"Please wait." She caught up with the older woman just as she reached the door to her sedan.

"I'm sorry," Jenna said, placing a hand on the other woman's shoulder. "We forgot today was your day to clean."

Jenna got a good look at the housekeeper's face and was slightly taken aback by the level of upheaval she saw there.

"Diane, are you all right?"

The older woman bobbed her head, swallowing with an effort, but appeared far from all right.

"What is it?" Jenna asked gently. She couldn't let her drive off in such a state.

"Nothing, hon." She tried to pull herself together. "I'm sorry I ran out like that. It was the uniform. Took me by surprise, that's all."

Jenna shook her head. "The policeman's uniform?" she asked.

"Yes. My husband was a policeman. Have I ever mentioned him?"

Jenna nodded. Diane had talked about him in passing, not necessarily in complimentary terms, but she didn't remember hearing his profession.

"He wasn't a good man," Diane said in a low, prim voice.

"I'm sorry," Jenna said. She could think of little else to say.

"It's okay. I'm long done with him now. But sometimes things sneak up on you, don't they? No matter how many years go by, the past never really lets you go."

She ran her hands up and down her arms, as if to ward off a chill. "It's sewn in, like patches on one of my old granny's quilts. You can run from it all you like, but it's part of you. Goes where you go."

Jenna's thoughts turned to Lars and the past he was so desperately trying to see, then to herself and the past she didn't know how to face.

"All you can do is your best," Diane said with a sigh. "Keep going until the good days outnumber the bad."

Diane got in her car and turned the ignition.

She raised a hand and sent Jenna a small wave along with a shaky smile.

As the woman drove away, her parting words echoed inside Jenna.

Could it be that simple?

"It could be . . . if you let it," Cassie whispered.

44

When Jenna let herself back into the cabin, Sergeant Allred barely spared her a glance. She closed the door softly behind her and tiptoed to her chair at the kitchen table.

Owen pressed one finger to his lips and pointed in the direction of the sofa, where everyone's attention was centered. Even Dr. Nordquist was leaning forward, perched along the edge of the recliner.

"Now that you've relaxed all the parts of your body and mind, Audrey, I want you to remember what I've said. We're going to walk through the events of the day just like we're watching a movie. There will be no pain. No hurt, no sadness, no regret. We're watching these things happen, not experiencing them. There is nothing to be afraid of. Do you understand what I'm telling you, Audrey?"

Jenna strained to hear if Audrey would give a response. There was none save perhaps a slight inclination of her head.

"Okay, then," Dr. Young said, still smooth and unhurried. "Let's try and go back to the day we discussed, Audrey. This day wasn't like other days, was it? Maybe it began that way, but something has changed. Something is different than normal. Can you see that day, Audrey?"

Dr. Young's attention was focused only on her patient as she studied Audrey's face for signs she was receptive to her suggestion.

"Can you tell me if you're able to see that day, Audrey? Just a normal day, beginning like any other, but this time like a movie on a screen.

A movie that cannot hurt you. Can you see the beginning of that movie, Audrey?"

Everything hinged on whether this was going to work. Jenna held her breath.

The air was thick with expectation.

The silence stretched, pulled taut by the load it carried.

"Yes," Audrey whispered in her high, girlish voice.

Jenna bit her lip. Dr. Young closed her eyes slowly, briefly, and her head tilted forward in relief.

"That's good, Audrey." The doctor's beat was steady, giving nothing away. "That's very good. Can you tell me, what day of the week is it?"

The silence was shorter this time, but no less fraught.

"It's Saturday," Audrey replied.

Jenna glanced in Lars's direction. His muscles were tense, and he strained to hear what might come from his wife's mouth next.

"That's good," Dr. Young said. "That's very good. Now let's fast-forward a bit, Audrey. Just a bit. Something is different today. Something makes this Saturday different from the rest. Can you take us to that point, Audrey?"

"Yes," she said.

"You're there now, then? This is an important place to be, and you've done very well. I'm with you every step of the way, and I want you to remember, this cannot hurt you. I'm going to ask you to start the movie from this point, Audrey, and tell me exactly what happens."

Audrey shook her head.

"I don't want to," she whispered.

Dr. Nordquist, who'd been sitting rapt, seemed to remember with these words that Audrey Jorgensen was his patient as well, and shifted in his seat. Dr. Young held up a hand in his direction, asking him with her eyes for the leeway to continue.

"I understand, Audrey. I do, but remember, this cannot hurt you. It cannot touch you. You are separate from this, and the words you speak are only describing the scene in front of you. Are you willing to try?"

For one terrifying moment, Jenna saw the whole thing collapse into a heap of worthless intentions.

"Okay," Audrey said. "I'll try."

"That's good, Audrey, that's very good. You are not alone, and there's no reason to be afraid. Now let's press 'Play' on this movie. Can you tell me what happens next?"

"I need to call my mother," Audrey said.

Beverly's brows drew together and she cut a glance at the doctor, but Dr. Young gave a miniscule shake of her head.

"All right. And what happens next?" Dr. Young prompted gently.

"The telephone. There's no dial tone, only voices already speaking," Audrey continued.

"And can you hear what those voices are saying? Can you tell us about the voices, Audrey?"

"*It's the kids . . . I can't leave the kids. You have to understand.*"

The voice that came out of Audrey's mouth was lower, stronger. The words resonated with indecision and worry. Just as they must have nearly three decades ago.

A picture floated up in Jenna's mind of Lars, his head in his hands, as he must have looked when he'd spoken them.

His stricken face had gone pale. If Dr. Young was right, Audrey wouldn't be touched by the hurt of hearing these words again. But there was no protection for anyone else.

"*I do understand, Lars. And I'm not in a position to judge. It's no easier for me. I just wish . . . Oh, I don't know what I wish.*"

This voice was higher, though still not Audrey's own. The shock of recognition on Lars's face said he knew exactly who it belonged to, though.

"'She's just so unpredictable, Nora. And things are only going to get worse once I file for divorce.'"

Owen turned his head slowly to stare at his father.

"'Can I see you today?'"

There was a pause.

"'I'll try.'"

The preternatural way Audrey had switched voices sent a shiver down Jenna's spine.

"Okay, Audrey," Dr. Young said after a quick glance over at Lars. "That's very good. You've done a wonderful job, and I think that's a good place to stop the movie for today. I want you to remember, when you come back to full awareness, that these words are just words, just images, and they cannot harm . . ."

Jenna lost track of what the doctor was saying as Lars slowly rose from the kitchen table and walked toward the front door of the cabin. After a searching, but silent, exchange with Owen, Jenna watched the younger man rise and follow.

The click of the door latch shutting behind the two was nearly impossible to hear, but Jenna felt it all the same.

45

The air was quiet after everyone left, but Lars's mind was a riot of noise and confusion.

Sergeant Allred had escorted Dr. Nordquist and Audrey back to the hospital, leaving Dr. Young to talk them through what would happen next.

"I know today's session was short, but my responsibility is to Mrs. Jorgensen. I don't want to push her too hard or too fast. We'll try to pick up from here for the next session."

Lars was standing in the driveway he and Jenna had cleared together that morning. He knew the doctor meant well, but her words were hardly penetrating.

She moved into his line of vision.

"I can see this is hard for you. Hard for you all. But after today, we know this just might work. Let that be enough for now."

He nodded distractedly. "Thank you, Doctor."

Owen walked the doctor to her car. Lars caught snippets of conversation.

"Whether we'll be able to continue will depend on how well your mother recovers. I'll speak with the hospital director and be in touch."

Owen closed her car door for her and watched her drive away. The distance that separated Lars from his son was only a matter of yards but felt insurmountable.

Lars heard the door of the cabin open and close. Jenna stood there, leaning against it, concern evident in the lines of her face and the tense way she held her body, like a spring coiled too tightly.

She looked like that often, whether she realized it or not. This time, that tension was for him.

Ice and snow crunched under Owen's boots as he slowly made his way back to him.

"Dad?" A question. One Lars had always known he'd have to answer one day.

"Jenna, get your coat," he called.

"O-kay," she drew out with a glance in Owen's direction.

"We need to talk," Lars said. "But I can't take another minute cooped up in there."

It turned out to be a bit more involved than simply "Jenna, get your coat," but after rooting around in the garage and sending the woman back inside the cabin to put on a few extra layers and borrow some woolen socks, they managed to cobble together what they'd need.

"What was wrong with my socks?" Jenna asked as she pulled on a pair of old hiking boots. They were big for her, but with two pairs of wool socks they would be fine.

"They were cotton," Lars said.

He leaned down to gather the equipment in his arms, missing the look of consternation that crossed her face.

"Cotton doesn't wick moisture away from the body," Owen explained to her. "And moisture in these kinds of temperatures equals trouble."

"Just existing in these kinds of temperatures equals trouble, if you ask me," she mumbled.

Lars turned around with his arms full.

"Snowshoes?" she asked doubtfully.

He raised an eyebrow.

"You know I've never used a pair of those before in my life, right?"

"We won't go far," he told her. "But if you don't think you're up for it—"

"I didn't say that," she interrupted. "It's just, aren't you a little . . . I don't know . . . *old* to be tromping around the countryside in snowshoes?"

"Just put those on, missy, and we'll see who's old."

He tossed her a pair of shoes, which she almost fumbled.

"I don't know how to do this!" she shouted as he walked out of the garage.

"Get Owen to help you, then try and keep up," he called over his shoulder.

Lars stopped at the steps to the cabin and slipped a pair of gaiters over his boots and pants, then attached his snowshoes.

He didn't wait for the pair of youngsters, but set out with his poles in hand.

Owen would know where he was headed.

It was no more than a fifteen-minute hike through a clear trail in the woods that lined the lake. The terrain had a slight incline, but Jenna should be fine, with Owen's help.

When he reached his destination, a familiar clearing in the trees, Lars pulled in a deep breath.

"Old," he muttered. He couldn't deny it. Like the rings of a tree, his age was etched on his heart and mind.

He walked toward the break in the evergreens that gave way to the best view for miles.

The ground was higher here, the lake lower, and there was nothing to impede on the vast expanse of lake and wilderness stretched out before him.

There were more houses dotting the landscape than ever before, but he tried not to begrudge that.

Progress happened. Time marched on, whether an old man liked it or not.

He heard the telltale crunch of snow as Jenna and Owen caught up to him.

"How'd she do?"

Jenna was trying to hide the fact she was slightly out of breath.

"Not bad," Owen said. "Only fell twice."

"No one told me these things don't work in reverse," she said, leaning her weight against her poles.

"Must have slipped my mind. The ravages of age."

"All right, all right," she said. "You've made your point."

He couldn't help a slight smile.

"Come look at this." He turned to the expansive view laid out in front of them. "I used to bring Owen up here as a kid."

"Been a long time," Owen said at his side.

"Too long," Lars agreed with a pang in his heart. He cleared his throat.

"It's breathtaking," Jenna said.

He studied her profile. Her expression caused him to take in the view with fresh eyes.

"I grew up around here, you know," he said, leaning against his own poles. "In a house in town. My dad was the only doctor for miles."

Owen, of course, knew this, but his son was patient.

"The cabin was an anniversary gift for my mom. She was the one who loved the lake. Summer or winter, it didn't matter. That's why it's outfitted for the cold while most of the other cabins aren't."

Lars took a deep breath and plunged on.

"Two years after the cabin was finished, Dad contracted smallpox while treating an outbreak upstate. There's no doubt my mother caught it from him. She died."

Jenna lifted a hand to her lips.

"In the end, Dad recovered from the disease. But the guilt—he couldn't get over that. He took a pistol, walked into the backyard, and shot himself."

Jenna gasped, but he didn't look at her.

"I was nearly sent to an orphanage in Minneapolis," he continued, "but the Bergman family took me in. Mrs. Bergman and my mother had been close. They had three daughters, and the youngest was about my age. She'd never liked me much, but she had a soft heart and took pity on the boy with no parents. She became my friend. My best friend, if you want to know the God's honest truth."

"Nora," Owen said suddenly. "Eleanor Lutz."

Lars nodded, unable to look his boy in the face.

"Probably I should have married her," he admitted. "But youth is stupid. At least I was."

He sighed and shook his head at the arrogant young man he'd been.

"I ran off and joined the navy instead. By the time I made it back to Raven, I'd given Audrey my heart and my hand. I was in love, and it was exciting, full of passion and life. I thought Nora would be happy for me."

Lars frowned, and an old image of the hurt on Nora's face when she'd met Audrey the first time rose in front of him. He could remember telling her, "She could really use a friend."

He closed his eyes tightly. He'd never deserved Eleanor.

"The hell of it wasn't that I'd fallen in love with another woman. The part she couldn't forgive was the time she'd spent waiting. She had more faith in me, and in us, than I ever did."

Lars leaned down and picked up a stick where it had fallen on top of the snow. He tossed it over the outcropping and watched it spiral through the air.

"She was married to Rudy Lutz within a year."

"Were you two . . . the whole time?" Owen asked.

"Having an affair?" Lars shook his head. "No, son. I loved your mother with every fiber of my being. And Eleanor barely spoke to me after that anyway. Not for a long time. She'd cross the street if she saw me coming."

Lars sighed.

"If I were a better man, I'd tell you I missed her. Her friendship, at least, but I had my hands full. I'd sold my parents' house in town to finance opening the garage, then you kids came along. And Audrey. I loved her, but my God, it was always a crisis. For a while I told myself she was just young. We both were. She'd grow out of it, but that never happened. If anything, time made things worse."

Lars picked up his poles and punched them again into the snow. He tilted them this way and that, fidgety and on edge.

"I'd come home to find a bunch of summer people in the house for a party. Some stranger offering me a beer, telling me to come on in." Lars shook his head. "The calls from the bank. 'Your account is overdrawn again, Mr. Jorgensen,' they'd say. And I'd find the house full of art supplies but no food."

"Sprinkles," Owen said suddenly, as if he'd just stumbled upon the memory. "Do you remember?"

"That damn pony," Lars said with a sigh. "How you kids cried when I sent him back. Audrey wouldn't speak to me for weeks. Barely got out of bed."

The memories were painful to revisit, but necessary.

"It wasn't until the fire that I forced myself to take a good, long look at what we'd become. What I saw scared me to death."

Lars turned to Jenna to explain. Owen needed no reminders.

"The kids were hungry, but Audrey was deep in one of her depressions. Owen was nine, almost ten. I was at work. He'd taken on a role he never should have been forced into."

"I almost killed us," Owen said.

"No," Lars said. "Owen was smart. He got his little brother and sister out."

"I remembered not to throw water on a grease fire, but I panicked when the flames started licking up the wall."

"They found the little ones outside, Francie holding Will, who was just a baby. Owen had gone back in to try to get his mother."

"She wouldn't come," Owen said. "She wouldn't come, and I wasn't strong enough to carry her."

Lars marveled at his son's presence of mind, his determination to keep them all safe. He'd been just a boy. A boy with too many burdens on his shoulders.

"Audrey needed help. Help I couldn't give her. It wasn't something that was going to get better on its own, and it was past time to face that. You kids . . . God, she loved you. Still does I know, deep down inside. But I couldn't trust her with you. It wasn't safe."

"I remember," Owen murmured, "walking home from school, never knowing what kind of day it would be."

"I didn't know what to do. I wrestled with it for a long time. Too long. And, I'm sorry to say, I turned to Eleanor. She was the best friend I'd ever had, and the most logical and compassionate person I knew."

"So it was just . . . friendship, then?" Owen asked.

Lars heard the grain of hope, and he wished he had the capacity to lie. But he wouldn't. He owed Owen the truth.

"If I'd been a stronger person, maybe it would have been. But no. She and Rudy were in trouble too. Not the same sort of trouble as your mother and me, maybe, but we found each other again in our weakest moments. I'm not proud of it, but I'm long past excusing my sins."

Owen said nothing. If there was condemnation, if there was scorn, Lars knew he'd earned it.

"Beverly knew. We'd talked things over. She was considering moving here, to be with you kids and your mom . . . after. Or if maybe it would be best to send Audrey to live with her, while you three stayed here with me."

The words clogged his throat, and Lars forced himself to push through it, to tell both his son, who was the most important thing in his world, and this woman who'd come to matter more than he'd expected, the most damning truth of all.

"But it wasn't just about the kids. It was more. I loved . . . I *love* Audrey. But I couldn't do it anymore. I wanted out, selfishly, for my sake. I was sacrificing your childhoods, and my own life, on the altar of Audrey's illness."

"Were you with her that day?" Owen asked.

Lars took a deep breath, then nodded.

"I told your mother I had to work. I did go to the garage, for a while, but I left to meet Nora. I had no idea Audrey heard that call."

He shook his head at his own blindness. It was easier to see nothing at all than to look his own guilt in the face. His father, faced with the loss of his wife to an illness he'd brought home to her, had known that.

"All these years, I never knew what set her off, sending her over that final edge. It was me."

Bitter regret threatened to engulf him.

"Dad," Owen said.

Lars felt his son's hand on his shoulder. Owen said nothing else, but Lars held tight to that one word and everything it meant. He held tight to it, hoping it could lead him home.

"I think I'll stay here for a while, if you two don't mind."

There was a pause. For a moment, Lars thought Owen might argue, then he said, "All right."

The sound of their shoes crunching through the snow barely registered, but Lars heard Owen say, "We'll see you back at the house. When you're ready."

Once the footsteps had faded, Lars let his shoulders drop, the weight of them too much, and wrapped his arms around himself. His legs would no longer support him, and he dropped to his knees in the snow. His head hung low and his chest began to shake as his face contorted.

He sobbed, silent and alone.

46

The heavy curtain of evening had drawn closed around them. Jenna pushed thoughts of the looming holidays away. *One day at a time. That's enough for now.*

When Lars returned, he was quiet and withdrawn.

"Keep an eye on him, will you?" Owen had asked before he left.

She didn't know how she was supposed to do that if he didn't come out of his room. At least he wasn't alone.

Jenna, after a shower that served no purpose other than to warm her and pass the time, dressed again in her secondhand pajamas. There was no one here she needed to impress.

When she walked back into the living room, running a comb through her wet hair, Lars had emerged from his room and built a fire in the fireplace. It was snowing again.

She wandered to the windows, drawn to watch the lacy layers fall with a childlike wonderment.

"It really is incredibly beautiful."

"Can't argue with that," Lars replied. "Apple cider or hot buttered rum?"

Jenna thought for a moment. "Buttered rum. I've never tried it, but if it's hot, I'll take it."

She snuggled into the sofa, curled her legs, and pulled a fleece blanket around her.

The rum was as hot as advertised, and delicious.

"Mmm," she murmured, as the liquid warmed her from the inside. "I could get used to this. Matt would have loved it here." Saying his name plucked a string deep in her center, the sound it made a haunting one.

"Your husband?" Lars adjusted the fire with an old iron poker.

She nodded, not trusting herself to speak.

"You had a happy marriage?" Lars asked. She felt his eyes on her.

She smiled a small, sad smile.

"Yes," she said. "We did. The kind of marriage our friends envied." *The kind of marriage it's easy to take for granted. Until it's gone.*

"No mean feat," he said.

She shook her head. "I can't take any credit for it. Mostly, it was Matt. He couldn't hold a grudge worth a damn. It's hard to stay mad at a man whose primary argument tactic is to hug you and apologize, whether he was to blame or not."

One corner of Lars's mouth curled upward and he lifted his glass. "A smart man."

She smiled. "That he was. Smart, kind, a fantastic father." Her smile faded, her memories jagged and painful. "He was a hard act to measure up to."

Jenna stared down at the rum left in her glass. She swirled it around.

When she glanced up, Lars was watching her, waiting to see if she had more to say.

Jenna took a deep breath.

"I used to have this fantasy about running away." She kept her gaze on the crackling fire. "Living alone in a little English village somewhere, with nothing but a cat and a garden to tend to. Which is stupid. I'm allergic to cats."

She risked a glance at Lars. He wasn't smiling. She sighed.

"I never would have sacrificed my marriage or left my kids. Not ever, for any reason. It was nothing more than a daydream to help get through the hard days when the kids were small. But it was always there, in the back of my mind."

She threw back the last of her drink.

"If I lived alone, I'd never feel like I was letting someone down."

"You can't beat yourself up for that," Lars said slowly.

She shrugged, pulling her knees up to her chin and wrapping her arms around her legs.

"Maybe, maybe not. But I can beat myself up about the business card. It was tucked into my wallet, folded up in the back. A card for a family lawyer."

Jenna shook her head at her own carelessness, and the hurt it had caused.

"I'd had it for years, since Ethan was small. I'd like to say I'd forgotten it was there, but that's not true. It didn't matter that I'd no intention of ever dialing the number. I didn't want a *divorce*. But I held on to the card. A talisman to a life I'd never lead, but one I could imagine so vividly."

"You didn't do it," Lars said.

"That's not much consolation," Jenna said. She let her legs drop. "Cassandra, my oldest, found it. She was looking for stamps, and stumbled onto my dirty little fantasy."

Understanding dawned on Lars's face.

"She knew what it was straightaway. The attorney was one of her friend's dads. She confronted me, and like an idiot, I got defensive."

Jenna squeezed her eyes shut, but she couldn't block the memory of Cassie's face, twisted in betrayal, as she'd hurled accusations Jenna had little defense for. She hadn't even bothered to try. Cassie was too young, Jenna had thought. She'd never understand the push and pull of all the responsibilities that came with being an adult, a wife, and a mother. Not until she experienced them for herself.

Jenna didn't even attempt to explain.

She thought she'd have time to make it right.

"It was just weeks before the crash. We were barely speaking when she died. And now I hear her voice in my head."

She leaned her head back against the sofa cushion and closed her eyes.

"I know it's not really her," she said, trying to reassure him. Or perhaps herself. "I'm too disgustingly sane to think I'm really communicating with my daughter from beyond the grave. But my subconscious, or whatever it is, has chosen to use Cassie's voice. Not Matt's or Sarah's or Ethan's. Only Cass. And the pitch is so perfect and so . . . so Cassandra." She sent him a heartbroken smile. "My daughter was amazing, Lars. And I let her down. All the way down. I can't forgive myself for that."

Lars finished his own drink and stared into the fire again.

"Karma is a nasty old bitch, isn't she?" he finally said with a sigh.

Jenna couldn't help but smile through the tears she hadn't noticed escaping down her cheeks.

"That she is, Lars. That she is."

47

Despite the success of Audrey's first hypnotherapy session, it was three days before Drs. Young and Nordquist were willing to move forward with a second session.

"Hannah's been on my back about being here for this," Owen murmured to Jenna when she noticed his worried expression that morning. "And she went to school entirely too easily."

Owen knew his daughter well, because Hannah strolled through the front door of the cabin twenty minutes later, looking defiant.

Jenna tried not to eavesdrop as the pair had a heated debate in the corner of the kitchen over her cutting class again.

Hannah Jorgensen's truancies weren't Jenna's responsibility.

The living room was set up exactly as it had been before, with the camera pointed at Audrey seated on the couch. Beverly had made the drive the night before, after the hospital notified them they were cleared to move forward. She was again seated at her daughter's side.

It might have been Jenna's imagination, but it seemed Audrey was more aware of her surroundings than she'd been before. *Or maybe that's wishful thinking,* she thought as Audrey slowly turned her head to look at the doctor who was speaking to her.

Fascinated, Jenna watched alongside the rest of the Jorgensens as Dr. Young walked Audrey through the relaxation techniques designed to bring her to a suggestible meditative state.

"That can't possibly work," Hannah whispered loudly to her dad.

"Hush, I'm warning you, or I'll take you right back to school," he told her.

Hannah kept further opinions to herself.

With gentle doggedness, Dr. Young brought Audrey to the point where they'd left off.

"Can you tell me about after the phone call, Audrey?" Dr. Young asked. "Without experiencing the emotions, I'd like you to describe to me in words what you're feeling when you hang up the phone."

"Scared," Audrey whispered, unaware of the effect she was having on the room. "I'm so scared. Lars is going to take them from me. I can't lose them. They're the only good things I have. I know I'm not the best mother. I know. But I'm *their* mother. I can't lose them."

"Oh, Audrey," Beverly murmured, forgetting herself. Dr. Young silenced her with a sharp shake of her head.

"Is your husband still there, Audrey?" Dr. Young asked, covering the interruption.

"He's at work. He says he's gone to work. Maybe he has. Maybe he's with her."

Jenna snuck a glance at Lars. He looked drawn.

"And your children?"

"They're with me, where they should be. Owen, though. Owen wants to play with his friend. I don't want him to go. I want them all here with me, close where I can touch them, but Owen doesn't listen. "*You told me I could!*'" Audrey suddenly said in a new voice.

"I did, I know I did, honey, and I'm sorry . . ." Audrey tilted her head and held out her hand, as if to place it on the cheek of a child who wasn't there.

"I try to hold him, but he pulls away. *'You're always sorry! You're always saying things, but your words don't match what you do! You're a liar, Mom!'*"

Audrey's words were a bucket of cold water down Jenna's back.

"He runs from me, out of the house," Audrey continued. "There's nothing I can do but watch him go."

Jenna reached out to place a hand on Owen's forearm and give it a small squeeze. He didn't look away from his mother.

"Owen is gone, then, playing at a friend's house? What do you do now, Audrey?" Dr. Young asked.

"I can't stay here," she said. "I can't stay. Everything will spin up and away again. Every time, it's like a tornado. It whisks me up with it, but when I come down, all the pieces are jumbled up and they don't get put back in the right place."

Audrey was picking up speed, and though her intonation stayed constant, Jenna wondered if the doctor's instructions were enough for Audrey to remain untouched by the memories.

"I can feel it starting to spin, in my head, and I'm afraid, so afraid when I come back down it will all be gone. Lars, the kids, all gone, and I'll be left wandering around alone in the broken pieces."

Dr. Young shifted in her seat. If Jenna could see the doctor's control of Audrey's state of mind was slipping, then Dr. Young certainly could sense it too.

"Let's slow down a bit, Audrey. Remember, this is—"

Just like a movie, Jenna thought as Dr. Young said the words. Only it wasn't, was it? These were real people, with real lives and real regrets. Whatever happened to the Jorgensen children may have been shrouded in mystery, but it was real.

"Let's start from there, Audrey, and keep it slow and steady," Dr. Young was saying.

"I have to go," Audrey said, her words back to the measured pace she'd begun with.

Dr. Young relaxed her shoulders slightly.

"I have to go, and I have to take the kids. I'll take them and hold them tightly through the storm. I know it's coming, but if I hold them tightly enough, they'll be with me when it stops."

But you were wrong, Audrey, Jenna thought, filled with sadness. *You were so wrong.* Pity for the woman stirred inside of Jenna for the first time.

No matter what had happened to Francie and Will, Audrey Jorgensen wasn't to blame. Her illness, perhaps, but not the woman in its grip.

"But Owen's gone. He ran from me and my heart is breaking. He doesn't trust me. But I have Francie and Will. I have my babies, and I have to go. So I leave him."

Audrey broke on the last word. Her shoulders began to shake as quiet tears overtook her.

"Audrey, I want you to take a deep breath and back away. Leave those feelings there where you found them. Just set them down like you would a glass of water in your hand. Can you do that, Audrey?"

But Audrey couldn't hear her. She was lost in a place the doctor's soothing couldn't reach.

"Audrey?"

"I leave him. I have to," she said. "I have to leave him."

"It's all right, Audrey. I'd like you to stop the movie now. Stop and step away, back to my voice."

"It's not all right," Audrey said. "I leave him, I do, but I come back. I come back and that's when it all slips away from me. I come back and he won't come. Why won't he come with me?"

Audrey's head came up, and Dr. Young's professional mask slipped. The doctor pulled back ever so slightly at the plea, though she recovered almost immediately.

"It's all right, Audrey," Dr. Young said, leaning in to coax her patient into relaxation.

But Audrey shook her head slowly from side to side.

"No," she said. "Nothing is ever right again."

48

A hush had come over the room while Audrey's session was taking place. Even as things were wrapping up, it remained.

Sergeant Allred had motioned Lars aside.

"This wasn't in the case notes. What's this about coming back? We thought she was gone."

Lars didn't have any answers.

"I've never heard anything about it," he murmured, shaken at the thought.

The men turned to look at Owen.

Dr. Young was standing a few steps behind Audrey while Beverly helped her daughter into the layers of warm clothing she'd helped her out of on her arrival.

Once she'd wrapped a bright-yellow scarf around Audrey's neck and placed a matching stocking cap upon her head, the effect of Audrey's aged features and gray hair stood at odds with her childlike demeanor.

She's a ghost of the woman she used to be. Lars remembered the sparkle in her eyes when she'd tap-danced her way to him. *A pale copy.*

They'd lost more than the children that day.

Beverly guided Audrey toward the door, but Owen stepped into their path.

Audrey raised her eyes slowly to meet those of her firstborn child. There was no recognition in her face. Nothing, not even a spark. She stared at her son as if he were a tree planted in her path.

Owen was no stranger to this. She'd never shown any indication she recognized him, even in the early days. It had been hard on the boy, Lars knew, though Owen never spoke of it.

He watched him now, his son, grown to a fine man despite it all. Owen opened his arms and pulled his mother, so small and unresisting, close to him, folding her into a hug. Audrey didn't resist, but the expression on her face didn't change.

She may have been recalling memories under hypnosis, but Audrey's mind was still deeply damaged.

Owen held his mother for a moment, then let his arms fall. Beverly wiped tears from her cheeks. She squeezed Owen's arm, then continued to lead her daughter toward the door.

Once Audrey had drawn past them, Sergeant Allred said, "I need to escort your wife and her doctors back to the hospital, but once Mrs. Jorgensen's secured, I'm turning around and coming right back here."

He placed his hat on his head and gave them all a look of warning.

"There are questions that need to be answered," he said.

When the sergeant shut the door, all eyes fell on Owen, who'd dropped his weight onto the back of the couch.

"I told myself I dreamed it," he said, staring at the floor. "Just a dream. I think I always knew that wasn't true."

"Why didn't you tell me, son?" Lars had to ask.

Owen shook his head. Lars's confusion was mirrored on his son's face.

"I don't know," Owen said. "I just don't know. Once I realized she was gone, I thought she'd come back. She'd always come back before. And then when I knew she wasn't, I thought . . . I thought it was my fault. If I hadn't yelled at her, if I'd only listened, done as she asked, it would have been okay."

All these years, Lars had been so busy dragging his own guilt around. He'd been blind.

"Owen, none of this, none of it was ever your fault. Not ever."

He took a step toward his son but stopped when Owen shook his head, warding off any efforts to be comforted.

"I know that now, but when you're ten . . . When you're ten and you scream at your mother and call her a liar. When you run away from her, and then the whole world caves in? It's hard not to think one thing caused the other."

Lars's heart skipped a beat when Owen looked up at him from such a desolate place. Hannah, nearly forgotten, stepped up and took her father's hand in her own. Owen pulled his daughter to his side and held her tightly.

"I couldn't tell you, Dad . . . I just couldn't. You were all I had left, and I didn't want you to hate me." The final few words were delivered in a whisper.

"Oh, Owen," Beverly said.

"Once enough time had gone by, I was able to tell myself it hadn't really happened. I'd imagined it, to make myself feel better about my mother leaving me behind. Mom hadn't found me walking along the road on the way home from Zach's, kicking at rocks and avoiding her. She hadn't cried and pleaded and begged for me to come with her. That I hadn't said I hated her, and run away again."

"Jesus, son," Lars said. He closed the distance between them in two large steps and pulled both Owen and Hannah into an embrace.

Owen allowed it for a time. Then he pulled back and stood, wiping suspiciously at his eyes.

"I have to take Hannah to school," he said, clearing his throat. "She can't miss any more time."

"The sergeant," Lars said.

"I'll come back. Once I get her where she needs to be. I'll come back and try to give him the answers he's looking for."

Left alone with the two women, Lars had nowhere to stow his worry. He busied himself making lunch. Jenna stepped into the kitchen to help, and he gave thanks he hadn't pulled a chatty woman off the ice. Sometimes, small favors were the only ones you were going to get.

Beverly stood at the window, an old hand at keeping her thoughts to herself.

The hell of it was no one had an appetite, so he slid the tray into the refrigerator for later.

At some point, people would need to eat. That was one of the few constants Lars had always been able to count on.

Owen returned before Sergeant Allred, though they didn't have long to wait on the policeman.

After the facts, as far as Owen could remember them, were laid on the table, the sergeant asked, "So you were on your way home from Zachary Clark's house when you last saw your mother. Do you remember how long you played that day, before you started back?"

The lines on Owen's forehead deepened. "I don't know exactly."

"Anything you can remember will help," the policeman prodded. "It was midmorning when you left. Did you have lunch there?"

After a moment, Owen nodded. "Yeah. Yeah, I did. I remember because I sort of invited myself. Usually I'd just go home for lunch—we only lived four houses down—but I didn't want to. I felt bad about what I'd said to Mom, but I was still mad too."

"Did you stay after lunch?" the sergeant asked.

"I did. I can remember Mrs. Clark being kind of put out over it. I think she had a headache or something. Zach and I promised to go outside and not kick the ball against the side of the house, and she let me stay for a while longer."

"A good while?"

Owen shook his head. "It's been a long time."

"Over an hour, would you say?"

Owen thought that over.

"Yeah, yeah, probably. I remember we ran down to the dock and fished for a while. Zach caught a northern." A ghost of a smile flitted across Owen's face. "Nearly lost his pole over that fish. I remember his dad coming down to help us get the hook out of the fish's mouth. He had to use the pliers, because it was buried deep."

Owen leaned back in his chair and looked up toward the ceiling.

"Funny the things that stick with you," he said. "I think Mrs. Clark came out to take his picture with it. He was damn proud of that fish."

"Do you remember going back inside?"

"No." Owen placed his forearms on the table and came back to the matter at hand. "No, I don't think I did. I'm pretty sure Mrs. Clark sent me home right after that."

"So you were walking along the road when you saw your mother?"

"Yeah," he said, full of regret again. "I was walking slow, trying to put it off as long as I could. I was about halfway there, I think. Then she was in front of me. She had that wild look she got sometimes, the look I hated. I can remember how jealous I was. I just wanted to run back to Zach's house, where everything was so boring and ordinary. I just wanted a boring mom."

Owen sighed and rose from his chair. He stuffed his hands into his pockets, paced back and forth a bit.

"She wanted me to go with her. She was being crazy about it, acting like the world was going to end if I didn't. I . . . I said terrible things. And I ran away again, this time toward home.

"I went to my room and threw myself on the bed. I remember pulling out my comics and . . . and trying not to cry. I was too old to cry."

Owen stopped and leaned his back against the counter, his arms folded in front of him.

"When everything hit the fan after Dad got home, and Mom never came back . . . I lied. I couldn't bring myself to tell everyone how hurtful I'd been." He raised his eyes to look straight at his father.

But Sergeant Allred wasn't interested in regrets. He looked down at the little notepad in front of him, then raised his head.

"Owen, I need you to think back. When your mother found you on the road . . ."

Owen tilted his chin forward, waiting for the rest of the question.

"Do you remember . . . was she in a vehicle? Was she on foot?"

Owen shook his head and there was no hesitation when he said, "No, there was no vehicle. Why would she have been in a vehicle? We were less than a block from home."

Sergeant Allred made a note.

"Okay, one more thing, and this one's important. Was your mother alone?"

Owen raised his eyes slowly and looked at the sergeant. Lars did the same.

"She was."

"She was completely alone?"

Owen nodded. "Yes."

"So when you came back into the house, did you see your little brother and sister?"

Owen's face tightened.

"No," he whispered. "No, I didn't."

"Think hard. Did you see them playing in the yard, or down by the lake? Were they in the house when you came in?"

Owen's eyes were wide. He shook his head.

"No, I'm certain. They weren't by the lake, because I would have seen them from the Clarks' dock. And they weren't in the house. I know they weren't, because Francie could be a pest, and she'd want to know what was wrong. I remember being glad I had the room to myself for once. We all shared. Bunk beds for me and Francie, and Will's crib was there too."

"Okay, this is really important, Owen. Are you absolutely sure you saw no sign of Francie or Will?"

Owen shook his head again, impatient this time.

"No," he said, with more force. "I'm telling you. Look around. The only place they might have been would be Mom and Dad's bedroom, and that doesn't make any sense. We weren't allowed to play in there. Mom never would have left them in there to go outside and find me, and besides, I would have heard them."

"You were upset," the sergeant pointed out.

Lars could answer that one himself.

"Have you ever been around a four-year-old girl and a toddler, Sergeant?" he said.

The detective looked toward Lars.

"Francie had a screech that could bring bears out of hibernation. I've never heard anything like it. And little Will, he wasn't much quieter. He loved his sister. Thought she was the funniest thing on earth. The two of them together were *never* quiet."

Sergeant Allred leaned back in his chair and placed the cap on his pen, which he set on top of the little notebook he'd flipped closed.

"This changes things," he said, somber and still. "Those two kids. They had to be somewhere while Audrey was trying to coax Owen into coming with her."

A sense of dread had settled into the pit of Lars's stomach.

"Somewhere closer than we ever thought."

49

It was late, but sleep slipped further from her grasp with each passing moment. Jenna was doubtful any of the Jorgensens were resting easy.

Questions flitted around her on silent bat wings.

Audrey's hypnotherapy sessions were working, but Jenna was more confused than ever.

Where *had* the children been while Audrey tried so desperately to collect Owen, the first and the last of them? And why, if Audrey had been so set on Owen coming with her, had she given up after her failed attempt on the road?

In Audrey's position, would Jenna have been willing to give up and leave Cassie behind, saying, *What the hell. Better luck next time?*

She found the idea not even remotely likely.

Of course, she was looking at it from the perspective of a mother under threat of losing her children. What if even that basic assumption was wrong?

Jenna forced herself to examine the very thing everyone was avoiding. What if, in some rational corner of Audrey's mind, she'd known that leaving Owen behind would be his salvation?

Wrestling with the unknowable, Jenna couldn't find an explanation that fit.

Unless the children . . . unless they were already dead. Jenna wrapped her arms tighter around herself, shaken by the possibility.

If the kids were dead at that point, did that mean Audrey was responsible? It was hard to see any eventuality that wouldn't play out that way, no matter how many directions Jenna twisted and turned the facts.

If Audrey's younger children were indeed dead, and at her hand, then there could be only one reason she'd come back for Owen.

To kill him too.

"You're making a lot of assumptions," Cassie interjected.

"Am I?" Jenna asked. "Am I really?"

"I think part of you wants Audrey to be guilty," Cassie said.

Jenna shook her head. "No," she denied. "I know what I said before, but I feel sorry for her. It's plain she loved her kids, even in the grip of a sickness she couldn't control."

"Maybe. But if Audrey's guilty, that helps you hold on to the black-and-white picture you've painted of the world, doesn't it?"

Jenna frowned. "What are you talking about?"

"If Audrey deserves the blame, regardless of how much pity you might feel, then you're justified in holding on to your own guilt. Because Audrey's the other side of your coin, isn't she?"

"Stop," Jenna said. "This isn't about me."

"Isn't it?" her daughter asked softly.

Jenna rolled over in the bed and fought back tears. She clung tightly to her grief. She wanted it chained to her, where she could touch and feel it, pick at it again and again so a scab couldn't form over the top of it.

If she wasn't vigilant, Jenna knew time would lay a fine dust over her memories. It would build, infinitesimally, layer by layer, until they became faded and their edges began to blur.

Her precious, beautiful children. Her husband, that sweet, giving man she hadn't appreciated enough but who'd inexplicably chosen her.

They deserved so much more than to fade away into what once had been.

Jenna faced a truth that had traveled all these miles and all these days, buried inside of her, wrapped in her dead daughter's voice.

She knew, in her heart, she didn't want to die.

But neither did she want to live, and regardless of what Cassie might have to say about it, that was the only alternative. Black or white. No gray.

The thought of living in a world where her family had been reduced to nothing more than faded memories was too much to bear.

"Not all stories have happy endings, Mom," Cassie whispered.

"But they should, Cass," Jenna murmured, her eyes still squeezed tight. "They should. And yours should have had the happiest of all."

50

"You're alone in the house now, with only Francie and Will. Owen's gone to play at his friend's house. Can you tell me, Audrey, without dipping into the emotions, just tell me with words . . . what happens next?"

"The babies," Audrey said. "I have to take my babies. I'll come back for Owen, I will. But I have to take the babies away and keep them safe from what's coming. I can feel it starting."

"And can you tell me how you do that, Audrey?"

"Go get your most favorite thing in the world, sweetheart," Audrey said, in a tone any mother would recognize. Jenna had used it on her own children, as had countless other mothers since time began.

"You're speaking to Francine?" Dr. Young asked.

"Yes," Audrey said. "I hold Will in my arms. He's getting so big now. Not a baby much longer. But he wants his nap, so I pick him up and he lays his head on my shoulder."

"Are you packing a bag, Audrey?" Dr. Young asked. "Do you have a plan?"

"No, there's no time. The storm is coming and Lars is going to take them. No bags, I tell Francie, just one thing. Your favorite thing, and she comes back with her Moonbeam and Will's favorite blanket, and I can feel the tears on my cheeks even though I'm smiling."

Dr. Young frowned. "Her moonbeam? What's her moonbeam, Audrey?"

"A bunny," Audrey said. "A little stuffed bunny I made just for her when she was small. It's dark blue, like the sky at night, and has silver stars for buttons down its front. She holds Moonbeam tight, and I tell her we're going on an adventure."

"An adventure to where?" Dr. Young asked.

The room held its collective breath.

Audrey leaned forward, and Dr. Young did the same.

Jenna's heart was beating in her throat.

"I can't tell you. It's a secret," Audrey said in a slow, exaggerated whisper. "We can't tell anyone. Especially not Daddy."

She held a finger up to her lips and whispered, "Shh."

Every set of shoulders in the room dropped, and Jenna exchanged a glance with Lars, who looked like he was balancing on a precarious edge.

Without considering the consequences, Jenna turned back to Audrey. "Can you show us?" she asked.

It was the first time she'd spoken during the sessions, and Dr. Young sent her a cutting glance.

"We've got to hurry, turtledove. And be very quiet. We don't want anyone to see us," Audrey said.

Then she rose, her eyes unfocused, and walked slowly toward the door.

The small crowd in the room stared, transfixed.

Audrey turned back to face them.

"Come on, slowpoke," she said with a small smile. "What are you waiting for?"

51

"Oh my God," Owen whispered as they came to a stop.

Jenna was seated behind him on a snowmobile she hadn't known was hidden beneath an old cover in the Jorgensens' garage. Her cheeks were stinging from the cold, though she and Owen had taken a slow pace, far back from the four figures that hiked in snowshoes through the drifts and the trees.

Jenna marveled they'd managed the herculean feat of getting the small group outfitted and on their way.

Dr. Nordquist, who'd been mostly silent during Audrey's previous few sessions, had finally found a place to stick his oar in.

"I really must protest," he hissed at his colleague. "This is highly irregular and shockingly unprofessional. You can't possibly intend to take a hypnotized patient out into the snow to go haring off to God knows where!"

The man's face had gone an alarming shade of red, and despite Dr. Young's proven ability to stand her ground, she appeared torn.

"Perhaps it would be best to begin again on another day." She looked apologetically in Lars's direction. "When we're better prepared."

Lars didn't pause.

"No," he said. "We do this today. I'm going to follow Audrey wherever she chooses to lead. Jenna, if you could help Beverly dress Audrey for the outdoors, I'd appreciate it. I'll be right back with what we need."

Jenna nodded, powerless to stop this train now that it was barreling down the track.

"Dr. Young, you can come with me or not. That is entirely your decision."

And with that, Lars walked out of the cabin.

Sergeant Allred exited on his heels, but if he thought he was going to talk Lars out of the madness, Jenna could only wonder if he was prepared to use the gun holstered at his side.

Audrey was pliable, though not necessarily helpful, as Jenna placed layers over her clothing and wrapped her yellow scarf around her neck. The doctor hadn't brought her out of her hypnotic state. Instead she'd asked her to wait. Jenna had no idea how well that would work, and wasn't entirely sure the doctor did either.

After a moment's indecision, Dr. Young also began donning her winter clothing. Wherever her patient intended to go, it apparently wouldn't be without her.

"Dr. Young—" Dr. Nordquist started again, sounding scandalized.

"Oh, shut up," Dr. Young replied, standing firm now that her decision was made.

The sergeant and Lars returned to the cabin together.

"I only have three pairs of snowshoes," Lars said. "Sergeant Allred has a pair for himself. Owen, you follow with Jenna on the snowmobile. Stay back a fair distance. We need to let your mother lead the way."

Lars looked apologetically in Beverly's direction.

"It's okay," she said. "You go."

He nodded, then looked Dr. Nordquist up and down.

"We don't have room for you." He dismissed the man while the doctor stood with his mouth gaping, looking like a fish.

And so they'd set off, the doctor, the policeman, Lars, and his wife, whom they supported along the way.

It had taken a few minutes for Owen to get the snowmobile from the garage, but there was a clear path to follow, and they soon saw the others in the distance.

Owen did as his father asked, keeping well back, following their trail.

They'd been doing just that for nearly half an hour before Jenna felt Owen stiffen.

"What's the matter?" she'd asked loudly over the whine of the engine.

For a moment, she thought he wouldn't answer, then she heard his reply.

"I know where she's going," he'd called back.

Jenna had no chance to ask more. Owen twisted the throttle, and they set off with more speed than she'd anticipated, forcing her to throw her arms around him while they caught up to the group.

They'd come around the opposite side of the lake from where Lars had shown Jenna such a spectacular view just days before. Here the elevation felt lower, and the stand of trees the group had disappeared into was thick, creating a wall that was difficult to see through.

Owen slowly took the snowmobile between the trees, following through an open space just large enough for them to fit.

He cut the engine, and the sudden silence was shocking. Everything was muffled, blanketed in white. Jenna wondered if her hearing had been left somewhere on the trail behind them.

She was relieved to hear Owen's soft exclamation.

Then Jenna heard a sound that stole her breath. It was a deep, almost grinding moan that seemed to come from everywhere and nowhere. It was followed by a sharp, thundering boom.

She flinched, and her eyes widened as she gripped Owen's arm. He glanced over his shoulder and caught sight of her expression.

"The lake," he said, gesturing with his chin. "It's just on the other side of those trees."

"The lake is making that sound?" she whispered.

He nodded, but his attention was on his parents.

The clearing was small, no more than ten feet by ten, and crowded with four adults standing side by side and the nose of the snowmobile jutting in.

Owen stepped into the snow and sank to his knees in the white powder.

"Stay put," he said to her unnecessarily. She had no intention of getting off the seat.

"Audrey, is this where you stopped?" Dr. Young was asking. She sounded different outside the confines of the cabin. Smaller. Less assured.

"You've got to stay here, turtledove," Audrey replied. "Be a good girl for Mommy, okay. We'll be safe here, where no one can find us. This place is magical, remember. Like I told you. Like the fairy tales."

"You and the children know this place, Audrey?" Dr. Young asked. She looked uncomfortable on the snowshoes, but she was handling the situation admirably.

Audrey smiled, glancing around, though Jenna thought she was probably seeing the place not as it was, but as it had been that summer so long ago.

"We play here. On the good days," she said. "We read stories and make up games. This is our place. Owen and I found it when he was little, but he never wants to come here with me now."

Audrey's smile lost its shine and slowly dissolved.

"And this is where you bring Francie and Will?" Dr. Young forged on.

"Yes," Audrey said, her voice soft and nostalgic. "Nothing bad can happen to us here."

Audrey opened her arms wide and slowly turned in a circle, clumsy in her snowshoes. A chill swept through Jenna that had nothing to do with the weather.

Suddenly, Audrey dropped her arms and looked frantically around.

"I have to get Owen," she said. "I have to bring him here, where he'll be safe with me and his brother and his sister. No one can take them from me while we're here."

Audrey looked from face to face, searching for something. Or someone.

Her gaze landed on Owen, who stood mute and unmoving.

She tilted her head and stared into his eyes, this man she didn't recognize as the boy he'd once been.

"I have to get Owen and bring him here too," she said directly to him, while a small smile played across her lips. "Then we'll all be safe, together. Happily ever after. Forever and ever. Amen."

52

Jenna sensed they'd gone past a precipice.

Once back at the cabin, a great many things hung between them, unsaid.

Sergeant Allred phoned for a patrolman to escort Audrey and her doctors back to the hospital, then stepped farther down the small porch to make other, more pressing, calls.

Beverly took one look at the faces of those gathered and caught Jenna's eye, gesturing silently toward the spare bedroom down the hall.

Jenna followed, then told her in hushed whispers what had taken place at the clearing on the far side of the lake.

Watching her face, Jenna marked the moment concern drained from Beverly and fear grew to fill the empty space.

"I think I should stay," the older woman said, holding one delicate, fluttering hand to her throat.

Jenna wished she had reassurances to give her. In the end, all she could say was "That would probably be best."

When the women reemerged, only the three men remained, having a somber discussion of their own.

Lars nodded gravely, then reached out to shake the policeman's hand.

"I'll be in touch," Sergeant Allred said, then took his leave as well.

"What is he going to do?" Beverly asked in a shaky voice.

Lars and Owen exchanged a glance, then Owen faced his grandmother and said, "He's going to coordinate a search of the area Mom led us to."

"A search . . . for . . ." Beverly couldn't go on.

"For Francie and Will, Bev," Lars added gently.

"But they searched before," Beverly cried. "If there was anything to find, they would have—"

But Lars was shaking his head. "Yes, they searched, we all did, but they could have been anywhere between here and Iowa, Bev. And there were sightings, remember?"

Beverly's fear was palpable, but she struggled visibly to rein it in.

"I remember," she agreed quietly.

There was so much more that could have been said. An infinite number of words and combinations of words that remained resolutely locked behind closed mouths.

All they could do was wait.

The Jorgensen family was well versed in the tortuous art of waiting. All of them, so stoic in their own ways. Jenna couldn't help but wonder how they'd fare if Sergeant Allred were to call with news that the remains of the children had finally been located.

Or—a potentially more disturbing thought—news they had not. That, after everything, Francie and Will Jorgensen were still, and possibly forever, lost.

Within hours, the phone rang. Everyone in the cabin stared as if it were a cobra rising from a basket.

Lars took a deep, girding breath and walked toward it.

"Yes," he said hoarsely into the receiver. A pause followed. The old man's sober face gave away no clues.

"Yes," he said finally. "I understand. Thank you."

He turned to Jenna and his family. He looked like he carried the weight of the world on his shoulders. He looked tired.

"They brought in a team to shovel the snow from the clearing." His voice was devoid of emotion. "Using ground-penetrating radar—" He stopped to clear his throat before he could go on. His eyes were pointed somewhere above their heads. "They believe they may have found indications of something buried beneath."

Beverly gasped and covered her face with her hands.

Owen stood and took a step toward his father, but Lars held up one hand and gripped the back of a kitchen chair with the other. His head dropped low, and Jenna's heart bled for him in places she'd believed drained empty and left for dead.

"They won't know for sure until tomorrow. They need to go back to the site with a grave heater before—"

But Lars had reached the end of his endurance. His voice broke cleanly in two, and he dropped to his knees on the kitchen floor.

53

The earth continued to revolve around the sun at the same pace it always had, but Jenna had rarely experienced a night so interminably long.

There were no hypnotherapy sessions the next day and little to do to fill the time.

Lars had spoken hardly at all since the day before. He'd waved off their concerns about his heart, saying only, "The damn thing is going to quit when it quits."

Standing at the windows, Jenna watched Lars, who'd gone out to the lake just before sunrise. He'd found a large bucket from somewhere and tipped it on its end to use as a seat. Occasionally he pulled a rock from his coat pocket to skip over the ice.

Mostly he sat. Silent, still, and alone.

Owen came to stand at Jenna's side. "It kills me to see him like this," he said.

It would have been hard to say if the devastation coming from Owen was more grief or self-inflicted guilt.

"There was nothing you could have done, Owen." It had been said before, but was worth repeating.

"I should have known." He watched his father, worry etched on his face. "I should have looked. I should have said something. There are so many things I should have done, Jenna."

She turned to face him.

"Owen, you were ten. You couldn't have known."

He leaned his shoulder against the window jamb.

"But I did," he said. "At least, I knew she believed that place was special." He glanced back out the window and gave a humorless chuckle. "Hell, it was special. That was where my mother became magical. Where all the forgotten dinners and the manic flights of irrationality and the bouts of crippling depression were gone. Like all that was the imaginary side of her, and when we were there, at the hideaway, that was what was real."

Jenna reached out and took Owen's hand into hers. She gave it a squeeze.

"I couldn't go back after they were gone. Without her and Francie and Will . . . I couldn't do it. Not for years. And then only once. It still looked magical, but it made me feel empty. I never went back again. And the whole time . . ."

Owen let go of her hand. He gave her a sad almost-smile before he pushed his hands into his pockets and walked away.

Without the desire to read, and with no one in the mood for a meal, Jenna cleaned the cabin instead.

It killed some time. Still the phone didn't ring. Owen left to run an errand, though she didn't ask if it pertained to the garage or his daughter.

Beverly stayed closeted in the spare room. Lars refused to come off the ice.

Jenna sprayed the counter with disinfectant and wiped it down a second time for good measure.

She was almost grateful to hear Cassie's voice.

"You're missing something, Mom," her daughter said.

Jenna glanced down at the countertop. It sparkled, as it should after the double treatment she'd given it.

"Not the counter," Cassie said impatiently. "Why are you cleaning anyway?"

"Because it needs to be done, Cassie," Jenna muttered aloud. There was no one in the room to give her a sideways glance.

"Mom, you're not paying attention."

Jenna regretted welcoming Cassie's company in that moment.

"Jesus, Cass, let me be." Jenna leaned one hand against the edge of the counter, and her head drooped on her shoulders.

"But *why* does it need to be done?" Cassie asked, unwilling to let it go.

Jenna had no idea what she was getting at.

"All that time you spent, plotting and planning for a novel you never wrote. What happens when, what comes next . . . And you never got it. You still don't get it."

Jenna blew out an irritated breath and shook her head, her eyes narrowing.

But Cassie wouldn't leave it alone.

"A story only matters if the people in it matter. The people. The plot is irrelevant. Secondary, as long as you allow the people to guide you where they can't help going next."

"What is your point?" Jenna's voice rose with a frustration she couldn't contain.

"Every character has their own agenda. Their own wants and needs and loves and hates and fears."

Jenna threw the sponge into the sink of soapy water, and suds splashed onto the countertop. "If you have something to say, just spit it out."

A knock on the door made her jump.

She straightened her blouse and tried to slow her racing pulse as she walked slowly to the door.

"Every character," Cassie whispered, just before Jenna turned the knob.

54

Lars saw the detective pull up and hurried to the house. Beverly, who'd heard the knock, emerged from her room. Owen, with impressive timing, arrived and parked in the drive just behind Sergeant Allred, completing the group.

They fanned out, the Jorgensens and Jenna, facing the sergeant, dreading whatever news he'd come to deliver.

Any doubts they might have had were swept away when he removed his police cap and held it in both hands.

"I'm sorry to keep you waiting, Mr. Jorgensen," Sergeant Allred said, looking Lars in the eyes.

"Say what you need to say."

"We've excavated the place where radar indicated a possible grave." The policeman took a deep breath and plunged on. "We've discovered what appear to be bones."

Beverly clutched Jenna, who wrapped an arm around the tiny woman, helping to support the weight Beverly no longer could.

"The medical examiner has confirmed they belong to a small child. I'm very sorry, Mr. Jorgensen."

Lars kept his legs beneath him, but he looked older than he had just moments before. He looked broken.

Owen stepped toward his father and placed one hand on his back and the other beneath his arm for support. Lars was shaking.

Despite the advance warning of what was coming, despite the hours they'd had to prepare, it was a massive blow.

"We'll know more once the ME has completed her examination, but I wanted to tell you personally."

Sergeant Allred rotated his cap in his hands. "I'm afraid that's not all."

Jenna's head jerked upward, and all at once it registered, the words the policeman had spoken.

"Child," he'd said.

A small child.

Singular.

Faintly, Jenna heard Cassie whisper again in her ear.

"*Every* character."

55

Jenna pulled the van into the driveway of the tiny cottage. It was painted a robin's-egg blue. From the outside, it looked cheery and quaint, particularly against the snow that blanketed the front yard.

Jenna took a deep breath and wondered, not for the first time, if she was crazy. But she didn't think so.

"You're not leaving, are you?" Owen had asked, the shock evident on his face when she'd asked for a ride into town to pick up her van. "Not now?"

Any ideas Jenna had been clinging to about somehow managing to skate through this town and this family without making any of those connections she'd wanted to avoid were shown, in that moment, for exactly what they were.

Delusions.

"No," she'd said, shaking her head. "Not yet. But there's something I need to do."

Owen bowed his head and scratched at the back of his neck. He studied her through lowered eyes full of questions.

"I wouldn't ask if it weren't important." She hoped that would be enough.

"Okay," he said at last. "I need to go pick up Hannah anyway. Let me . . . I'll just let Dad know."

Her first stop had been the Raven Public Library.

"Mrs. Shaw," the librarian began when she spotted her. "I'm afraid we may have gotten off on the wrong foot before."

Jenna shook her head and tried to wave off the woman's words, but Eleanor Lutz wouldn't be dissuaded.

"I spoke with Lars and . . . I owe you an apology. I behaved quite rudely before. That's unlike me."

"Help me now, and we'll call it square."

Eleanor straightened her spine and peered more closely at Jenna. Whatever she saw must have convinced her the matter had some urgency.

"What do you need?" she asked with a librarian's innate efficiency.

It didn't take long to find what Jenna was searching for. She was quickly gathering her things, her mind already out the door, when Eleanor Lutz placed a hand upon her shoulder.

"I did love him, you know," the librarian said, holding her head high even as a blush colored the apples of her cheeks. "I love him still, I suppose. But it was impossible, after everything."

Jenna reached up and squeezed the older woman's hand.

"Thank you for your help," she said softly.

Eleanor only nodded, then briskly stepped back into librarian mode.

"Of course, Mrs. Shaw."

Jenna left the library practically running for her van, a slip of paper tucked into her coat pocket, thanks to the help of the internet and Lars's childhood friend.

Hastily scrawled upon it was an address.

An address for a tiny robin's-egg-blue cottage.

The drive had taken just over an hour. A considerable distance to commute several times a week.

Unless you have a good reason.

Diane Downey looked tired when she answered the door. Her hair was down, and she was wearing pajama bottoms and a stained T-shirt.

Her eyes were puffy, like she'd cried a great deal in the last few days.

Her hand came up, her fingers fanning over her lips upon seeing Jenna.

"I've been expecting someone, but I have to say, I never thought it would be you."

Jenna schooled her features into a benign expression and chose her words with care.

"Can I come in?" she asked.

Diane took a deep breath and stepped back, holding the door wide for Jenna to enter.

"I doubt I could stop you," she said. "Not now that you've figured it out."

She shut the door behind them.

Jenna glanced around the room. It was cozy, and neat as a pin. She turned back to the woman she'd come to see, who was considerably less neat. "Only parts of it," she told her. "Will you tell me the rest?"

Diane hesitated.

"It's been a long time coming, wouldn't you say?" Jenna said in a quiet voice.

Diane gave an immense, world-weary sigh. "Twenty-nine years," she murmured. "You'd better have a seat."

56

"When I said my ex-husband wasn't a good man, I meant that. Have you ever been mixed up with a truly bad man?" Diane asked.

Jenna shook her head.

"I could have guessed that," Diane replied. "There's an air about us, a constant kind of nervousness. You don't have that." Diane peered closely at her. "You have sadness, but no fear. You know who you are, Jenna, even if you don't like it much."

Jenna shifted in her seat, uncomfortable with the turn of the conversation.

"I won't get into ugly details," Diane went on, staring into the distance. "He was abusive, and he had a badge to back him up."

Jenna's brow furrowed. The path forming in front of them was hazy, but she could be patient.

"There came a day I knew in my bones that if I stayed, he'd kill me eventually. So I ran. There's a cabin on the other side of the lake. It belonged to my second cousin. Gary didn't know anything about it, so it was as good a place as any to hide while I tried to get my life sorted out."

The first missing piece fell into place.

"I'd never been there before, but it was summertime, and it was beautiful. I was sitting on the tiny front porch, trying to heal, when a small child came wandering out of the woods."

Jenna held her breath. This was what she'd hoped and prayed for, tapping her fingers against the steering wheel while she drove the minutes and miles to get here, warning herself not to get her hopes up.

All for this.

"'You've got to come,' she said, running up to me. 'Please. Oh, please.'"

Diane was lost in the memory, and Jenna watched, fascinated, as she was pulled along into the current of the past.

The little girl tugged Diane by the hand, straining and insistent as only a child can be.

"Please, miss. Please come," she begged.

The child had dark hair, with a slight wave covering one eye, but the eye visible was full of apprehension.

Diane stood without a word, powerless over the sensation of that small, warm hand in her own. She would have followed this child wherever she led.

Through the woods, down a path, they traveled. The child urged her forward, pulling when she felt Diane might be falling behind. Her little face turning to her, making sure the stranger she'd found was still there.

Diane heard the sobs before she saw the woman hidden in a copse of trees. She was kneeling, holding a bundle to her, rocking back and forth.

"Mommy," the girl said, dropping Diane's hand and running to the woman. Diane felt the loss of the warm hand as a hole that had been carved there. She shook herself from her daze.

"Ma'am," Diane said, coming back to herself. "Ma'am, are you all right?"

Stupid Diane. Just as stupid as Gary always says. Obviously the woman wasn't all right.

"Ma'am," Diane pressed, leaning down and placing a hand on the woman's back. "Are you hurt?"

The ravaged face that turned to meet hers was full of a desperate fear she recognized all too well.

"He won't let me keep them!" the woman cried, her features contorted with pain and tears. "He'll take them away from me. He'll take them and I'll never see them again."

The woman was hysterical. Sobs quaked through her body as she clung to what Diane realized was a second child in her arms, wrapped in a blanket.

She was hugging the child to her chest, rocking back and forth.

"Help me," the woman pleaded. "Oh, please God, help me!"

Diane could have no more turned and walked away from this little family than she could have pulled her still beating heart from her chest.

"Of course," she said, trying to soothe the frantic woman. "I'll help you. I'll help. Shh, it's going to be okay."

It took time, but Diane managed to calm the woman somewhat. All while the little dark-haired girl watched, sitting on the grass and hugging her legs a few feet away.

Diane supported the woman beneath her arms as she stood, and supported her still while they walked the distance back to the borrowed cabin.

The little girl led the way, glancing back at them now and again, worry on her face.

The girl had good reason to look so concerned. Despite the hysterics of the mother and the constant rocking back and forth, it hadn't escaped Diane's notice that the baby in the woman's arms had yet to make a sound.

◆　◆　◆

"He was dead," Jenna said. It wasn't a question.

Diane bowed her head and gave a quick, sharp nod.

Jenna struggled to comprehend. She didn't have enough pieces to make a full picture. Not yet.

"Can I ask . . . Why didn't you call the police?"

There were countless lives that would have taken an entirely different path if the woman had just picked up the phone, dialed three little numbers.

Diane's face twisted and she stood, rubbing her hands up and down her arms. Jenna watched her pace the room, to the window and then back to the sofa. She watched and she waited.

Finally, Diane took a deep breath and spoke.

"I'd like to tell you it was because there wasn't a phone in the cabin. And there wasn't. Or I could tell you it was because I'd taken all the money out of our joint account when I ran from Gary and I was terrified of facing him again, which was true too.

"If it were only that, I probably would have done what any rational person would and found a way to contact the police straightaway."

Jenna leaned her elbows on her knees and clasped her hands together. She tilted her head to stare at the woman who'd affected so many, so deeply, with this one irrevocable decision.

"But that wasn't all?" Jenna asked, sensing the need to be gentle, even as she grasped for understanding.

"Oh no," Diane said with a humorless smile. "Not by a long shot."

Diane ran her hands down the backs of her thighs before she took her seat again on the sofa. She sat primly, her back straight, despite her disheveled appearance.

"I had a daughter, you see." Her voice was nearly a whisper. "I had a little girl of my own. She'd passed away less than six months before that day. Leukemia."

Jenna sat back in the chair and let out a pent-up breath.

"She was my child, only mine," Diane continued. "Gary had nothing to do with her after conception. She was my . . . my everything."

Diane's eyes bored into Jenna's, silently begging her to see.

Unstoppable, thoughts of the bottomless cavern that had opened inside of Jenna when her family was taken rushed in.

"When that child materialized from the edge of the woods," Diane went on, "for a moment—one brief, miniscule moment—I believed, with every ounce of my being, that she was Paige. That she'd come to find me. To take me back with her."

Comprehension had finally dawned.

"Of course," Diane continued, "it wasn't Paige."

The quiet child with the large eyes may not have been her daughter, a fact Diane had realized within moments, but the child and her mother needed Diane's help.

She found the sensation, after years of caring for her own child, a familiar one.

"You can't tell him," the woman was saying, over and over. She was more coherent now, but barely. Still she clutched the bundle to her chest, refusing to set the second child down.

"I can't go back, I can't go back there. He'll take them all and I'll never see them again," she kept repeating.

"Shh," Diane said, trying to soothe the woman. "I won't tell your husband, I won't. No one's going to make you go back." She stood beside her, rubbing circles along her back. "It's going to be all right. Just breathe. That's right, breathe deep."

Diane's gaze returned, unwillingly, to the girl. That explained why the child had sought a stranger rather than going home. Diane could see the woman's state was upsetting her daughter.

Somehow, she convinced the woman to lie down on the bed.

"Just rest, then we'll figure out what to do next."

"You won't send me back?" the woman asked fervently.

"No." No matter what, Diane could never do that. It wasn't difficult to infer, given the woman's extreme fear of returning home, who exactly was the villain here.

The woman's eyes were unfocused, but she nodded. Diane didn't have to imagine the horrors playing across the woman's mind. She'd lived through her own for many years.

When Diane left her in the cabin's only bedroom, the woman was still clutching the bundle to her chest. Diane couldn't conceive of taking the baby from her arms.

The little girl sat, quiet and alone, on a chair while her legs dangled beneath her, too short to reach the floor. She was so heartbreakingly beautiful Diane could hardly bear to look at her.

Averting her eyes, Diane turned to the cabin's poorly stocked kitchen. She found a packet of powdered hot chocolate of indeterminate age and busied her hands making the girl a cup.

"My little girl was about your age, you know." She immediately regretted the words. If the girl asked where her daughter was, or what happened to her, Diane wouldn't be able to hold it together.

The child didn't ask.

"Can you sing to me?" she asked instead, in a thin, wavering voice.

Diane's heart ached, and she fought back tears. The last thing the child needed was to see another adult weeping. It would scare her to death.

Instead, she stirred the cup of chocolate in front of her until she had a better handle on her emotions, then walked to the table and set it down in front of the child. She took a seat in the chair beside her.

"Here you go."

The dark-haired beauty stood, ignoring the drink. Then she closed the short gap between herself and Diane and climbed into the woman's lap.

Diane's heart fell wide open.

"Sing to me?" the child asked again, laying her head against Diane's chest.

Diane couldn't sing, because to sing, she would have had to open her mouth, and if she did that, nothing would escape but an endless howl of wrenching pain.

Instead, she brought her arms up and encircled the child in a feather-light grip, and she hummed.

She hummed every song she knew, while she closed her eyes and shed silent tears onto the top of the girl's head. She hummed and she rocked the child and she grieved for the daughter she'd lost.

Diane was content to stay that way for eternity. The girl had fallen asleep snuggled in her arms. She should lay her down and deal with whatever came next.

The problem was, Diane didn't know what that was. The woman and the girl clearly couldn't go home. She'd given her word.

We'll have to run. It's the only way.

It was irrational. It was borderline insanity. She could think of nothing else.

She had the money she'd taken from Gary. It wouldn't last forever, but it would get them away from here, where people were bound to be searching before long.

It wasn't much of a plan, but it was something. Diane rose, intending to place the child on the couch, but found she didn't want to give up her warmth.

There had been no sound from the bedroom, and Diane hoped the woman had fallen asleep as well. She needed to rest. Maybe rest could take the haunted look from her eyes.

It was a slim hope, one Diane clung to all the same.

She gingerly sat on the couch, allowing the girl to continue sleeping.

I can give this up when she wakes. She closed her eyes and breathed in the child's woodsy scent. *I can. Until then, I'll just hold her. It won't hurt to hold her just a while longer.*

When Diane woke, the woman and the baby were gone.

She and the child searched, running from the cabin down the path into the woods. They didn't call out, though—the child because she was crying too hard and Diane because she'd never learned the woman's name.

They ran instead to the only place she could think to check.

The small copse of trees that sat beside the lake.

Dusk was beginning to fall as they rounded the corner. She took in the tiny clearing at a glance.

The woman wasn't there, but there was no denying she had been.

She'd spent a great deal of time there while Diane and the woman's daughter had slept, blissfully unaware.

The woman must have wandered through the woods and picked every flower she'd come to, because the clearing was bursting with them. They hung from branches. The ground was littered with them. Blooms that were still fresh, but would inevitably wither and fade.

Love was evident in the careful bed of leaves and flowers that had been arranged just so. A mother's love.

On that bed, the poor broken woman had placed the body of the child Diane hadn't been willing to take from her arms.

In this place of beauty she'd created with her own hands, a mother had laid her child to rest.

The woman was gone.

Diane's heart pounded as she took in the scene in front of her. The woman had disappeared and left behind her children. One who would never take another breath. The other, though. The other was clinging to Diane's leg, hiding her face from what she couldn't bear to look at, crying like she'd never, ever stop.

The other. A little girl who was very much alive.

A ribbon of shame ran through Diane at the way her heart leapt.

She'd lost so, so much. She'd lost everything.

Ignoring the shame, Diane made a decision standing there, one she would never be able to take back, even if she wanted to.

Diane refused to lose this child too.

Quickly, before the light faded, Diane returned to the cabin with the girl. She'd seen what she needed in the small garage when she arrived.

But first, she walked into the cabin and opened the suitcase she hadn't yet unpacked.

She'd brought little with her when she fled her husband and his fists. A few changes of clothing, not much more. At the bottom of the case, where she knew it would be, her fingers found the crinkle of tissue paper.

She'd wrapped it so carefully, the first thing she'd placed inside the suitcase that would travel with her to a new life.

She tucked the tissue-wrapped parcel under her arm, then took the girl by the hand, and they headed back into the woods.

In the other hand, Diane carried a shovel.

When they'd drawn near to the copse of trees, the girl broke away from Diane, rushing to pick something up from the ground.

"Moonbeam," she cried, hugging her prize tightly to her and nuzzling it with her cheek. "It's Moonbeam!" She held up a stuffed bunny for Diane to see. "Mommy made her for me."

The girl's smile wrenched at Diane's heart.

"Sweetheart, can you sit right here with Moonbeam for a few minutes? Auntie Diane needs to do something."

The child looked up, and her happiness dimmed. "Are you going to see my baby brother again?"

Diane knelt and tucked a strand of hair behind the child's ear. "I am."

There was so much more she could have said, but she wasn't sure how much the child would understand, and she couldn't bear to frighten her again.

"Will you stay here? I'll be right on the other side of those trees. Just shout and I'll hear you."

The girl sat and clutched the little bunny her mother had made for her.

Diane turned to walk through the opening in the trees when the child called out to her.

"Promise you'll come back?" the girl cried.

Diane walked back to the child and knelt again.

"I promise." She opened her arms wide, and the girl lunged into the offered hug. Diane held her and stroked her tangled dark hair. "I won't leave you," she whispered. "You'll see."

The child nodded, but her worry showed.

There was nothing for it. She wouldn't bring the child into the trees with her, not this time.

Diane needed to do this alone.

Once she'd stepped into the small clearing, she looked around, burning every detail onto her mind.

Then she began to dig.

When the time came, Diane slowly unwrapped the tissue from the only memento she had of her own daughter's short life. It was a soft cotton blanket, hand sewn with love while Paige had grown in her belly, safe still from the world.

She held the cotton, worn and faded from many washings, to her face and breathed deep. She thought she caught the faintest scent of her daughter.

With precise motions, and before she could change her mind, Diane laid the blanket in the bottom of the small grave she'd dug, lining the earth.

Then with a strength and determination she hadn't known she possessed, Diane took the lifeless baby boy into her arms. Gently, she laid him upon her daughter's blanket, praying Paige's spirit would find him wherever they were now. That she would take him under her wing.

As the last sliver of sun dropped below the horizon, Diane gathered as many of the flowers the child's mother had chosen for him as her arms would hold.

She let them fall into the grave, blanketing the boy. With a final prayer but without tears, because she simply had none left, Diane covered the boy in earth.

She buried the baby in that lovely, secluded place his mother had chosen.

Then she turned her attention to the precious gift the same woman had left for her.

Because somehow, Diane knew the woman wouldn't be back. As incomprehensible as it was, Diane had seen the woman's eyes. There was something crushed inside of her. If Diane had any doubts, all she had to do was remember the clearing and the baby she'd left behind.

57

"We left."

Diane was standing in front of the fireplace mantel, touching one finger to a white ceramic bird that sat atop it.

"We went to Arizona. I'd always wanted to see Arizona." Diane sighed and walked back toward Jenna, who was wiping tears from her cheeks.

"I changed her hair. A short cut and some home dye. I kept her back from school an extra year, and I gave her my daughter's name. All it took was a phone call or two, and a new copy of her birth certificate was mailed to me. After all, I was her mother. No one thought to check if she'd already died."

Diane leaned her head back against the couch and closed her eyes. "It was surprisingly easy," she said in a tired voice.

"And your husband?" Jenna asked. "Weren't you worried he'd find you? There's no way you could pass Francie off as Paige to him."

Diane opened her eyes and sat up. "You're a perceptive one, aren't you?"

Jenna didn't miss the sour note of bitterness.

"I *was* worried," Diane continued. "It was the money, you see. I knew he was too lazy to come looking for me for my sake. Probably glad to see the back of me, but I'd stolen from him. That, I knew he wouldn't let go."

"So what did you do?" Jenna asked when Diane said nothing more.

"I sent it back to him, didn't I?" she replied. "What else could I do? Things were tight for a while, but I'm not afraid of hard work. I'm afraid of a lot of things, but not that. And I didn't see another choice."

"And that worked?"

Diane nodded. "I never heard from him again. For a while I worried he'd track me down, looking for a divorce. It kept me up nights, but in the end, it never happened."

Diane gave her an appraising look. "You happened instead." She stood and began pacing the room again.

Jenna had more questions, but time was slipping through her hands.

"Do they know yet?" Diane asked suddenly, still facing away from Jenna.

"No. I needed to make sure I wasn't wrong."

"How did you know?" Diane asked.

"When you came into the cabin that day," Jenna said truthfully, her mind too jumbled to play games. "You were shaken. We could all see that. You told me it was the policeman. The reminder of your ex-husband."

Diane studied her.

"But you barely glanced at Sergeant Allred. There was someone else in that room you were trying to avoid."

A shadow of a smile passed across Diane's lips, though not a happy one. "When I saw Audrey, I was terrified she'd recognize me."

Jenna considered the woman. "I don't think she would have," she said. "She doesn't even recognize Owen. But you didn't come back after that. You should have come to clean today. You didn't. In the commotion, it almost went unnoticed. But you had to have a reason for staying away."

Diane stared at her. "That was all?" she asked.

A strange desire to comfort the woman who'd done this terrible thing came over Jenna, but there was nothing she could do. Diane Downey had made her bed.

"The photograph of your grandson. The one you showed me the first day we met?"

Diane reared back as if struck, then reached a hand behind her to guide herself onto the sofa again.

"He's chewing on something. It's impossible to tell what it is from the photo. It could be a blanket. But it's not, is it?"

"Moonbeam," Diane said with a sigh.

"It's the ear of a midnight-blue stuffed bunny named Moonbeam. A precious family toy, passed down from his mother."

Giving in to the inevitable, Diane began to cry.

"They're going to have questions. So many questions," Jenna said softly, almost apologetically. "Questions they deserve answers to."

Diane nodded, sniffling and trying to curb the flood of tears. "Yes. But, Jenna, can you let me tell her first? Please," Diane begged. "Let me be the one to tell her."

Another person might have dismissed the plea, but Jenna recognized it for what it was.

A mother's need to cushion her child from an inevitable and unimaginable hurt.

58

Darkness had long overtaken the day by the time the minivan pulled into the driveway of the cabin. Its headlights illuminated circles across the yard and house before they came to rest on the back of Lars's truck.

Jenna was keenly aware of the hour and the exhaustion of the woman sitting in the passenger seat.

"You'll stay here, like we talked about?"

Diane inclined her head, then leaned it back against the headrest, her eyes closed.

"I'm not going anywhere, if that's what you're worried about." She sounded hollow. Empty.

Jenna didn't doubt that was true, even though she was about to step out of the van and leave the other woman waiting there alone. Diane had told her she'd accepted long ago that if this day ever came, she wouldn't run from the repercussions.

Though the aging housekeeper had been in no mood to talk as they'd driven the miles back to Raven, Jenna couldn't help but ask, "Would you do it again? If you had the choice?"

The interior of the van was dark, lit only by the unnatural green glow of the dashboard instruments, and Jenna couldn't make out the other woman's face.

Diane shifted in her seat and turned her head toward the passenger window. The silence dragged on long enough that Jenna thought she wasn't going to answer.

"I'm aware of the pain I've caused," Diane said at last. "I may be the only person on earth who can really know what I stole from that man by keeping his child. Even Lars . . . he knows there was a hole in his life. I know the exact shape of it."

Another pause, then Diane exhaled sharply. "What I did was wrong. But I'd be lying if I said I was ever strong enough to give her up."

Jenna blinked at the unvarnished honesty.

"I'm done lying."

Jenna asked no more questions, and the rest of the drive had passed in tense, expectant silence.

"I don't know how long this is going to take," Jenna said. Now that she was here, she was second-guessing herself.

Diane folded her hands in her lap. "It takes as long as it takes." Her unnerving calm was at odds with Jenna's agitation.

"I don't think I'm the right person to do this," Jenna said, gripping the steering wheel.

The other woman watched Jenna as she sat exposed with all her nervousness on display.

"Go on," Diane said. She sounded almost motherly. "You're bringing him a gift."

Jenna reached out a hand and took Diane's in her own. She gave it a gentle squeeze.

Then Jenna took a deep breath and clicked off the headlights. She left the engine and heater running to ward off the cold, then stepped out of the van.

Jenna's footsteps were steady as she crunched through the snow. When she reached the porch and found Owen waiting, her doubts fled.

"You came back," he said.

She gave him a small smile. "I said I would."

"Is there someone with you?" Owen asked, peering into the darkness where the shape of Diane seated in the van could faintly be made out in the moonlight.

"Yes." Jenna threw a glance over her shoulder. She could sense the other woman watching them, waiting. "But we'll get to that."

"Jenna, what's this about?"

"Let's go inside," she suggested. "I have something to tell you. Something you all need to hear."

He cast a final glance at the figure in the darkness, then opened the door and followed her inside.

While Diane remained alone in the eye of a hurricane of her own making, inside the cabin the storm raged.

As Jenna slowly and methodically laid out the story placed under her guardianship, the reactions among the Jorgensens swung wildly from one extreme to another.

Once the tale was told, Jenna surveyed the effects her words had wrought.

Beverly Jorgensen was seated on the couch, clutching her great-granddaughter to her. Hannah's head lay on her nana's shoulder, her eyes stunned. She looked so young, her face scrubbed clean of her normal dramatic makeup, and too awash in shock to maintain the guise of an indifferent teenager.

Both faces were blotchy from the tears they'd shed while clinging to each other for support.

Owen stood with his back against the wall, his arms folded in front of him. His eyes were trained on the shattered glass littering the floor. He gripped the prescription bottle he'd run to fetch from his father's bathroom when it was unclear whether Lars's heart would withstand the strain.

And Lars. Lars, who'd risen partway through Jenna's telling and gripped the edge of the mantel, while his shoulders shook with emotion.

When Jenna told them in hushed words of Diane's actions in the clearing, his knuckles had whitened and his body tensed.

With a groan of unimaginable pain, Lars swept his hand down the mantel, sending picture frames and candlesticks flying. Glass shattered and slid across the floor into darkened corners.

Everyone flinched, and Hannah couldn't hold back the tears that started anew. She buried her face in her great-grandmother's side, the only sound her muffled, choking tears.

The seconds ticked past. Owen walked swiftly out of the room, then returned moments later with the bottle of pills for Lars's heart. His father waved him away as he struggled to get himself under control. Jenna looked helplessly at Owen, unsure if she should go on.

The worry in Owen's face didn't fade, but he raised both hands, as if to say, *There's no going back now.*

"Diane," Lars said in a slow, hoarse voice, his back still turned to the room, "lives seventy miles from here. You're telling me she *buried* my son, *stole* my daughter, and raised her as her own . . . *seventy* miles away from me?"

Lars turned to stare at Jenna. The fierce outrage emanating from him stole her breath, and she pulled back.

Swallowing the lump in her throat, Jenna nodded.

"Yes," she said.

"That woman . . . ," Lars said slowly, then stopped. *"That woman,"* he said again, his voice rising. He made a visible effort to get himself under control. Softer now, but no less fearsome, he said again, "That *woman* has a great deal to answer for."

Jenna looked around the room. It hardly seemed the right time, but would there ever be a right time? She took a deep breath and plunged forward.

"I . . ." Jenna hesitated. "I don't have all the answers, but . . . I've brought someone who does. Diane is waiting in the car."

All eyes swiveled to stare at her.

"You . . . you brought her here? You brought that woman *here*?" Beverly asked, incredulous.

Jenna held up her hands. "I didn't know what else to do."

"I want to see her." Lars straightened from his slump. "I want to look her in the eyes and ask her myself . . ." He trailed off, a war waging across his face.

Jenna nodded. She stood and walked toward the door.

With her hand on the handle, Jenna turned back.

"I've met her," she said gently to Lars, who'd begun pacing the room, oblivious to the glass that crunched beneath his feet.

Lars grew still and turned to her. She watched an enduring hope bloom upon his face.

"Francie?" he asked in a torturous whisper.

Jenna nodded, not bothering to hide the tears that began to spill down her cheeks. She smiled through them instead.

"She's beautiful, Lars," Jenna said. "She's married now. A mother herself. She has a little boy named Tommy."

Lars's face crumbled, the words hitting his heart with the force of a wrecking ball. He choked back tears of unexpected and unreserved joy.

His daughter was alive.

Diane Downey looked small and old as she faced her accusers. That the accusations were justified made it no easier to witness.

"Why?" Lars demanded. His voice was abrasive, but the burning edge of it had lessened to a smolder. "Why did you come here, insinuate yourself into our lives? To gloat? What kind of sick games have you been playing? You let me believe my daughter was *DEAD*!"

Diane flinched, her shoulders shrinking farther inward.

"Well?" Lars demanded.

Diane glanced up, her gaze flitting around the room, an animal trapped, despite her willingness to walk through the cage door.

"I couldn't give her up," she finally said, dropping her eyes to her lap where her hands gripped each other. "I truly believed you were . . . I let myself believe you were the problem. I *had* to believe that."

Lars could barely look at Diane, and Jenna watched his fists clench, then loosen and clench again. He wasn't a violent man, but this was pushing him to his limits.

Owen studied Diane, clearly trying to understand.

"But why did you come here, Diane?" Owen prodded. "Why not get as far from here as possible?"

"I came because of you, Owen."

Diane stared at him, pleading for something Jenna wasn't sure he could give. Absolution, maybe? Forgiveness? Simple understanding? Nothing was simple anymore, and may never be again.

"Paige—" Diane stopped, corrected herself. "Francine, I mean," she said, the girl's given name obviously difficult for her to say. "She talked about her brother. At first, I thought she meant her younger brother, but when I saw the news reports, I knew . . ."

Diane had the attention of everyone in the room as each struggled to grasp what she was saying.

"I subscribed to the local paper," she went on. "Even once we'd made it to Arizona. I paid to have it delivered through the mail. I read about Audrey's reappearance, the search for the children."

Diane stood, unable to sit under their microscope any longer. She moved to the windows, where Lars had stood and looked out so many times, wondering where his children were.

"Then the ruling of the judge, declaring Audrey unfit to stand trial. I told myself I wouldn't have let her be sent to prison, I would have come back if that happened, to stand for her and tell the story she couldn't manage. I like to think I would have."

She turned to face them. "But that didn't happen. She was sent to the hospital instead, her mental state in question. I convinced myself that was the best place for her, that she'd get the care she needed. You must understand. She was terrified of returning here. Absolutely terrified."

Her lips tightened into a grimace. "But even that wasn't enough for me to risk bringing Paige back," she went on, unconsciously slipping into use of the name she'd called the child for nearly thirty years.

"It was Owen," she continued, facing the windows again. "The newspapers ran photos of Owen and Lars, the family Audrey left behind. His eyes were so sad, so lost."

Diane turned and took a step toward Owen. Her hand fluttered as she lifted her arm slightly, wanting to reach for him, but she let it fall back to her side. Her fingers fiddled with the hem of her shirt.

"I believed, to the depths of my soul, you'd been left abandoned in the care of a monster."

She crossed her arms, tucking anxious fingers beneath them.

"I'd justified stealing Paige away with the belief that I was keeping her safe. I reminded myself of that every day, reinforcing my own reasoning, as circular as it was. But what kind of person would I be if I saved one child while I left another alone to face whatever hell Audrey Jorgensen had been running from?"

"So you came back," Owen said, face-to-face with the ugly secrets of a woman who'd been like a mother to him. His illusions were shattered. Jenna watched him struggle to sift through the wreckage in search of truth.

Diane nodded. "I couldn't sleep nights, worrying about you, a boy I'd never met. Finally, I gave in. You were twelve then, almost thirteen. It was such a risk, bringing Paige so close to home. I knew I'd have to be vigilant, always, to keep you apart, keep her safe." Diane shook her head slowly. "It was crazy to even consider it, but I couldn't let it go.

I was so afraid I'd find you damaged beyond repair, living here alone with your father."

"Dad never hurt me," Owen whispered. "He never would. He never raised a hand to my mother or to us."

"I know that now," Diane conceded, raising her shoulders, then letting them drop. "All I can say is, the mind can be a powerful force. I'd convinced myself of things that weren't true, then fell into my own trap."

"And once you realized?" Owen asked.

Diane busied her hands by dusting an imaginary speck from the back of the chair nearest her. She avoided Owen's probing gaze. "I couldn't give her back. I just couldn't. She'd adjusted, even to being back in Minnesota. She'd come to think of me as her mother, come to think of herself as Paige. I wasn't strong enough, and . . . and I'd come to love you, too, by then, hadn't I."

She tilted her trembling chin defiantly upward. "It was so incredibly selfish, but I . . . I can't apologize for that."

"I remember that day." Lars's voice strained beneath the weight of an immense anger. "You walked in through the door, right past me, and set your little bucket of cleaning supplies on the counter. 'I hear you're in need of a housekeeper,' you said."

"And I was right," Diane said. "I've been wrong about many things . . . so many. But not that."

"I thought Eleanor sent you," Lars said.

"I thought you were some sort of fairy godmother," Owen said quietly.

Diane's face crumpled into sorrow. "Oh, Owen, I wanted to be," she said. "I wanted so badly to be here for you if you needed someone."

Owen was torn, and it was evident for all to see.

Diane hung her head and waited for whatever judgment he would pass.

Lars sprang to his feet, and Jenna was afraid she'd made a terrible mistake, bringing Diane here. Lars hovered over the woman who'd done this unspeakable thing, who now wouldn't meet his eyes.

"Lars," Jenna said, pleading, though for what she couldn't say.

He didn't look at her. His jaw was clenched and tight as he stared down at his own hands, gnarled by work and grief and time.

With obvious effort, he shoved those hands in his pockets, perhaps to keep them from circling the woman's neck. He turned his back to Diane, and Jenna let out a breath she didn't realize she'd been holding.

"He did need someone," Lars said, his voice low and hurting. "I was a poor excuse for a father to him."

"Dad—" Owen said, shaking his head.

"Yes, you were," Diane said sharply, cutting Owen off. A remnant of the old Diane, for the briefest of moments.

Lars glanced around, shocked at her outburst.

"I'm sorry, Lars," she said. "I'll certainly have to answer to God for what I did to you . . . But the state of this place. The state of *you*."

Diane's face was a reprimand all its own.

"It took you years to get your act together," she said.

Lars peered at her, and Jenna held her breath again.

The anger flared once more, then banked. Pain washed in to fill the space left behind. Slowly Lars squeezed his eyes closed, and his shoulders slumped forward in defeat.

It was a sliver, the first and barest hint of acceptance, and Diane's composure crumbled beneath it.

"I'm sorry." Ugly tears began pouring from her. "I'm so sorry."

Owen took one jerky step in her direction, then stopped himself short, but the needful onslaught of tears was too much for him. He sent his father an apologetic glance, then moved to the older woman's side. He took her in his arms, and the sobs grew louder.

He held her, patting her gingerly on the back until the tears had given way to hitching, gulping sniffles.

He led her to the recliner, guiding her to take a seat.

"I'm so sorry," she said again, once the worst had passed. "I knew. I think I knew as soon as I arrived. I told myself it was better this way. You weren't the parent that child needed. But I knew."

She sniffed and scrubbed her hands across her face.

"You were no monster. Neglectful, maybe. Hurting. But you weren't a bad man."

Her voice trembled. "You didn't deserve any of this."

Lars gave a great, deep sigh, taking his turn to stare out the windows into the snow-covered darkness beyond.

"Maybe," he said hoarsely. "Maybe not."

Jenna blinked. Diane slowly lifted her head to stare at his back.

"I may not have been a monster, Diane . . . But I . . . I was careless," he said. "I was careless with what I'd been given. And a careless man is a bad man, too, in his own way."

Silence fell at his pronouncement.

Lars cleared his throat, but his voice cracked anyway when he spoke again.

"Is she . . . is she happy?" he asked in a tremulous whisper.

Jenna's chin quivered and she pressed her knuckles hard against her mouth, afraid to break the fragile spell that had conjured such a lovely and delicate hope.

"Did she grow up happy, Diane?"

The housekeeper broke into tears again, but she managed to nod through the snot and the sobs.

"Yes," she said, smiling and crying at the same time. "Yes, she's happy."

"Oh God." Lars let out a sharp exhale. "God," he murmured, gripping the back of a chair for support. "Thank you," he whispered, his voice raw. "Jesus, whatever else . . . thank you for that."

"Sit down, Dad." Owen led him to the sofa before the old man's legs went out from beneath him.

Beverly, who'd been as quiet as Jenna and Hannah through it all, finally spoke up. "Have you told her?"

Diane jerkily inclined her head. She gulped back more tears and stared at her shoes. "She was . . . understandably upset."

Jenna had been with Diane when she broke the news and thought that was the understatement of the night.

"She asked for some time. I hope you'll respect that, but . . . she wants to meet you."

The pools that formed in Lars's eyes were as abiding as any ocean and just as deep.

"There's something else, though." For the first time, Diane showed a hint of fear. "Something you need to know."

"Does Mommy hate me?"

"Oh, honey," Diane soothed. "No, she doesn't hate you."

Months had passed since the girl had been delivered into her arms. She'd tried to explain to the child that her mother had left her with Diane to keep her safe. That she needed to play pretend now. Play pretend that Diane was her mother.

"You can call me Mama, if you want," she'd said. "That way, it's different than your mommy. Because she wants me to keep you safe while she can't."

It was hard to guess how much the little girl understood. She was so young. The news reports confirmed Francie Jorgensen was only four years old.

Diane could only hope that, with time, she'd forget. That this new life they were making together would paper over her old life, her old family.

The importance of that happening couldn't be underestimated, because even with the child's hair cut shorter and dyed a light auburn, they had to be careful.

No distance would be far enough if the child slipped in front of the wrong person and admitted Diane wasn't her mother at all.

Pushing the near-constant stream of worries from her mind, Diane knelt before the little girl she'd grown to love so ferociously in such a short span of time.

"Your mommy couldn't possibly hate you, sweetheart. Not ever."

"But she hasn't come back." The child's voice was as thin as a reed.

"Oh, love." Diane ran her hands down the girl's arms. "She's just doing what she believes is best. Don't you worry about it for one more minute, okay?"

The little girl nodded, and Diane hoped she'd let it go, at least for the moment.

"Will is dead, isn't he?"

The child's words stole Diane's breath. She pulled the poor, sweet thing into her arms and hugged her tightly.

Her voice wavered when she said, "He's gone up to heaven to be an angel now, love."

Nothing existed but the warm weight in Diane's arms.

"Is that why Mommy left me?"

Diane pulled back and lightly placed her finger beneath the child's chin, tilting her head upward to meet her eyes.

"No, honey. Your mommy just couldn't take care of you anymore. She wanted to, she just wasn't able to. So I get to take care of you now and be your mama."

"She's not mad at me?" the little girl asked, seeking comfort and confirmation in her new mama's face.

"Of course not, sweetheart. Why would she be mad at you?"

Tears began to pool in the little girl's eyes.

"Because she told me to be good and quiet and look after my baby brother and she'd be right back." The words picked up speed and fell from her mouth in one long stream. "But he woke up from his nap and he didn't want to be good and quiet. I told him to shush, that Mommy would be right back, but he was fussy and crying."

Diane's heart skipped a beat.

"You were watching your baby brother?" she asked slowly. "All alone?"

The child nodded gravely, wiping her sniffles against the back of her hand.

"Mommy said she'd be right back, with Owen this time, but Will didn't understand. I just wanted him to stop crying."

She shook her little head back and forth, pleading for Diane to understand. "I didn't mean anything bad."

Tiny pearls of baby teeth winked in the light as the child's lower lip began to tremble.

"Oh, baby. Of course you didn't." Diane pulled her into another hug. "Shh now. Shh."

But the girl started to cry in earnest, words spilling from her mouth, words that could never be unheard.

"I took him down to the water," she said in her tiny voice. "He liked to play there. It would make him giggle and laugh and he'd be happy, even if he wasn't very quiet."

Oh God in heaven. Dear God.

"And it worked. Mommy would be proud when she got back with Owen, and we'd play pretend and tell stories, and I could be a princess. Then Willie saw the frog, and it croaked and jumped, and he giggled, but when I tried to catch it for him, it hopped away. Will started to cry really loud then."

Diane could do nothing but hold tight as the little girl let loose the story she'd kept locked inside all this time.

"Mommy told us to be quiet, though, and Will crying wasn't quiet, so I told him to stay put and if he'd stop crying I'd catch the frog for him. But it just kept jumping and leaping and I couldn't catch it, no matter how hard I tried."

Oh Jesus, help me, Diane prayed.

"And when I got back, Willie was floating in the water." The little girl's voice started to rise. "I thought he was sleeping, but he didn't wake up. And when Mommy came back, she couldn't wake him up either. And I don't want him to be an angel! I just want him to be my baby brother again!"

The poor lost child cried and cried while Diane rocked her back and forth, giving what little comfort she could.

"Shh now," Diane murmured. "Shh. It's all over now. Over and done, just like a dream. Just like a bad dream, but you're awake now and Mama will make it all better. Shh. Just a dream, Paige."

Diane had been unwilling to refer to the child as Francie, even in her mind. It was too dangerous. But she'd been unable to call her Paige often. Saying the name had conjured the face of another little girl, one whose loss would always be part of her. But it was time to let that dream go too.

"Just a dream, love. A dream of a little girl named Francie, but you're Paige now, and Mama's going to be here for you always. It's going to be all right."

It was far from the last time Diane would say those words. In time, the words became more. It took time and persistence, but those words eventually became a new reality for Diane and her daughter, Paige.

59

"All this time," Lars said with a stunned breath. "All these years, I thought Audrey . . . When they found Will, I thought Audrey . . . Oh God. I thought Audrey hurt them. I was so afraid Audrey had killed our babies."

Lars squeezed his eyes shut, unable to stop the tears.

"It was an accident," Diane whispered. "A terrible, terrible accident."

The word *accident*, delivered with such sorrow, rang like a church bell inside of Jenna.

An unidentified voice on the telephone. "Mrs. Shaw, there's been an accident."

Her friends. "Such a tragic accident."

Her husband's family. "Mechanical malfunction. An accident."

Whispered conversations, all in black. "Such a shame. An accident."

The words flew about, blackbirds in a cage, trying to break free.

Cassie's voice, so close, in the middle of it all.

"Mom. It was an accident."

Across the room, a father and son embraced each other, and great-grandmother and great-granddaughter did the same, while an old woman cried tears of guilt and regret.

Jenna, dizzy with vertigo, turned and fled.

She was grateful for the clash of frigid air. Her feverish body was burning her from the inside out.

She gripped the post of the porch, her chest heaving, fast and loose. She concentrated on the fog of breath condensing in the air in front of her and began to count the puffs.

One. Two.

Buckle my shoe.

This old man, he played three.

A memory of Matt's voice echoed from a great distance. "What exactly is involved in playing knick-knack, paddy-whack anyway? And why does it need to happen on my knee? The old man sounds kind of sketchy."

A strangled laugh broke from her and floated away into the night.

The tears, the hated tears she'd been holding back for so long. The pressure of them was building, straining their bonds.

She grasped for a peace she didn't know if she'd ever find again.

"I miss you, Matt," she whispered, sending the message on a wing of hope into the wintry air. "I miss you all so much."

The words were woefully inadequate, but somehow the act of saying them aloud helped Jenna find a tiny thread of sanity. She clung to it, holding tight with both hands.

The sound of the cabin door opening and closing entered her consciousness.

"First rule of Minnesota winter, missy," Lars said. "If you're going to have an emotional breakdown outdoors, in the middle of the night, you've got to dress for it."

He draped Jenna's puffy orange coat around her shoulders. She hugged it close and gave him a tremulous smile.

"I'm sorry," she said. "It was just . . ."

"A lot to take in," he finished for her. "It's all right."

Lars cleared his throat and spoke again, "I recall I told you once I don't believe in debts."

She tilted her head and observed his profile. There was something new there. Something had shifted inside Lars Jorgensen at his core.

Jenna studied him. One corner of her mouth lifted slowly once she hit upon what it was.

There was a peace that hadn't been there before.

"A lot can change in the course of a day, Jenna Shaw," he said. "I owe you a debt I can never repay."

Jenna smiled then, a slow, sad smile. "Can I get that in writing?"

He let out a snort of laughter and raised his gaze to the sky.

"Look, Jenna," he said suddenly, pointing a finger up and to the north.

Jenna followed his line of sight and caught her breath.

"Is that . . . ?" She trailed off, awestruck at the sight.

"The northern lights."

A buzzing warmth flooded her as she stared, transfixed, at the dazzling display.

A play of green and violet hung in the sky, as if painted there by God's own hand.

"That's a sight, isn't it?" Lars said on an amazed breath. "Rare to see so far south."

Jenna thought of the words she'd spoken into the darkness. Maybe Matt had heard her after all.

"You don't owe me a thing, Lars," she told him softly. "Not a single thing."

He took her arm in his and they stood, side by side, watching their own private miracle.

60

"How do I look?" Lars asked for the third time as he fiddled with the top button of his shirt. "I should have worn the suit."

"Dad, that suit is from 1982, and it makes you look like an undertaker," Owen told him. "You look fine."

Jenna sent him a smile of encouragement. "Take a breath."

He nodded shakily, and his cheeks puffed as he blew out a long exhale. He shoved his hands deep into his pockets.

"What time is it?"

"About two minutes past the last time you checked." Jenna reached up and placed her palms on his chest, smoothing his crisply ironed shirt.

"Trust me, she's as nervous as you are," she said. "But from what I saw, she's a warm and compassionate person. She's going to love you."

His eyes were big and filled with wonder as he bobbed his head at Jenna's words. Her heart swelled for him. She cleared her throat and busied herself with rearranging the lunch that had been prepared.

Beverly shooed her out of the kitchen, her birdlike hands waving through the air.

"Find somewhere else to hover, Jenna, for goodness' sake."

Jenna backed out of Beverly's self-designated domain, holding up her palms in acquiescence.

The older woman had been flitting about the cabin all morning, fluffing and dusting and finally focusing her boundless nervous energy on putting together an impressive buffet lunch.

They could always take the leftovers to the church kitchen, Jenna supposed, surveying the copious amounts of food.

"And just where has Hannah run off to? Owen, that girl—"

"She'll be here, Grandma," Owen said, rubbing a hand down his grandmother's back. "It's going to be fine."

If he'd said those words once, he must have said them a dozen times that day, a voice of reason among them.

"I'm going to wait outside." Lars rose suddenly from the chair he'd only just sat in.

"No, Dad—" Owen reached out, but Lars had already shut the door behind him.

Owen sighed and grabbed his coat and his father's.

Jenna gave him a smile. "It's a big day."

He nodded, and Jenna saw a hint of his own nerves.

"Yeah," he said. "Yeah, it is."

Owen opened the door to follow his father but stopped dead at the sight of Diane's sedan, followed closely by a gray SUV, pulling slowly into the driveway.

"They're here," Owen said.

"Oh my God, Jenna," Beverly cried. "Did he say they're here?" She patted her hair as she hurried to the door.

"We probably shouldn't crowd her—" Owen gave up when he saw the uselessness of the words.

Lars stood stock-still as Diane stepped out of her car and sent him a small wave.

Jenna was glad Diane could be there that day.

In the weeks since the housekeeper's truth had been revealed, Diane had aged, but also seemed lighter somehow. Relieved of the burden of lies she'd carried for so long.

Inevitably, Sergeant Allred had taken Diane into custody. There was no statute of limitations on kidnapping in Minnesota. There were additional charges to sort through related to the burial of Will and obstruction of justice. Diane had gone willingly.

Her eventual fate was still up in the air, but given she posed no immediate threat and wasn't a flight risk, the judge had granted bail.

And while Diane's relationship with the Jorgensens remained tenuous, her daughter had asked for her to be there today.

No one was inclined to deny her.

Diane walked to the passenger window of the SUV and spoke for a moment with someone in the vehicle.

The anticipation on the porch was thick and insufferably heavy.

Beverly, standing at Jenna's side, reached for her hand, though her eyes never left the vehicle in the driveway. She needed to touch someone, anyone, and Jenna would apparently do.

Owen stood behind Lars, who hardly seemed to be breathing.

Finally, the driver's side door opened and a tall man unfolded himself from the seat. He saw the welcoming committee standing on the porch, waiting, and raised a hesitant hand in their direction before he reached to open the door to the back seat.

At the same time, Diane took a step back and the passenger door opened.

Owen placed his hand on his dad's arm, wordlessly supporting the man who'd waited almost thirty years for this day.

Jenna caught her bottom lip between her teeth. It was nearly unbearable to watch Lars's face as his daughter stepped out of the car, yet Jenna found she couldn't look away.

He took a slow step forward, then another, descending the steps of the porch. Little Francie, now a grown woman, walked toward him and shyly tucked a strand of dark hair behind one ear. Lars drew closer, and his steps quickened.

They met in the middle of the icy driveway and stared wordlessly into each other's eyes. Lars held out his hands, and she placed her own in his, finding a connection neither had ever dreamed to have.

When Lars opened his arms wide, silently offering his long-lost child who'd finally come home his unreserved acceptance, Jenna caught her breath. When the woman who would always be Francie Jorgensen, somewhere deep inside, stepped into his embrace and hugged him tightly in return, Jenna couldn't stop the tears that fell.

It was one of the most wondrous and precious sights she'd ever been blessed to witness.

How many minutes passed no one could have said, certainly not Jenna. But at the precise moment she thought she had a handle on the emotions flooding her, the tall man from the driver's seat took a step forward.

"This is your grandson, Thomas," he said, shifting the baby seated on his hip, who clutched a midnight-blue bunny that was love-worn and threadbare. It had silver stars for buttons.

Lars threw his arms open again with a teary laugh, full of such warmth and gratitude, such utter joy, that it was contagious, spreading outward in ripples until there wasn't anyone present who wasn't smiling through their own tears.

Even the baby gurgled happily and waved his prize around.

"Come in," Lars said to them all. "Please, come in."

With nods all around, the group began to move toward the cabin, wiping tears from their cheeks.

Francie's arm was woven through her father's, but she stopped. She searched out and found Diane, who followed a few steps behind.

The younger woman held out her free hand, which Diane tearfully accepted, and together, the family that never had a chance to be and the family that never should have been walked side by side.

◆ ◆ ◆

After a round of tearful introductions on the porch, Beverly ushered the whole crowd inside.

Jenna hung back.

"Well, come on, then," Beverly said, as she urged her inside. "You're part of this family now, too, whether you like it or not."

Owen, who was standing between the two women, smiled and swept one arm low. *After you,* the gesture said.

Beverly's proclamation caught Jenna off guard and brought up conflicting feelings, but she stored them away to pull out and examine later.

She'd drawn even with the threshold when Owen placed a hand on her shoulder.

Jenna peered at him, but his gaze was trained toward the road.

"I believe there's someone here to see you," he said.

Jenna turned. She heard a car door slam, then saw the top half of Hannah Jorgensen walking toward the cabin, passing along the far side of the parked vehicles in the driveway. Hannah quickly waved back to the driver who'd given her a ride as the unfamiliar car pulled away.

Happiness lit the teenager's face and her laughter traveled over the snow, reaching them before she did.

Jenna had no idea why the girl was so pleased, but she doubted it was the thought of seeing Jenna.

"What are you—"

Jenna stopped short as a blurry streak of pale yellow bounded around the front of the cars and made a wide turn in her direction.

A familiar euphoric barking filled the sky as all the breath left Jenna's body.

She dropped to her knees just in time to catch the golden retriever as he leapt up the steps and found his way home again, safe in her arms.

"Beckett," she cried, and thought she heard Cassie echo the word. She hugged the exhilarated dog, running her hands over his downy fur, while he showered her with the million kisses he'd missed the opportunity to give.

"Oh, Beckett," she said, her chin trembling. "Buddy. Oh, buddy, I'm so sorry. I'm so, so sorry."

The tears hit her with a great, crushing wave. All of them. All the tears she'd tried so desperately to hold back for months and months.

But she'd waited too long. The dam she'd built, stone by stone, to store her monumental grief was cracking. She heard it spread and sensed the enormous weight and roar of what was coming for her on the other side.

She was powerless as it washed over her with the force of a shifting continent. She had no choice but to let it come, wave after wave. Tears for a phone call out of the blue, tears for a funeral all in black, tears for a carved wooden box. Tears for the eyes of a beloved dog, watching her mournfully as he was left behind. Tears for a family, an entire family that no longer was, and the separate, distinct, and amazing individuals it used to be.

And Beckett was there for her through it all, his love unconditional. His fur soaked up her grief, and his tongue lapped the tears from her cheeks.

His forgiveness was complete.

EPILOGUE

Jenna hadn't mentioned where she was going.

Not that it was a secret, but this was something she needed to do alone, so she held even the words that would describe her intentions close.

She'd risen before dawn. On a normal day, she'd click a leash on Beckett's collar and the two would set out on a run. Jenna mostly to combat the hours she spent in a chair with her fingers tapping a keyboard, and Beck for sheer pleasure. Some days Hannah would join them. The teenager had warmed to Jenna. Sort of. Though her affection for Beckett was probably at the heart of the girl's newfound tolerance.

The dog had taken to Minnesota. When the snows began to melt and spring blossomed again, Jenna found herself marveling at the resilience of everything around her. In a fit of spring fever, she was nearly brought to tears by the first blooms she spotted on the ground.

Nearly. But Jenna had cried enough tears for five lifetimes once she'd fallen headlong into her grief. She'd always known it was too big for her, that it would destroy her with its scope.

And it did.

What she hadn't anticipated was coming through the other side. Yet she had. Wounded, bloodied, and battered, Jenna had endured.

Today was not a day for a run.

With her bag slung over her shoulder and Beckett padding beside her, Jenna walked the length of the dock she'd helped to install once the ice had thawed.

Mornings on the lake were a benediction, a prayer to the close of night.

The mournful call of a loon traveled across the water. It echoed through the thin layer of fog.

Beckett gave a soft bark. His tail wagged and his back end wiggled suspiciously from side to side as he contemplated something in the water beside the dock.

"Beckett, no," she said with a gentle note of warning. "No chasing fish. Not today, buddy."

An ancient aluminum fishing boat was moored along the edge of the dock.

"Beckett, come." She patted the side of her leg. He needed no more encouragement. He bounded past her and leapt into the boat. Jenna stepped in after him.

Going through the steps Lars had insisted she learn, Jenna slipped on the life jacket that was stored in the boat, then primed the little motor attached to the back.

The first time Lars walked her through these steps, he'd gotten a laugh out of watching her try to pull the rope to start the motor, before she'd glared at him and asked what was so funny.

"I've wired it for a push-button start," he admitted, as she blew back the hair hanging in her eyes.

"Funny," she said. "I hope you enjoyed that."

"I did, as a matter of fact," he agreed with a chuckle, then directed her to the little red button that brought the engine to life.

Jenna started the motor and let it idle as she unwound the ropes that held the shallow boat to the dock, then slowly, patiently, navigated away from the shore toward the center of the lake.

The light steadily brightened. The sun winked over the horizon, hinting at its own brilliance. Jenna cut the motor and drank in the silence.

A flock of geese called from overhead, and Beckett woofed in reply.

Jenna smiled wistfully, grateful every day for the delight he found just in being alive. For the insight of Owen in bringing him back to her.

"We had to do a little snooping, I hope you don't mind," he'd said. "The Davises were sorry to let him go, but they send you their best."

The months had brought changes to this small place. Lars had asked Jenna if she would consider staying. She'd agreed.

She sold her family home without ever returning. There was nothing left for her there. Just walls and the empty spaces between them. Shadows of what used to be.

Her former neighbors had been happy to pack her laptop and photo albums and have them shipped to her. The real estate agent she'd hired to handle the sale of the house had sent a photo of the new owners, a young couple standing in the front yard, waving for the camera.

They were expecting their first child.

Jenna wished them a future full of happiness and a wellspring of hope large enough to see them through the tough times.

Paige, as she preferred to be called, and her small family had become fixtures in their lives. She and the rest of the Jorgensens had forged a new relationship over the remains of the old, like a phoenix risen from the ashes.

There were a few awkward moments. Paige refused to hear a word against Diane, standing by her after her arrest. Diane's lawyers had suggested a plea bargain, and the district attorney, recognizing the difficulty of trying such an emotionally charged case, had agreed.

Lars could understand his daughter's support of the woman who'd raised her, a woman she still thought of as her mother, but when he learned Paige was an Arizona Cardinals fan, a remnant of the few years she'd spent in the state with Diane, he found that a difficult pill to swallow.

"That woman has a great deal to answer for," he'd muttered.

After several heated discussions, Lars gave up, transferring his hopes to his new grandchild, who was the adorable recipient of a tiny Minnesota Vikings T-shirt and matching purple pants.

Lars savored those times, Jenna knew, though they were bound together with a ribbon of sadness. Audrey had been released from the Minnesota State Secure Psychiatric Hospital. Paige visited her first mother at the private treatment center she'd been transferred to, under the care of Dr. Nancy Young, but there were no happy endings for Audrey. Though she was no longer a ward of the state, Audrey Jorgensen was the lost one now. The only one who'd yet to find her way home.

Little Will Jorgensen's bones had been laid to rest in the Raven Cemetery. At long last, Lars Jorgensen knew where his children laid their heads. All of them.

Jenna took a deep breath, pulling the peace around her into her lungs like incense. She'd chosen this place with care.

The perfect place to die.

She'd intended to sink to the bottom of this lake, weighed down by the unendurable despair she carried with her.

An old man, one old bastard of a man, was the only thing that had stopped her.

Jenna knelt in the bottom of the boat as the sun crept upward and the fog danced its slow dance over the water.

She slid the carved wooden box from her bag.

Beckett gave it a sniff, then let out a soft whine.

"It's okay, bud." She gave him a reassuring hug.

As she unhooked the brass latch, Jenna said a silent prayer.

Her cheeks were wet when she lifted the lid of the box and tipped the contents over the side of the boat to swirl into the water below.

She had a few tears left after all.

"Goodbye, my loves," she whispered, wiping her cheeks and trailing her fingers in the dark water as the cloud expanded.

Jenna was the sole guardian of the memories her family had left behind. She would carry them always, wherever life took her. They would fade with time, and grow ragged around the edges, just as she feared they would. She would treasure them all the same, a precious, precious gift.

Jenna had no second thoughts about bringing the ashes here, to a place her family had never been.

Because this was a place of beauty. Full of sorrow and hope. Of pain. Of healing.

Cassie whispered in Jenna's ear for the last time.

"A place of forgiveness."

ACKNOWLEDGMENTS

I owe a debt of gratitude to the incomparable team at Lake Union Publishing. Danielle, Christopher, Gabe, Faith, and all the rest, thank you. Thank you, always, to my fairy godmother, Miriam Juskowicz. Thank you to my agent, Katie Shea Boutillier.

Thank you, Jim and Sue James, for your gracious generosity in sharing your time and expertise. Any mistakes are mine and mine alone.

Thank you to Nicole for the longest-running lunch date (*cough* therapy session) ever.

Thank you to my family for your patience, your love, and your unwavering support.

Last but never least, thank you to the readers who hung in until the end. This one came from the heart, and my greatest hope is that it touched yours.

ABOUT THE AUTHOR

Eliza Maxwell is the author of *The Unremembered Girl*, *The Grave Tender*, and *The Kinfolk*. She writes fiction from her home in Texas, which she shares with her ever-patient husband, two impatient kids, a ridiculous English setter, and a bird named Sarah. An artist and writer, a dedicated introvert, and a British cop-drama addict, she enjoys nothing more than sitting on the front porch with a good cup of coffee.

Made in the USA
Middletown, DE
17 October 2020